his
hollow
heart

USA *TODAY* BESTSELLING AUTHOR
RACHEL LEIGH

SOME ARE BORN TO SWEET DELIGHT.
SOME ARE BORN TO ENDLESS NIGHT.
  -WILLIAM BLAKE

For Sara
For everything.

PROLOGUE

ELEVEN YEARS OLD

Bella

COLORS BOUNCE off the walls in a prism, as the light catches the crystal suncatcher hanging in the window. I blink a couple of times, adjusting my eyes to the brightness. Rolling over to my side, I see the empty bed next to me. I sit up abruptly and notice all of the beds are empty. Each one made perfectly. An old comforter tucked around every corner of the twin-size mattresses. One flat pillow lying centered at the top of each bed.

The sudden realization that today is *the day* has me flinging off my blanket. My bare feet hit the old wooden floorboards that creak as I hurry over to my armoire closet.

Pulling down my pink poufy dress—my only dress—I hold it out and cringe upon inspection. It'll have to do. Even if it has been worn so many times that the lace on the hem now hangs in stray strands. The white flowers now resemble more of a crescent moon, and the hole in the armpit reminds me not to raise my left hand today.

I often find myself gawking at Lucy, the neighbor girl, who is the same age as me. She always wears the most beautiful dresses. Rainbow colors, with sparkling gems sewn

1

around the waistline. Cal always makes me feel better by saying, "*You don't want to be like those people. They wear their happiness on the outside, they don't feel it where it counts.*" But there is one dress Lucy wears often. It's baby pink with a floral lace overlay. She looks like a princess when she wears it, and every time she does, I watch her from across the yard and daydream that it's me. Living her life, hugging her parents. Cal thinks it's ridiculous, but there's not much that isn't ridiculous to him. Yet, he always has a way of helping me see the bigger picture. No matter what happens, I hope I never lose myself in *things.*

Cal told me that one day he was going to buy me all the dresses in the world, just to prove to me they don't hold my beauty.

After I'm all dressed and feeling content with my appearance, I brush my teeth in the shared bathroom and run my fingers through my cedar-brown curls, getting them stuck at the end and ripping through the matted mess.

Quiet baby steps lead me to the top of the staircase as I listen to see if they're here yet. The laughter of the other kids leads me to believe that I didn't miss them. If I had, it would be quiet. There would be tears. And, there is no way that Callum would have left, nor let them leave without waking me first. We made a pact, after all.

Part of our deal was that we'd do whatever it takes to stay together. If he is chosen and I'm not, he said he'd moon the visitors just so they didn't pick him and if that didn't work, he'd kick the guy in the balls. I told him I'd simply scream at the top of my lungs until they no longer wanted me. I mean, it's a solid plan. No one wants to adopt brats.

Callum and I came to The Webster House together four years ago. I was only seven years old; he was three years older. We've watched so many potential parents come and go during our time here, that we'd almost given up hope.

Only kids come to The Webster House—no babies. The youngest being Elizabeth, or Bibs as we call her. She's eight now, and I worry that she will still have many more years here. Everyone wants a baby or a toddler. Someone they can mold and hear their first words of "mom" or "dad." I'm not sure I could ever refer to another with that title. Especially since my only knowledge of a mom is someone who leaves you alone to raise yourself, so she can drink and do drugs, even at the tender age of four years old. Dads are just something I've read about as a fictional entity.

I often fantasize about having one. He would be tall, with dark hair, and muscular arms that he would sweep me up in as he plants kisses all over my rosy cheeks. He'd twirl me around in a brand-new baby pink dress as the bottom half catches the wind. I'd be his little girl.

Only, time is passing quickly. My days of being a little girl are numbered. So are the years I have left to build a solid relationship with new parents. Today is likely my last chance. Today, we welcome a family who is looking for a son and a daughter. I've heard through the cracks in the walls that they do not want babies or toddlers. They want older kids and they are ready and willing to provide them with a loving home.

Today is the day that Callum and I begin to live—really live. Public school, dances, sports, a life outside of these walls. I've always wanted to take piano lessons. I've learned a little by teaching myself on the old piano in the dining hall. It's missing a few keys, but it's better than nothing.

Tonight, we will celebrate the first day of the rest of our lives. Maybe even with blueberry pie—our favorite.

"Psst." I hear from down the hall.

I look left, and right, to be sure that the coast is clear. Callum and I have our own secret hiding space. We call it a secret, but everyone knows about it. They just know not to enter. Not only is there a big sign that reads "Keep Out OR ELSE" on the front of the knee-wall door, Callum also uses threats and punishment for all who enter.

Occasionally, we let Mark and Layla in, since they are the same age as us, but they've both proven to be tattletales and have shared some of the secrets meant to stay inside the small, squared space. For instance, when Callum broke Mr. Beckham's window last fall with a curveball. We made a pact that we'd take his wrongdoing to the grave. That was until Mrs. Webster told us that if no one comes forward then we had to spend the entire weekend in our rooms. Mark and Layla broke the pact. They never admitted it, but we knew.

"What are you doing?" I drag my eyes up and down the hall to be sure no one is out here. When I'm sure the coast is clear, I duck my head and enter the crawl space. "I thought our parents were on their way."

That's what we call them. *Our parents.* Because, we just know that they will choose us. We've had this planned ever since we learned of their visit over a month ago.

Callum sweeps the air with his hand and walks over to the petite dormer window. He presses his palms against the wall on each side. "They're late."

I can immediately tell by his tone that he's upset.

"They're still coming, though, right?" I walk to his side, taking notice of his gray slacks that are far too short. His long-sleeved button-up shirt is tucked only in the front and missing a middle button. A pain stabs at my chest. "Cal, tell me they're coming."

He shrugs his shoulders, then kicks at the wall. Hard, loud, and frightening. I wince at the sudden shock of his outrage. Most of the kids here are scared of Callum. He's a bit rough around the edges. I've seen his heart, though. He has one in there; he just doesn't share it with the world. In a way, it makes me feel privileged. Everyone else gets bitterness and a sour attitude; I get the sweet stuff.

In one swift motion, Callum spins around. "Bella," he grips my shoulders, "promise me, again. Promise me that you will never leave me."

My body tenses under his aggressive hold. My heart's racing, palm's sweating. Something is wrong. "Cal, what's this about? What happened?"

At first, Callum was like the big brother I never had. The older we get, though, the more grateful I am that he *isn't* my brother. The last couple of months I've seen him in a different light. When he walks into a room, butterflies freefly through my stomach and my heart rate excels. I continuously shake off the notion that I could possibly have a crush on my best friend, because this is the same boy who has slept in my bed countless nights due to his recurring nightmares. We're friends. Nothing more. Nothing less.

It's also the same boy who beat up Mr. Beckham's preppy fourteen-year-old son, Trent, because he lifted my skirt once. He literally beat him to a pulp. Blood painted the Beckhams' well-manicured lawn a dark shade of red.

"I just need to hear you say it. Tell me I'll always have you." He pulls me into his chest, wrapping his arms around my head in a gentle, yet abrasive hold. Our hearts beat in sync. Rapid and unruly. Shattered pieces meant to mend together. But, I can feel him slipping away, even as he holds me so tightly.

"What did you do?" I know this can't be good. Callum is always getting in trouble, and if he did something to mess this day up, so help me…I can't even think about it.

Everything is fine. We're minutes away from our new life.

"I screwed up. I really screwed up this time." He pulls away and looks me in the eye. "I've always got you, right?"

The desperation in his voice slices through my happiness. An uncertainty for our future. The burden of a decision that decides our fate.

The slamming of a car door has us both back at the window. "They're here." His eyes close, then open slowly. "I'm gonna need that promise now, Bella."

I don't even think. I just feed him the words that he craves. "I promise, Cal. Until kingdom come. It's you and me. Always."

1

TWELVE YEARS LATER

WITH THE LIFE I know behind me, I look over my shoulder, and my heart splinters in two. A large sign stares back at me, *Thank you for riding with Falcon Ferry*. It slowly disappears into the abyss as the ferry leaves the dock.

Destination: Elizabeth Islands

My hand rests on my luggage bag. One bag with everything I should need for the next six months. A single tear drops down my cheek when I pull the image from memory of Mom and Dad waving goodbye from the driveway hours ago. I brush the dampness away with the back of my hand and swallow hard, anxiety overwhelming me.

I've never even left the state without them. When it came time to choose a school, my heart longed to accept the offer in the Piano Department at Juilliard, but the miles between here and there seemed too long. Not to mention, I couldn't afford it. There was a scholarship, if I really wanted to go, but how could I when I had so much lost time with my family to make up for? So, I decided on an interior design degree at a local university. Yet, here I am—leaving. Six months secluded from civilization.

My parents are empty nesters now. Mark is away at law school in New York, and I doubt he'll ever move back to our hometown in Rhode Island.

This temporary move is a good thing, I keep reminding myself. I never would have imagined that I would be leaving our small town and moving eight hours away. But, this is an offer that anyone in their right mind would take. I don't claim to always be in the right mindset, but that's exactly what I did. I jumped on it.

With little time to prepare, I didn't even make a list of everything I needed to bring. Just threw some clothes into a suitcase and left the next morning. Normally I would have sat on it for days, weeks maybe. I have no idea why the president of Ellis Empire would want little old me working on the design of one of his exclusive hotels, but he does. So here I am, starting a new chapter in my life, one I never even knew I wanted, but one I can't wait to begin.

A phone call interrupts Selena Gomez's voice through the speakers of my earbuds. I take the call with a chuckle, "I haven't even hit the interstate."

"Just turn around, babe. It's not too late to change your mind."

Taking a deep breath, I say what needs to be said, "This is going to be good—for both of us. I promise."

I've been with the same guy, on and off, for the last three years. We've hit so many bumps in the road that I barely even notice them anymore. We've come to the point in our lives where I think we are headed in separate directions, and I'm not sure that what we have is strong enough to survive the pull. He proposed last week, and I still haven't given him an answer, even if deep down, I know what it will be.

"When you get tired of this job, come home. I've told you, you don't need to work. Let me take care of you."

Holding my breath, I count to five in my head. *One. Two.*

Three. Four. Five. "We've been over this, Trent. I need my independence. I have to go, we're hitting rough waters. Talk soon." I end the call and blow out an exasperated breath.

I'm leaving a lot behind, but if things go as planned, I'll be finding something even better—myself. My own identity. With zero connections on the island, my past doesn't have to follow me.

"Excuse me, miss?"

My eyes flutter open as someone shakes my shoulder. Smacking my lips together, I hope I wasn't drooling. I pull out my earbuds and set them in my lap, then look up at the big burly guy in front of me. "I'm sorry, what?"

He doesn't even smile, just stands there with a scorned look on his face. "We've docked. You may exit the boat now."

"Wow. That was fast." I drop my earbuds into my purse, along with my phone, and grab the handle of my suitcase. "Thank you very much." I smile politely at the asshole.

Dragging my suitcase behind me while Mr. Grumpy watches, I make my way down the ramp.

Surprisingly, there aren't many people. I've got no idea where I'm going from here, but I was told there'd be a gentleman waiting to transport me to the hotel where I'll be staying.

My eyes sweep the small crowd and I spot him. A tall, lanky man holding a white piece of paper that reads Isabella Jenkins. Seeing it makes this feel all the more official.

Here we go. I'm off to an island in the middle of nowhere with choppy cell service, no car, and strangers as co-workers. It's intimidating as hell, being the new girl at any job, but this isn't just any job. It's *the* job.

I approach the man with heightened nerves. There's still

time to back out, but if I take this boat ride, it's pretty much written in stone. Sure, I can leave if I want. But, that would make me a quitter and I'm not known to quit.

He lifts his chin from me, then looks down at the sign with questioning eyes. I give him a nod and he smiles. Breathing out a sigh of relief that he's not as much of a browbeat as the guy on the boat, I greet him. "You must be my ride out of here."

"And you must be Isabella?"

"That would be me."

"I'm Jeffery, and I'll be your escort. Here," he takes the handle of my suitcase, "allow me."

"Thank you," I tell him as I walk next to him, down the waterfront sidewalk.

Jeffery looks at me and quirks a brow. "Are you excited about your stay at Cori Cove?"

"Nervous is a better word. It's a big change."

"I can imagine. Working for Mr. Ellis does sound quite nerve-wracking."

Gee. Thanks for the encouragement. "You don't work for him, then?"

"Not quite. Mr. Ellis doesn't get many guests on his island, but when he does, I escort them from the docks. I'm not on his payroll, though."

"Interesting." Now I'm curious how many people will be working at the hotel. Jeffery refers to them as guests, but the hotel isn't set to open until next year. From my understanding, there's a lot to be done. Positioned all over the world, Ellis Empire is known for their gorgeous castle-like hotel chain.

Mr. Ellis, who is a billionaire, purchases these very old castles—most of which are on private islands—completely guts them and turns them into these magical kingdoms. A one-night stay at one of his hotels is said to cost around two-thousand dollars, depending on the location.

Jeffrey waves his hand, gesturing me toward a tiny little boat that actually resembles more of a raft with a motor. "After you, Ms. Isabella."

I hesitate, unsure if I'm ready to risk my life. "Is this…safe?"

Jeffrey laughs at my hesitancy. "Of course it is. I've been doing this for twenty years. You're in good hands, dear."

His warm smile calms my nerves slightly as I take his hand and allow him to help me step into the boat. With only three seats, it's quite small. I suppose something larger isn't needed, since it's just me taking this trip.

"How long is the ride?" I ask him, hoping that it's not too far.

"A short ten minutes."

Okay. I can do ten minutes.

I've never been a fan of water. Don't care much for swimming. Went on a boat once with my parents and Mark and threw up all over the side of it. I prefer that my feet stay on solid ground, especially since I'm somewhat of a ditz and tend to do myself more harm than good.

Jeffrey looks over his shoulder. "Ready?"

Biting hard on my bottom lip, I nod as the motor purrs to life.

What starts off as a slow tug, quickly turns into us skating over the water at full speed. It looks as if we're driving straight into the fire glow of the sunset. My hair catches in the wind as I hold tightly to my suitcase. My heart is settling in my stomach, but the breathtaking view calms me slightly.

A few minutes pass and we start to slow down. I look past Jeffery at the immaculate structure in front of us. "Is this where we're going?"

Jeffery looks over his shoulder with a crooked smile.

"Welcome to Cori Cove, Ms. Jenkins. One hundred private acres surrounded by water with a castle sitting as the heart of the island. Also known as your home for the next six months, or longer, if you decide to never leave."

"Oh, I doubt I'll stay forever. Though, I might not mind this short escape from civilization."

2

WE COME to a stop at a long dock that stretches out over the water. There's a small tin boat without paddles, but that seems to be the only way off the island, aside from public transport. Jeffrey steps onto the dock and offers me his hand.

I smile warmly. "Well, thank you for the ride." Jeffery is a stranger that I've known all of thirty minutes, and I can't help but feel like he's my last encounter with another person, outside of Cori Cove, for a very long time.

"Up the dock, follow the steppingstones and you'll see the main doors. Mr. Ellis is expecting you." Jeffery checks me with a smile. "See you in six months, Ms. Isabella."

I just stand there. Watching as he pulls away. The little orange boat becomes nothing more than a speck in the wide-open water. Once it's faded from view, I turn around and look up at the castle staring back at me.

Made of stone and ashlar over a century ago, the castle stands tall and fierce. Likely weathered by storms and neglect, its wear only adds to its beauty. The turret on the very top of the castle catches my eye and I can only imagine how gorgeous the view is from up there.

From what I've read about the monumental castle of Cori Cove, it hasn't been inhabited by people for over forty years. Passed down from generation to generation by an English family, the Bromleys, I believe. The last owner opted to forgo the legacy and sold it—to Mr. Ellis, I assume.

The sun is dipping low in the clouds and there's only minutes of daylight left. I get a grip on my suitcase handle and begin walking down the dock. Each step has me feeling all the more permanently affixed to this place.

It's only six months. It is not a life sentence.

I've never been bold. Never taken risks or chances. I've got no idea what to expect as I walk at a leisurely pace toward the front of the structure. There is not much information regarding the Ellis family online. All I know is that the former Mr. Ellis passed away around seven or eight years ago and his son has taken over the business. I'm imagining a burly man with a beard and a 'better than thou' attitude, though, who am I to speculate? This man doesn't know a thing about me outside of my resume filed with the job search company I desperately sought out. Waiting tables at the local diner can only take someone so far and there isn't much demand for an interior designer in Hickory Knoll. So, here I am.

The scent of wet cement fills my senses as I walk up the steppingstones. Each one is half-buried in the dirt while the other half is covered in lime green moss. There's some sort of engraved design on them, but I wouldn't be able to make it out even if I dug them up.

I do take note of the two-lined engraving on a slab of cement sitting on two knee-high pillars.

Welcome to Cori Cove.

Where secrets hide and desires lurk.

That's an odd welcome sign.

When the stones end, I step onto the broken cobblestone beneath a granite arch. From here, I'm able to see the front entrance. Two very wide double doors with paint chipping away. It seems there's a lot of work to do, starting with the entryway. I envision antique wooden doors with black, wrought-iron, U-shaped handles. Fresh steppingstones and a new sign out front. That one is just creepy. *Secrets and desires?* Guests would assume they're walking into a swingers' resort.

Swallowing hard, I reach for the handle on the door, but to my surprise, it's already opening. "Good evening, Ms. Jenkins. We've been expecting you." From the other side of the door, an older gentleman greets me with a thick Boston accent. He's wearing a black butler's suit with one hand behind his back and the other on the door. His fluffy white beard is peppered with streaks of black and his blue eyes are soft and inviting.

"Hello. And thank you. I'm happy to be here." It's partially true. I am excited for the job. As long as this unsettling feeling diminishes quickly, I'll be fine.

I step inside as he holds the door open. As I'm looking around at the very large open space, the door closes with a thud, startling me.

The butler takes my suitcase and motions for me to follow him. "Right this way. Mr. Ellis is expecting you."

Gripping the strap of my purse, I follow behind him. It's apparent the hotel still at the construction point. It's damp and that smell of wet cement returns. Straight in front of me is stone-arcading supported by columns. It's completely open to the outside, allowing anything or anyone to come in and out. It looks as if it leads to the backside of the property. There's a puddle to the left and I look up to see an actual hole chiseled in the concrete ceiling. I guess the settlers didn't believe in drywall or boards back then.

The walls are completely bare, with only a clay-like color that actually resembles clay. No paintings, no decorative hangings. Not even a glamorous chandelier. I hope this place at least has electricity and running water.

Following behind the butler, we round a few corners and stop at an elevator. To my surprise, it's not old, nor stone. It looks like it was just put in. With two very wide stainless-steel doors. We step inside and it smells like fresh paint and fresh wood.

I watch as my guide presses the number eight on the panel, which appears to be the top floor.

When we come to a stop, the doors slide open and I follow his lead. The hallway is dim, lined with lanterns hanging from the cement wall. All lit with dancing flames.

I look around and it's like we've stepped into an entirely different castle. The floors are clean, without a crack to be seen. The walls are coated with a layer of glossy epoxy and that smell...it's weirdly familiar—lemongrass and a hint of mint—it smells like the home I lived in as a child.

Unease swarms in my belly. A blast from the past. A lifetime of memories hit me at once.

Me. Him. Us. Then and now. What we were and what we're not. What we'll never be.

It doesn't happen often, but every now and then, Cal gets into my head and reminds me of the choices I've made. I tried to find him a couple times but never had any luck. For years, I wondered what his life had become. Did he get out? Find a family? Is he married with kids? Is he even alive?

With my mind wandering back to another time, I don't even realize that the butler has opened the door to a room. He stands there with his hand pressed to it. "Ms. Jenkins? Is everything okay?"

I snap out of my thoughts and acknowledge him, "Yes. I'm sorry."

"As I said, this will be your room."

I take a step forward, and gasp when I see the beauty behind the door. "This? Is mine?" I look at him for assurance, because it's far too spectacular. This isn't just a measly hotel room. It's a room built for a queen, or at the very least, a princess. French doors that lead to a private balcony made of the original stone structure.

Bright, white paint covers the stone walls. A king-size bed sits in the center of the room with a large baby pink canopy overtop. The white lace that lines it dips into small *V*'s and every centimeter of fabric is precisely cut. The canopy alone must have cost a fortune. The bedding matches in color, dressed in a soft satin.

There's a large vanity with a stool and a matching white dresser on the opposite wall. A large, white, wooden jewelry box catches my eye. As we pass by, I lift the top and a balle-rina pops out. A tune begins playing and I shut it quickly because of the familiar sound.

The butler steals my attention as he lugs my suitcase across the hardwood floor.

I follow behind him as he walks toward, what I take to be, a walk-in closet.

"This is all yours, Ms. Jenkins."

I'm staring into a room that is big enough to be a bedroom. But that's not what takes me by surprise. It's the dozens of ball gowns. Every shade imaginable. On another wall are shoes—heels, flats, pumps, sandals. I grab a pair and hold them up—even tennis shoes?

"There must be some mistake. Why would all of this be in my room? I'm just a measly interior designer."

"Mr. Ellis makes no mistakes." He sets my suitcase upright and leaves the closet.

I set the shoes down and walk briskly behind him. "Excuse me, what did you say your name was?" I grab his arm and go to spin him to face me as confusion washes through me.

"Peter. Peter Blake."

I drop my hand and bite my bottom lip, trying to understand what all this means. My thumb shoots over my shoulder. "Are those his wife's clothes?"

"Mr. Ellis is not married," he says point-blankly.

"Daughter?"

"No kids."

"Hmm. Okay. Could you please take me to him? I just feel as if he's mistaken about my stay here." The assistant I spoke with was very specific about my duties. This is a job, not a vacation.

Peter folds his hands in front of him and nods, very properly at that. "Of course."

As we continue down the hall, it begins to feel more and more like we're in a finished home. There's an open sitting room that's decorated immaculately. All-white furniture, a gray shag rug in front of the larger couch. Fresh flowers in a vase sitting on top of... I stop walking, gawking at the grand piano in the room. It's beautiful. Hand-carved wood, stained in a cherry finish.

"Ms. Jenkins?" Peter quips.

Right. I peel my eyes off the piano and scurry down the hall behind him.

A new smell invades my senses—garlic. "Is there a kitchen on this floor?"

"The kitchen is on the first floor, not to be mistaken with the main entrance on the ground floor. Dinner is being served shortly."

"Do you stay on this floor?" I feel redundant asking so many questions, but this is nothing like I'd imagined.

"The live-in staff stays on the sixth floor."

Isn't that what I am, though? Live-in staff?

At the risk of driving this man crazy with all my questions, I offer some light humor. "I suppose your room wasn't equipped with enough dresses to attend a lifetime of balls?"

He doesn't respond as he continues on his path. Guess he doesn't do humor.

Peter stops in front of another door at the very end of the hall. "Here we are."

He just stands there, looking as if I'm expected to open the door and shout, *"I'm here."*

Finally, he taps his knuckles to it.

"Come in," a gruff voice trails through the sliver of an opening between the floor and the door. The vibration of his voice climbs through me and leaves me feeling anxious to put a face to the sound.

Peter turns the knob and pushes the door open. Cautiously, I step around him and look inside. A door at the end of the room closes and Mr. Ellis is nowhere in sight.

My eyes skim the room. There's a very dark feel to it. A large desk is placed in front of a wall-sized window. Above it is elegant stained glass with the design of a tree and fallen leaves. The roots are the focal point of the artwork. Spread along the entire bottom, ending where the glass meets the window beneath it.

There's an antique artifact sitting on a tall, black pedestal of a naked woman with her hand on her chest that looks like it was made from limestone. Beside it is a large black couch that looks like it's never been sat on. Then, there's a square, glass table with a chessboard on top of it. The walls are white, aside from an accent wall that is black and displays a large, vintage-looking clock. It smells like black currant and spice and it's most definitely a man's office.

My body jolts when the door closes and I realize Peter

has left. My legs begin to feel weak and wobbly as I stand here alone.

"Hello," I call out, looking toward the other closed doors in the room.

"Have a seat. I'll be out in a minute."

That voice again. It's masculine and stern. Sexy and mysterious.

I walk over to the desk and take a seat in the leather chair in front of it, opposite the chair I presume to be his. It looks more like a throne made for a king. There are chess pieces jutting from the back corners. All black, leather, with snake heads on the ends of the arms. It's actually pretty creepy.

The door that Peter just walked out of opens back up, causing me to look over my shoulder. A man walks in. He's not dressed in business attire. Instead, he appears sharp in a pair of beige shorts and a tucked-in polo shirt with a Manila folder placed under his arm. Slicked-back, blond hair, gorgeous blue eyes, and a muscular build.

"You must be Bella," he says chipperly as he joins my side. He extends his hand and I return the gesture.

He's the first to call me, Bella. While that's what everyone I'm close with calls me, my legal name is Isabella. "I am. You must be Mr. Ellis."

"Oh no," he chuckles, "I'm Byron Davis, his attorney."

My brows shoot to my forehead. "Attorney?"

"That's right. Mr. Ellis is tied up on a business call at the moment, so we're taking this time to finalize contracts."

"Oh, right." I nod. When I got the call for the job from Mr. Ellis's assistant, she mentioned paperwork and contracts.

Opening the folder, Byron shuffles through some documents and pulls out a small stack. "Go ahead and have a seat. This shouldn't take long."

Once he finds a pen, he hands it to me and points to an X

on the paper. "You're welcome to read through them if you'd like."

I've never been one to read through legal documents and it hasn't bit me in the ass yet. I'm getting a job. I'm staying on the job site. And I'm getting paid more than I would ever ask for. I press the pen to the paper and sign my name. He flips a page and I sign again, and again, and again.

"That should be all. I'm excited to see what you and Mr. Ellis do with the place. You'll see me around from time to time."

"Thank you," I say to him. He tips his chin and turns to leave the room.

As one door shuts, another opens. I look over my shoulder, and that's when I see him.

At least, I think it's him.

3

STARING BACK at me is a gorgeous statue of a man, standing at least six-foot-three. Black, disheveled hair. Skin that doesn't look like it's seen sun in years. Eyes so dark they're almost black. He's wearing a black suit, tailored to fit him perfectly. There's a bit of scruff on his face, but it only adds to his appeal.

A strange feeling washes over me. There is something oddly familiar about him. *Have I met this guy before?*

"Hello, Bella," he says, standing afar and taking me in while I do the same. Those two words are like music singing to my soul. I can't pinpoint exactly what it is, but I feel like I've known him for years.

I should get up. Greet him properly. Though, I don't move as he comes closer. His eyes boring into mine, as if they're searching for something.

Swallowing hard, I take in a deep breath to try and steady my racing heart. "It's nice to meet you." I finally stand. Stepping around the chair, I meet him face to face.

"This is a beautiful place." Breaking the gaze I hold on him, I give the room a lazy sweep. Looking into those eyes is dangerous. They have the ability to turn off all logical thinking, while paralyzing my whole body.

With his feet planted firmly to the floor beneath him, he folds his hands in front of him. "It will be."

His voice, again, sends a rapid-fire of electricity through me.

It's apparent he's a straight-to-the-point man and doesn't mind that he's making me feel highly intimidated at this moment.

Tension sizzles between us as we stand there silently. Even if I was standing here completely naked, I'd still feel the same level of exposure I'm feeling right now.

Say something, Bella.

I go with the first thing that comes to my mind. "I met your attorney and signed the contracts."

He gives a subtle nod, keeping the same blank expression on his face. Not even a tug at his lips.

"Okay," I drop my shoulders, "I'll just see myself to my room and we can get started in the morning?"

Nothing. Not a hint of a smile, nor a frown. This man is completely zombified, and even if he is freakishly handsome, it's sort of creeping me out.

I press my lips together firmly and walk to the door.

"You've changed."

His words catch me by surprise. I turn around to face where he stands. Puzzled, I question his statement. "I've changed?"

"Your eyes." He takes a step closer, examining me all over again. Each step has my heart sinking deeper into the pit of my stomach. "They once spoke to me. I could read your thoughts with just a look."

That strange feeling washes over me again. *No.*

It can't be.

I push away the bizarre thought. Tilting my head, I look

into his eyes, probing for the reason behind the familiarity. It's uncanny. But I refuse to believe that the man in front of me is Callum.

Concentrating on his face, I dig deeper. Dark brown orbs that wear a lifetime of pain. I see loneliness. I see hate for the world he's forced to live in. I see him—Callum. Fourteen years old, standing at the dormer window in the attic. The same eyes that looked back at me as I drove away. His stare shot through me with more force than a silver bullet. Much like this moment.

He comes closer, eating the foot of space between us. Looking down on me, his warm breath clouds my logic. "We meet again, Bella." The way my name rolls off his tongue makes me dizzy.

"Oh my God!" My hands clap to my mouth. I'm speechless. It really is him. In an instant, I throw myself into his arms while he remains impervious. His arms are draped at his sides, his expression still as serious as ever. "I can't believe it's really you." I can't think straight. The words I'm choking on as they come out of my mouth are barely audible. I pull back, looking up at him. "How? How did this happen?"

His eyes bore into mine, though, they're different. Everything about him is different. What once was a tall and lanky boy with glasses and in desperate need of a haircut, now stands before me as a muscular grown man with facial hair and a jawline that could chisel glass.

"Fate," he finally says. One simple word that speaks a thousand different volumes.

"Fate?" Am I naive to think that fate brought us back together?

I'm sure Cal can see the rapid beating of my heart as we stand mere inches apart. Yet, he fosters the same hard glare he's had since the second I looked at him. Proof that fate did not bring us back together. He orchestrated this. He brought me here.

"You've had a long day of travel. The cook has brought dinner to your room. Go eat and get some sleep. We'll talk tomorrow.

"But, I—"

"Tomorrow," he says sternly.

I nod in response. Hesitantly, I take a few steps back and turn around to leave.

When I reach the door, I glance over my shoulder. Cal has given me his back as he fidgets with his phone.

Tomorrow.

4

"SMILE, Callum. This is a good day. You finally get a home," Mrs. Webster says as I sit nervously on the porch, waiting for my new parents to pick me up.

I haven't smiled in almost a year and I'm not sure that look is possible at this point. I'm not upset that I'm finally getting out of this hellhole, but I hate people, especially ones that know my misfortunes. I've been pitied for far too long and I'm ready to take the world by the horns and ride out of this bitch on my own. I don't need anyone.

A vehicle comes down the gravel driveway and it's not what I expected at all. The sun bounces off the fresh coat of wax on the shiny black car, blinding me. I turn my head, squinting my eyes while still trying to look. It's most definitely a Mercedes, though I'm not able to make out what kind. Maybach, maybe? I might be washed-up goods, but I know cars. In fact, reading a book every day for five years has made me exceptionally smart, even if I don't apply my knowledge to my schoolwork.

"Here we go." Mrs. Webster grabs my dingy black bag that holds the only things I need. My writing book, my memory box, and a clean pair of underwear.

I run my fingers over my bald head, remembering that I have no hair left. Bibs thought it would be a good idea to freshen me up with a haircut before leaving, and she royally fucked up so Mrs. Webster had to shave it all off. I look like Mr. Clean, waiting for a flood in these pants, and I wouldn't be surprised if the car turns back around and leaves us standing here in dust. Who the hell would want me? Especially someone who drives a car that nice.

An elderly man steps out of the back seat and I'm confused as fuck. He's old enough to be my great-grandfather. Why would he want a rebellious teenage boy living in his house?

This process was a bit different for me. Most of the kids meet their adoptive parents before pickup, but not me. It wouldn't surprise me if Mrs. Webster sold me just to get me out of her damn house. Not that I care. At least I'm getting out.

"Hello there," the gentleman says. He offers a hand, but I just look at it, then slide my eyes up to his. They're warm and welcoming behind his glasses.

"Aren't you a little old to be adopting a kid?"

The man chuckles, and Mrs. Webster swats my arm. "Forgive him. He's a jokester."

"It wasn't a joke."

"I'm Peter," the man says, trying again with the hand.

Instead of giving it a shake, I bump my fist to his hand. "Callum. But you can call me, Cal." I snatch my bag away from Mrs. Webster. "Let's get the hell outta here."

Mrs. Webster grabs my attention as I walk away. "Callum?"

I turn around and give her one last look. "Take care of yourself."

And then it happens—I smile. "I plan to."

When you enter the world alone, you have to take care of yourself. No one else is gonna do it for you.

My body shoots up in the bed as I pant, trying to catch my breath. I look behind me at the sweat spot on the black, satin pillowcase.

I prepared myself for the possibility that the nightmares would get worse, but in reality, nothing can prepare either of us for what's to come.

5

I SHOULD HAVE DUG DEEPER. Asked him how he found me and why he brought me here. It certainly wasn't for my expertise in interior design.

God, I'm such an idiot. Here I thought that this successful man saw my portfolio and was impressed with my skills and actually wanted me to work on the scheme of his hotel. I thought this was my big break. Freedom from the chains that hold me down. My guilt-free escape from a small town where you only grow as big as your parents.

Unless? Unless Cal was searching for a designer and just happened to come across my info at the job agency and he was impressed, only to learn that I was a blast from his past. Maybe he wants to rebuild the friendship we once had. Or maybe he wants more.

He's a godly form of man, that's for sure. I'm not sure I've ever even talked to a guy as sexy as him. I've always been a pretty forthright person, but Cal stole my breath away and left me unable to comprehend a sentence, and that was before I realized it was him.

My best friend grew up fucking hot as hell, and filthy fucking rich.

Stop thinking, Bella.

A beam of light casts through the glass doors that lead to the balcony, reminding me that it's now morning and I haven't slept. I'd credit it to being in a ginormous castle that's been desolate for forty years, but that doesn't even faze me.

It's him. The way he looked at me like I was a stranger who came on his property uninvited. He barely spoke, yet when he did, goosebumps danced across my skin.

Tugging the comforter aggressively, I curl into a ball on my side. My eyes wide open as I stare into the closet. He bought me dresses. Cal knew how much I loved them, and he bought them just for me. Why?

I know that I never forgot about him, but I was certain he'd forgotten about me. We spent four short years together at The Webster House. Four years compared to the twenty-six of his life. So why now? Why me?

Tossing back and forth, I try to drown out the pounding at the door, hoping for just an hour of sleep. When it continues, I drag myself out of the bed and pull on my robe that's lying on the footboard.

When the knocks become more forceful, I pick up my pace as I make my way across the room. "Coming," I holler. Turning the crystal knob of the Victorian door handle, I pull it open. "Peter. Good morning."

Peter graciously folds his hands together in front of him. "Good morning, Ms. Jenkins. Mr. Ellis has requested your presence in the dining room."

"Really?" I rub a fist into my tired eyes. "What time is it?"

"Six a.m."

I nod. "Six a.m.? Okay. Please tell him I'll be there shortly."

Why are we up this early? Surely, this won't be the normal business hours?

Everyone is so formal here and I can't help but feel inferior. I'm not fancy, proper, or even well-mannered. I use informal words and have the mouth of a sailor.

Peter leaves and I close the door behind him. I could really use a shower, but I don't want to keep Cal waiting. Besides, more than anything, I need answers.

I quickly throw myself together with my hair twisted into a bun on the top of my head. I opt for a black skirt and a cream-colored, knitted sweater. Hopefully it's appropriate for the occasion. Then again, it's six o'clock in the morning, so Cal shouldn't expect much from me.

I make my way down the hall. I remember passing a dining room on the way in, so hopefully I'm able to find it on my own.

There's a chill in the air this morning, but I'm not sure if it's due to the weather, or the ghost of my past lingering around me.

Two minutes later, I find myself looking into a large sitting room. The one that has the piano. It's been at least five years since I've even played. There was a time my fingers danced across the keys for hours a day. Cal would sit beside me while he wrote stories in his notebook and most of the time, we never spoke, we just enjoyed each other's company.

Once I left The Webster House, I took lessons for a couple years. Even played in a musical during freshman year, but I was never a fan of the attention. Slowly, the passion fizzled out and was replaced by school and friends.

Tiny hairs on my neck prick when someone comes up behind me. Not just anyone. It's Cal. I can feel him standing there. Stray strands of hair hit my face with each exhale he makes. "Do you like it?"

I don't turn around as I gaze into the room. "It's beautiful."

"Steinway 1942. When I got her, she was pretty dinged-up. A few coats of lacquer and she's as good as new."

My jaw drops open and I turn around to face Cal, not realizing he's so close. Our noses almost collide and I take a few steps back. "Is it… Did you—"

Cal nods, knowing exactly what I was going to ask. It's the same piano I used to play as a kid.

"When The Webster House was shut down by the county, everything was auctioned off. I was able to get a few priceless things out of that mess."

I knew Mrs. Webster was convicted of sex trafficking about five years after I left. Apparently, the older girls were forced to "work" on the weekends. I only knew of one girl who was placed there at the time and my heart broke for sweet Bibs.

I look up at Cal, tears threatening to break free. "I wish I could have done something to help those girls."

Had I stayed, maybe I could have protected them. Bibs was eventually placed in another home until she was old enough to leave two years ago. I reached out to her last year. She's having a hard time with life but getting by. I promised her we'd keep in touch, but time sort of got away from me.

Cal holds his stare on me. "Maybe you could have." He steps around me and walks into the room, hands in the pockets of his black dress pants. "But you chose to leave and now you have to live with that choice."

He's right. I did make the choice to leave. A few steps forward bring me into the room. There's a large window that overlooks the mountains on the island. "You would done the same thing." He can lie and tell me he wouldn't have, but he'd have left too.

His fingers trail featherlike over the closed lid of the

piano as he walks around it. Finally stopping, facing my direction. "That's where you're wrong, Bella. I made a promise and I keep my promises."

One hand still in his pocket, he waits for a reaction from me. But I don't even know what to say. I decide to go with the response he's likely waiting for. "I'm sorry, Cal."

"It's Callum. No one calls me Cal." No smile that tells me he's fucking with me. No wink, no flutter of his lashes.

What happened to the boy I used to know?

"But, I've always called you Cal."

"You called your friend Cal. I am not your friend."

Like a knife straight to the heart, my hands fly to my chest as I try to catch my breath. "Are you angry with me?" Chances are he'll lie and say he's not, but he's distant and cold. It's apparent he's harboring some bitterness toward me.

As he should. No matter how I feel about the choice I made and no matter what my reasoning was, he'll never understand because he didn't have to make the choice. I did. I was the one in that position because Cal was reckless and troublesome. If I'd left it up to him, we'd have been in that home until we were eighteen years old. I would have been sold to the highest bidder on the weekends. Not him.

"How can I be angry with someone I don't even know?" He stalks toward me and when I think he's going to stop and elaborate, he keeps going. Leaving me standing in the room alone.

I pivot around and watch him walk away, but not before hollering at him over his shoulder. "You got a good life, Cal. Look at all this." My arms wave around the room. He doesn't even acknowledge me. Just keeps walking until he disappears down the hall and into a room I take to be the dining room.

He *did* get a good life. Cal has anything anyone could ever dream of. If anything, he was better off without me.

My black flats traipse across the floor as I walk briskly down the hall. Following the same path that Cal did, I find him taking a seat at the head of the twelve-foot, oblong table. The room looks like something out of a magazine. There's an entire row of windows with stained-glass panels. A large crystal chandelier hangs from the ceiling. A dozen cream-cushioned chairs organized perfectly around the table.

I stop in the doorway, cross my arms over my chest, and lean against the doorframe. "What did you mean when you said you don't know me?"

Cal jabs his fork into a perfect triangular piece of pancake and stuffs it into his mouth, watching me intently as he chews. "Sit down. You need to eat."

Taking a stance, my feet stay planted. "I'm not sitting anywhere until you tell me what you meant."

"Suit yourself. Your hunger only hurts you, Bella."

"My name is Isabella. Only my friends call me Bella, and if I remember correctly, you're not my friend."

The corner of his lip tugs up as he looks down at his plate and bites back a smile. Maybe he's human, after all.

He may be human, but he's still stubborn as an ox. Against my better judgment, I walk into the room, my eyes glued to him as I lift the lid on the tin platter and grab a pancake with my hand.

Cal looks from me to the tongs sitting beside it and I, ever so gracefully, drop the pancake onto a plate with a smirk. Lathering it up nicely with syrup, I scoop some scrambled eggs and a few pieces of bacon, then sit down about four chairs away from him.

As much as I'd like to return his stubbornness, this food smells damn good.

Once I've taken a couple bites and my hunger begins to subside, I try again. "Why do you feel like you don't know me?"

Cal pats around his mouth with a cloth napkin, then sets it back in his lap.

"Should I know you?" He sticks another bite of pancake into his mouth.

"Well, yeah. It's me, Cal. We spent every waking minute of the day together for four whole years. For the longest time, you knew me better than anyone."

It's true. Cal knows my dreams, my secrets, the lies I've told. He's heard the stories of my harrowing childhood. And, I know his. Cal has always been quiet, but he let me in and, in some ways, it made me feel special.

Granted, it's been twelve years, but to say he doesn't even know me is crazy. We weren't just friends who shared the same house. We were so much more than that.

"Four years that meant nothing." He drops his fork on the plate and pushes it away from him.

"What are you talking about? It meant everything. Just because I left, doesn't mean I didn't care about you."

"Well, thanks for clearing the air, Bella. Everything is fine now." His chair slides back abruptly as he gets to his feet and attempts to leave.

Oh no, he doesn't.

I jump up, almost tipping my chair over. With syrup still on my lips, I round the table and step in front of him. "You're not walking away again. Not until you tell me why I'm here. How did you find me? If you're so angry with me, why not just let me live my life as if…"

"As if what, Bella?" He steps into the space between us. "As if I didn't exist?"

"No," my head shakes, "that's not what I meant." My shoulders drop in defeat. "I just want answers. Yesterday I thought I was meeting an older man with a beer gut who fell into money. Thought I'd be fixing up a hotel and making my own money. Then I come here and find this extravagant room made up for me with ball gowns, shoes, and the piano. This wasn't a coincidence, was it?"

"Well, you got one thing right. I do have money. Lots of it. But, I certainly don't have a beer gut and most definitely didn't fall into it. It was earned. I bled for everything I own." His lip curls, brows dipped into a tight V. "In response to your previous statement, just because it looks like a good life, doesn't mean it is. The light you see on the outside only shines because of years of darkness on the inside."

His chest is heaving by the time he finishes. I can tell I've hit a nerve and dammit, I don't want to. I just want to make things right. No matter what he thinks, I do care about him. Probably more than he will ever know.

"You're right. Perception is everything. Maybe it's time you consider the fact that I left because I wanted to avoid the darkness. Why does that make me such a bad person?"

"I never said you were a bad person. You wouldn't be here if I thought you were."

My breath hitches as I search for the answer to the question that's been lingering since last night. "Why am I here?"

"To work. For me." Cal's cold fingers brush my cheek before tucking a stray strand of hair behind my ear. "Now eat."

"What happened in the last twelve years that made you this way? Why are you so bitter?"

Cal drops his hands to his sides and bares his teeth as he speaks, "If you even have to ask that question, then you're more of an idiot than I thought you were."

"Oh, so now I'm an idiot?"

His eyebrows elevate, the tension between us coiling with each breath. "You really don't get it, do you?"

I do get it, but no matter how I explain my reasoning, I know it'll never be good enough. "I messed up, Cal." My chest rises and falls quickly as I confess my own sins. "I was scared that you'd just keep getting in trouble and we'd be stuck there forever. I had no time to think about it, so I reacted."

"Without even a goodbye? Was I that insignificant to you?"

"It would have been too painful. I was worried I'd change my mind. You were the only person in the entire world who ever gave a damn about me and no explanation at the moment felt fitting. So, I just left."

I never even packed my things, just grabbed the photo of my mom and wore the stringy dress I'd put on that morning. There was nothing in that house I wanted to take with me— except Cal, but that was impossible.

"Then maybe you should try and see things from where I'm standing. Because you were the only person in the entire world who ever gave a damn about me, and you left me. You may not have been the one to deal me this shitty hand called life, but you stretched that hole inside of me and because of it, I entered a new world of suffering. A world that you now get to live in."

A tear falls from the corner of my eye, and I sweep it away. "So, what? You want to own me? That's impossible. You can't just keep me here."

Cal's breathing becomes heavy, his eyes glowering at me. "Want to?" he grinds out. "I already do own you." Two hands grab me by both arms and slam my back against the wall, stealing my breath. "You see, this was no accident, Bella. I brought you here and I *will* keep you here."

For the first time ever, I'm scared of Cal. Like really fucking scared. "Why do you want to hurt me?" I choke in an outbreath.

"Because you hurt me." His gaze dips downward and he lets out a low grumble. "For the past twelve years, I've wondered what you look like, what you smell like, what makes you smile, and most importantly, what it feels like to be inside of you. Your tight walls clenched around my cock."

Bile rises up my throat, and I swallow it down. "Please move."

His eyes ride back up to mine as he positions his hand between my legs, trailing his fingers up my inner thigh under my skirt. "Tell me, Bella, have you been fucked in the last twelve years?"

I don't answer when he blows out a menacing laugh. "Of course you have. You're what, twenty-three now? A body like this doesn't go untouched for that long."

Without denying or confirming his assumption, I roll my eyes and look away from him.

Cupping my crotch, he presses his fingers against my entrance through the fabric of my panties. "Please, Cal. Don't do this." Tears fall carelessly down my cheeks and I swallow hard.

Warm lips graze the shell of my ear. "You want me to stop?"

I nod repeatedly in response.

His head comes back up and he looks at me while I continue to cry silently. "Then why are you so wet?"

My heart begins racing as tingles trickle through my entire body. Pressure builds inside of me and it's burning hot. I'm disgusted with myself for being partially turned on by his forward behavior. "I...I'm not."

Cal pushes my panties to the side and begins rubbing circles feverishly at my entrance. His eyes skate down to my mouth and he leans forward, darting his tongue out and licking a tear off my lips. I'm completely caught off guard when his mouth collides with mine. I squirm and try to pull back, but it does no good. I might as well be shackled in chains and handcuffed to this wall.

The taste of syrup and salty tears seeps into my mouth

when his tongue enters. "Mmm," he hums, "You taste better than I ever could have imagined.

"Stop," I whimper into his mouth. "Just stop."

He finally pulls back, looking at me, and it's like he's had an epiphany of some sort. His eyes are suddenly full of awareness, and perhaps, guilt. He drops his hand from beneath my panties and they fall back in place. He goes to speak, but says nothing, before turning around and storming out of the room.

6

MY FEET DON'T STOP MOVING as I slam my bedroom door shut behind me. Pacing the length of the room, up and down, back and forth.

Stop. Just stop.

Those words were deafening. A wake-up call and a slap in the face at the same time. What the hell am I doing? I need to get some control over myself before I completely lose my mind and hurt us both in the process.

I should go downstairs, relieve some stress and clear my head.

No.

I'm done with that. I made a promise to myself that it would end the minute she came to the island.

Sweat gathers at my hairline, even though it's only sixty degrees in this room. Always sixty degrees. Never more, never less.

"Fuck," I bellow, gripping the sides of my head and tugging at my hair. My fingers dig deeper, nails scraping my scalp as memories of the past flood my mind.

"My name is Callum," I shout loudly at the crazy bitch standing in front of me.

"No, honey. You're just confused." She brushes my hair back with warm fingers. Her eyes are lit up like she really believes I'm her dead son standing in front of her. "Now, go eat your breakfast, so Peter can bring you to school."

My voice rises as I do everything Vincent forbids me to do. "I don't go to school. Wanna know why? Because you crazy people don't let me. You keep me locked in this house, pretending I'm someone I'm not, just so you don't have to face the truth."

Her hand presses flat against my forehead. "Are you sick, Caden?" Her eyes dart to my open bedroom door and she hollers, "Vincent. Come in here, please."

Vincent is my adoptive dad, and standing in front of me is my adoptive mother, who is three crayons short of a full box. I know exactly what the rules are. I also know what's coming from breaking them, but I hate this. Pretending to be someone I'm not, just so this lady can keep living in a fantasy world.

For the most part, I do as I'm told, but every now and then, I get fed up and this is one of those moments.

My heart rate excels as Vincent's footsteps come closer down the hall.

"Daddy will take you to the doctor and we'll make you all better, Caden."

Slapping her hand away from me, I scream, "I'm not Caden!"

That's all it takes for me to be gripped by the back of my shirt and anchored off the ground. Delilah continues to ramble nonsense to Vincent about how she thinks I'm sick and have a fever, but neither of us pay any attention as I'm being carried out of the room.

"I didn't mean to—"

"Shut your damn mouth," Vincent growls, taking me down the hall. The collar of my shirt digs into the skin of my neck and I can

41

feel my throat restricting. He stops outside my bedroom door and messes with the thermostat.

"No. Please. Not that. I'll do anything. I'll tell her I'm Caden. I'll let her read me a story. Just please, don't do that."

Vincent kicks the door open and tosses me inside. My body comes to a rolling stop in front of my bed and I sit up quickly as I watch his shiny black boots coming toward me. "I'm sorry," I cry out, "it was a mistake."

I keep scooting, trying to bide as much time as I can, although my punishment is inevitable. I open my mouth to speak, but nothing comes out as the back of Vincent's hand pierces my cheek. The sting lingers, but it's quickly replaced by the pain in my stomach as the point of his shoe meets my side.

"If you wanna be Callum, you can go back to that shack of orphans you came from. In this house, you will be Caden."

"Stop. Just stop," I beg of him.

The kicks continue, targeting every part of my body as the air in the room thickens to the point of suffocation.

Once I'm unable to move, or speak, Vincent finally leaves.

The door closes and each lock on the outside echoes through my body.

An hour or more passes and I'm finally able to push myself off the floor and strip out of my clothes. The temperature continues to rise until I'm vomiting on my own legs. It's at least one hundred and twenty degrees at this point, and I'm barely able to keep my eyes open.

So I shut them, drifting away to another lifetime. One I created just for myself. A castle on a private island where no one can touch me. Maybe she'll join me. Maybe I'll make her.

Delilah took her life the night before my eighteenth birthday. I think part of her knew I wasn't Caden. It was just easier to pretend I was. After all, that's the only reason Vincent adopted me—because I was a loser with nothing but a name, and the spitting image of his offspring. The next day, when I turned eighteen, everything changed.

I never knew Caden, but I knew everything about him. I lived his life, took over his room, and was given his name—not legally, though. Apparently, he died only months before the Ellises took me in. Delilah was always crazy, but the death of her son pushed her over the edge. She refused to accept he was gone, and Vincent refused to let her. So I played the part of the dutiful son, just biding my time until I could make Vincent pay.

And pay he did.

7

LAST NIGHT I had assumed it was only me, Cal, Peter, and
Cal's attorney on the island. Now it's been confirmed that
there's a Michelin star chef, a housekeeper, and a couple
security guards.

I haven't spoken to Cal since he assaulted me at breakfast,
so I've taken it upon myself to get familiar with the property,
even though the job feels moot at this point.

Peter is showing me to the back yard while I take notes
on a clipboard. It's an open exit with no wall covering or
doors. There's another arch positioned overtop where the
cement continues. A round glass table and a couple wrought-
iron chairs sit around it.

We step outside and I draw in a deep breath of fresh air.
"This is gorgeous," I say to Peter as he walks beside me.
"Could use a little upkeep, but there is so much potential
back here.

"Little is too weak of a word. I'd say massive is more
fitting."

I chuckle. "Okay. Massive.

"I envision a wet bar made of stone with pillars that extend up to an overhead canopy."

There's a curtain wall in the distance that looks like it goes beyond the length of the castle. To the right, I see a wooden bridge that doesn't seem stable enough to hold a small child, let alone an adult. I walk closer to see what's beneath it, and it looks like it's a man-made pond, though it's very small and only runs under the bridge. It's very pretty, though, and I can only imagine what it could become.

I continue to babble as we walk. "A separate garden area with wildflowers and fountains. Maybe a pond with goldfish. All of this with the breathtaking view of the mountains that rim the backside of the island. The possibilities are endless."

A gust of wind sends chills down my spine. Peter had mentioned a storm heading for the island, which had me a little nervous, until I remembered that this place has weathered storms for over a century and it's still standing tall.

Looking up at the sky, I take it all in. For a brief moment, I feel at ease. That is, until I level my eyes and see Cal standing five feet in front of me.

"Lunch is ready," he deadpans.

I don't even humor him with a response. Tilting my head, I look back up at the sky where a flock of birds flap hurriedly, likely fleeing the storm that's coming.

"Peter," Cal says, "please see Ms. Jenkins to the dining room."

Peter acknowledges him with a nod.

Once Cal is gone, I look at Peter. "You don't have to escort me. I can find my way." It's obvious Cal is angry with me. Hell, he might even hate me. After the way he fondled me, I should hate him.

Maybe my coming here is some sort of revenge scheme he's cooked up. After the tension during breakfast, I'm not sure that I'm ready to have a quiet meal with Cal again, at least not yet.

"Boss's orders. Besides, it will be my pleasure."

"I'm actually not very hungry." It's a lie. I didn't eat much at breakfast and I'm actually starving.

Peter shrugs a shoulder. "Mr. Ellis makes the rules. I only follow them."

Once I finish up my walk through the yard, or what will eventually be a yard, we head back inside. Peter follows behind me, hot on my trail. Instead of going to the dining hall, I go straight to the first floor where the kitchen is to get a plate of food directly from the chef.

"Ms. Jenkins, I do think you should have lunch with Mr. Ellis. You wouldn't want to anger him on your first full day."

"Oh, I think I've already angered Mr. Ellis." I smirk as I pull open the stainless steel door to the kitchen.

Just as I'm about to step inside, in my periphery, I see Cal coming out. Ignoring him completely, I go into the kitchen. Peter hangs back and I can hear his chatter from outside the door. "I tried but she's a mulish one, that girl."

"That she is," Cal hisses, jerking the door open. I step to the side, hoping to hide from him like a child, but it does no good.

Cal grabs me by the arm hastily. "Hey! What are you doing?" I attempt to jerk my arm away, but his grip tightens as he walks me out the door. "Let me go." I jerk again to no avail.

"You are here on a contract and that contract states that your living quarters are upstairs. Your lunch is waiting." He gives my arm an aggravated shove and heads toward the elevator.

My arms cross over my chest and I scowl at his backside. "And what if I don't?"

Cal eats back up the space he just took and gets right in

my face. "Then you're breaching your contract. Do I need to tell you what happens when a contract is breached?"

I swallow hard. He's dead serious right now.

"Cal?" I say his name in question. "Why are you doing this?"

I'm upset that he's behaving this way, but more than anything, it hurts.

He doesn't respond, just breathes fire into me as he clenches his jaw.

"I can't live like this for six months. If you expect me to work for you and abide by *your rules*," I air quote, "then I want answers."

He's silent for a moment before he exhales a drawn-out breath. "We can discuss the terms of your contract if you have lunch with me."

My head shakes. "That's not enough."

"Fine. We will discuss the terms of your contract and I'll tell you why you're here."

With my head held high, I walk to the elevator and press the arrow going up.

At least he's giving me something.

I don't have to turn around to see if he's coming. Something tells me that Cal will be one step behind me for the next six months.

Hugging my chest, I position myself in the corner of the elevator and avoid eye contact. It's too painful to look at him this way. Never in my wildest dreams did I think Cal, of all people, would treat me as if I were menial.

The elevator stops and Cal gestures for me to go first. Silence descends down the hallway as we walk to the dining room. I take a seat in the same spot I sat in for breakfast, sinking down in the chair. Whatever is under those lids smells damn good but lifting it up and eating right now means eating my pride as well, and I'm not ready to do that.

Cal pulls out the chair at the head of the table, his eyes fettered to me. Two arms lie flat against the table and he blows out a breath. "What would you like to know, Bella?"

I hate the way he says my name. It sounds so formal. Everything about Cal is serious now and my heart hurts when I think about what he must have endured to become the man he is.

I decide to start with the most obvious question. "Why am I here?"

Being the finicky person he is, he doesn't answer my question right away. Picking up a glass of caramel-colored liquid, he gives it a swirl, ice clanking against the small glass. He takes a sip, darts his tongue out at his lips and I catch myself watching each precise movement that he makes.

His eyes lift, catching mine. There's a glint of a smirk on his lips and it infuriates me.

Finally, he sets his glass down and levels with me. "You're not an easy person to track down, even for a man of my stature. I always knew I'd find you. I just never expected it would take this long. If it weren't for your submission to the job agency, it may have taken me another twelve years."

"So you *were* looking for an interior designer?"

Cal spews a devilish laugh. "My family name has been refurbishing rags to riches for over a century. Vincent Ellis's great-great-grandfather started this empire and it's been passed down from generation to generation. We certainly weren't in need of a twenty-three-year-old girl with an undergraduate degree and zero experience."

Pins poke at my chest. A sensation that I wasn't expecting. I'm actually rendered speechless.

"Come on, Bella. You have to have known that we employ top-tier designers from all over the world."

Clearing my throat, I choke out, "I suppose you're right. I

guess I was a fool to think that was real." I'm on the verge of tears but trying really hard to fight them off.

Cal pushes his chair back and comes over to where I'm sitting. Slouching down in front of me, his eyes smolder. "Cry, Bella. I can see you need to. Let me see those tears. Show me you're not the heartless bitch I take you to be."

I gasp at his words—completely caught off guard. "Excuse me?"

With knitted eyebrows, he watches me as if he's waiting for me to completely break down. Instead of giving him the emotion he wants, I push him back. "Screw you!"

He catches his fall, anger rippling through him. The shade of his eyes shifts from dark to crow black. Grabbing me by the wrist, he squeezes so hard I can feel the quickening of my pulse against his palm. "You wanna know why you're here, Bella? You're here because I caught you. My own little toy to pocket and keep. Running is no longer an option. The life you lived outside these walls is over. You're mine now and there isn't a damn thing you can do about it."

My bottom lip trembles. I've never been afraid of Cal before, but, at this moment, I've never feared anything more. "Why are you doing this?"

With flared nostrils, he sharpens his tone. "You did this."

His fingers are still wrapped tightly around my wrist, so much so that I can see the paleness in his knuckles. I pull back slightly, but he doesn't budge. No longer able to hold it back, tears fall from my eyes. Sliding down my cheeks and onto his cold, strained fingers. "I had no choice. You ruined everything that day by getting into trouble. In a split second, everything had changed and I had to make a choice."

His jaw clenches, lip curled. "And now you get to live with that choice."

My head shakes. "I want out of the contract. I'll go home and you can just forget about me."

"The same way you forgot about me?"

I'll never be able to make him understand, mostly, because I don't understand myself. I'm happy with the life I was given, but it took years for the guilt of leaving him to subside. Oftentimes, I ask myself if I would make the same choice if I had the chance to do it over again. And I don't even know if I would. That right there is the reason why I can't justify my leaving him.

My chin hits my chest as the tears continue to drop. "I never forgot about you. I thought about you every second of every day that first year. As time went on, you slipped further and further away. But, I never forgot and I never stopped caring about you."

Cal places his thumb on my chin, tipping it up. "I can guarantee after your stay here, I will never slip your mind again." His thumb slides across my lip, catching a tear before he pries my mouth open and jams it between my lips. The saltiness of my own woes hits my taste buds. I don't even try to force his thumb out of my mouth as he watches his own movements. "As for the contract," he continues, eyes locked on my mouth, "there is no escaping it."

Turning my head, I pull back and his hand drops. "All contracts are expungable at a cost. How much is it? Double the salary?" I don't have that kind of money to buy back my freedom, but I'm beginning to think that I'd find a way to come up with it if it meant I could leave. Cal isn't just angry with me; he hates me. Mentally and emotionally, I can't live like this for six months.

"That's where you're wrong. I have the best attorney in the nation and he was very clear in the contract that there are no provisions that give you the right to end the contract. If you do, I have the right to sue." Cal pushes himself to his feet. His palms clamp down on the arms of the chair and he leans forward, invading my personal space. "It won't get that far, though, Bella. I've ensured you will be staying here. If you don't, your perfect little family will lose everything they own." Warm lips press to my forehead. "Welcome home."

"What does my family have to do with this?" I sniffle. "What have you done?"

"It's not about what I have done. It's what I could do." Cal leaves me sitting here, devastated in a mess of my own tears. That man's heart is as stone-cold as the foundation of this castle.

8

"COME ON!" I hold my phone up, trying to get a signal. I've gone to every corner of my room and still nothing. I even went as far as dangling over the balcony and almost falling to my death. There's Wi-Fi in range, but it's protected and Peter played dumb when I asked him for the password. I could bite the bullet and ask Cal, but I doubt that will do any good. Besides, I'm in the middle of my own pity party and plan to avoid him for the next six months—as if that's possible.

It's apparent I'm not here to work. Cal calls himself my boss because those are the terms used in the contract, but the only thing he wants to micromanage is my emotions. If I had to guess, he wants me to feel like complete shit for leaving him. He's spent years dwelling on it and blames me for everything bad that has happened to him. Does he not realize that bad things happen to everyone? Even me?

The more I think about it, the more I believe Cal has been living in the darkness of his past for the last twelve years. Of course I feel bad for leaving like I did, but I was a kid. He's behaving as if I was an adult who made an adult decision. It's not fair.

Screw it. I'm getting that damn Wi-Fi password. With heavy steps, I cross the room and jerk the door open. I'm taken aback when I see Cal standing there. "Umm. Hi," I say, walking backward as he walks in, "can I help you?"

He doesn't respond, just looks around the room like it's his first time ever stepping foot in here. "I have to take a trip to Naushon this evening. I'll only be gone a couple hours. You'll have dinner in your room." He stops beside my bed and scoops up a pair of my clean panties. He holds them up as they dangle from his index finger, observes them, and drops them back down like they're contaminated.

I take long steps to his side and tuck my panties under the blanket of the unmade bed, pressing my hands against the comforter. "Why are you leaving?"

His head lifts and he looks me in the eye momentarily. "I have business to tend to." Glancing away, he takes in the rest of the room. "I'll send Paulina, the housekeeper, in to tidy up your room, but I expect you to be a little neater. We're not kids anymore, Bella."

A low grumble climbs up my throat. "That's a little hypocritical coming from someone who's still holding on to the past of their childhood." Tightening my upper lip, I step out the open doors onto the balcony. The grainy stone beneath me scrapes against my bare feet. My fingers wrap firmly around the stone banister as I look at the dark clouds rolling in. It's such a dreary day as it is, and now I've got my former best friend harping on my cleanliness, or lack thereof. He knows I've always been a bit of a slob.

Cal comes up behind me and my breath hitches when his hands plant on either side of mine. His chin is practically resting on my shoulder. "Maybe it's not the past I'm bitter about, maybe it's the present. Or both, perhaps."

His vocabulary has changed drastically. Like someone that just stepped out of a historical English novel. Cal never used words like 'perhaps.' He talked in slang such as 'gonna' or 'wanna' and now it's 'going to' or 'want to.' Everything about him has changed. He's gone from cold to ice. Angry with the world, to downright loathing it.

My eyes stay focused on the sky as if I'm speaking directly to the clouds. "You're the one who brought me here. If you don't like it, let me leave."

"Is that what you want?" His breath tickles the back of my neck as he speaks.

I'm not even sure how to answer that, so I go with the truth. "I'm not going to pretend this reunion has been a happy one. I always hoped I'd see you again, Cal, but I never could have imagined you'd treat me this way." I want to tell him how bad it hurts. Like a knife in the chest that twists and turns every time he talks down to me.

"You didn't answer my question. Do you want to leave the island?" Placid fingers sweep my hair to the side. Eyes shut, head tilting, as Cal's lips ghost the crease of my neck. Each breath sends chills riding down my body. My mind goes back to that foggy state it was in when I laid eyes on him less than twenty-four hours ago. Only this time, it's because I won't allow myself to think.

I'm not sure if I want to leave. Cal shouldn't be making my body demand attention from years of neglect. The pulsating between my legs, the prick at my nipples. He certainly shouldn't be the reason for my dampened panties and the cause of me having to clench my thighs. He just showed up out of nowhere. A missing piece in my life that is trying to find a place to fit while tossing other pieces to the side.

Pushing the sleeve of my shirt down, Cal exposes my shoulder. My eyes open quickly when his lips graze the skin. "Answer me," he demands, in a no-nonsense tone.

"Yes. I want to leave," I say on a clipped exhale.

Cal's mouth leaves my shoulder and he pulls my shirt back up. "That's a shame. But, unfortunately, you signed a contract, and I don't barter with employees bound by their signed contracts."

I snap around, facing his bemused smile. "I want a copy of that contract."

Cal places his hands behind him. His shoulders drawn back. "Not a problem. I'll have Byron bring a copy tonight."

With slumped shoulders, I ask one of the many questions gnawing at me. "Am I really here to work, Cal?"

"Yes. I will take your opinions on the design of the rooms on floors two through five. I may use your ideas; I may ignore them."

"And the pay that was agreed on in the contract?"

"You'll be compensated, per the agreement."

Biting the corner of my lip, I find myself lost in so many thoughts. "For six months?"

"For as long as it takes." Cal grins at me as if he has a plan already set in stone. My insides shiver when I think of what that plan might entail—me, as his plaything.

"Do you really plan on opening this up as a resort, or do you just plan on making this my own personal prison?"

"Someday, there will be guests." Grazing my cheek with the back of his hand, he licks his lips. "Make sure you eat your dinner tonight. The last thing I need to come home to is a hangry houseguest."

"Employee," I correct him. "I am not a houseguest."

"Tomayto, tomahto." His hand drops and he walks back inside my room.

"Cal, wait," I holler as I snatch my phone off the bed. He stops in the doorway, presses his hand to the frame, and looks at me with impatient eyes. I scroll to my Wi-Fi settings and hold it up as I walk toward him. "I have no service, but there's a signal in range. Could I have the password?"

His hand grips the door handle firmly. "No," he deadpans before slamming the door shut.

"Please," I shout, grabbing the handle and ripping the door back open.

I step into the hall where he's already halfway down. Jogging after him, I catch up and walk in step with him. "Please, Cal. I have a family. People who will worry about me if I don't stay in touch."

"Must be nice," he quips, continuing on his way.

Grabbing him by the bicep, I try to stop him, but he just keeps going, causing me to stumble over my own two feet. I hit the hard floor on my knees and begin sobbing where I sit. "Why are you doing this?" I scream so loudly that my words bounce off the cement walls. A lantern flickers beside me, then slowly fizzles out. "My fiancé knows where I'm at. He's planning to come here to visit at some point." My face drops into my hands and the tears keep falling.

It's partially true. I did tell Trent he could come for a visit. I was under the assumption I'd be staying in the hotel where I'd be working.

I'm completely caught off guard when Cal grabs me by the wrist and jerks me up. My wobbly legs give out as I fall into his arms. Fingers grip my chin relentlessly as he gets right in my face. "Then I'll fuck you and make him listen while you scream my name."

"Why are you doing this to me?" I whimper through heavy breaths.

"Because I lost you once and I will not lose you again."

"You can't seriously think you can just keep me here."

"You'd be surprised at what I *can* do." His eyes dance across my lips as my heart beats rapidly in my chest.

Even as he spews his threatening and hateful words at me, my traitorous body reacts. I blame fear for my life. Desperation to flee this place and never return. At this moment, I think I'd do just about anything to escape—even if it means giving all of myself to him.

When his eyes slide back up, I shake the thoughts away. Bile rising in my throat for even thinking that way. One more second in his close proximity and I just might vomit all over his shiny black shoes.

My chin is released, but we're still standing only inches apart. "When did you say yes?" Cal asks, his angry tone shifting to a more curious note.

"Say yes?"

"You referred to *him* as your fiancé. When did you accept his proposal?"

"Right before I left," I lie. I didn't say yes, but Cal doesn't know that. Maybe if he knows I'm spoken for, he'll drop this ridiculous idea of keeping me here as his prisoner.

Rigid cords tense along Cal's neck as he gnashes his teeth. "Why?" His voice rises to a near shout. "Why the fuck would you do that?" Shivers cascade down my body as he grabs me by both shoulders. "You're a damn fool, Bella."

Scowling back at him, I refuse to cower. "I've done perfectly fine living my life the way I see fit for the past twelve years." I attempt to walk around him, but his hold only strengthens. "I think I can make my own choices."

"Of all the guys," he tsks. "And you had to choose the one I hate the most in this world."

My eyes widen in surprise. *He knows.* I don't say anything else because whatever I do say will only make things worse. No part of me wants to hurt Cal, even if he is out for my blood as his revenge.

Cal turns around and looks down the hall, giving me his back. "I guess I should have seen it coming. You were always into shiny, pretty things. It's no surprise you'd marry into the uptight Beckham family."

"We were just kids then. Trent has changed. He's very smart and kind. He—"

"Shut up!" Cal spins back around, slapping a hand over my mouth, forbidding me to speak. "He's scum. A piece of shit on the bottom of my shoe."

Cal's fingers dig into the side of my cheek as he walks me back up against the wall. My head rests between two lit lanterns, the only source of light in this dim hall. Sliding his hand down my waist, chasing the shudders, he keeps going until he's reaching low with his hand on my inner thigh. I tremble as his hand drifts up, cupping my crotch through the thin fabric of my leggings. Angry eyes stare back at me. Dark, empty eyes that bore into mine and chase away any logic.

Our noses brush as his fingers grate at my entrance through my pants. "Does Trent make your legs shake the way I do?"

"You're disgusting," I growl, turning my head to avoid looking at his fixed glare.

With one hand pressed firmly to the wall on the side of my head and the other groping me, Cal draws in a deep breath of the air between us. "Tell me, Bella, do you enjoy being fucked by the guy who tore us apart?"

My eyes bolt to him. "What are you talking about?"

"Oh, he never told you? What about that brother of yours? Did he ever once mention their seditious act all those years ago?"

"You're lying," I spit out. "You just want me to hate everyone but you. Well, guess what, Cal?" I enunciate his name with a smirk on my lips. "I love them and I hate you." The words just drip from my mouth, out of both anger and fear. The truth is, I'm not sure I could ever hate Cal. There's a reason he is the way he is. We've both had to work extra hard to find our place in this world and something tells me, Cal had to do overtime.

Cal moves his hand, and when I think this game of cat and mouse is done, he slides it down the waistband of my leggings. The muscles in my stomach clench and I take in a shaky breath. His dark eyes glisten with mischief. "Love. Hate. Is there really a difference?" His fingers slide up and down my sex, rubbing at my entrance, for just a second, before he removes his hand from my pants. "You say you hate me, but I think you're loving this just as much as I am." His fingers shove into my mouth, causing me to gasp. I squirm, trying to get away, but I'm forced to taste myself on him.

Finally, Cal backs up, freeing me from his clutches, so I use this opportunity to get as far away from him as possible.

Walking hurriedly down the hall, I go back to my room and slam the door shut. There are no locks, and I'm certain that was no accident.

Eyeballing my phone, I think hard. I have to find a way off this island.

9

I'VE PACED the length of this room at least a dozen times. My thumbnail is down to the skin since I've been chewing relentlessly on it. I'm slowly going crazy, that's all I can come up with. Playing out every scenario in my head, they all come back to me being stuck here. It's certainly crossed my mind to try and hide on Cal's boat when he leaves tonight, but it's easier said than done. For one, there are guards. I know of two, but there could be more. Chances are, those guards are here just for me.

The only option I can come up with is trying to get to the small boat I saw by the dock when I arrived yesterday. There were no paddles, but I'll use a damn broomstick if I have to. I vaguely remember passing by an island, just beside this one, that looked inhabited. It would take me twenty, maybe thirty minutes on a boat without a motor. All I know is if I stay here, Cal will hurt me more than he already has. He will tear me down, probably rape me, and possibly kill me. I've come to the realization that my friend is no longer inside of him. The Cal I knew is gone, and I'm not sure if he's ever coming back.

Creeping down the hall, I listen intently for any sound that could mean someone is coming. Cal left a couple hours ago and said he'd be gone until dark. It's only five o'clock in the evening, so I have another hour, at least. I pass by Cal's room and curiosity gets the best of me, so I give the handle a turn, but it's locked. Of course it is.

Leaving everything behind except for my phone and the clothes on my back, I take the elevator down to the lower level.

The puddle I saw coming in has dried up to just a damp spot on the cement floor. I look up and see the hole has been filled and smoothed over. I wonder if Cal did that. I don't take him to be a carpenter or even a handyman. It's possible there are more people staying here than I thought.

There's a door off to the side I never noticed before. It's different from the other rooms in this place. This one has the old skeleton keyhole but also a modern-day password keypad.

Everything about this place is a mystery and I just need to get the hell out of here and off this island and never look back.

A gust of wind ripples over the backside of the castle. The overgrown bushes out back blow so heavily they practically cover the opening. Hugging myself, I head out the same way I came in. Pushing the large door open, I step out onto the cobblestone, looking out at the water in front of me. My eyes quickly dart to where the boat was and I breathe a sigh of relief when I see it's still there.

Hope washes over me. It's not going to be easy in these heavy winds, but it's either die trying or be at the mercy of a man who'd love nothing more than to shred me of any dignity I have left. Before the door closes behind me, I turn around and push it back open. Skimming the open area, I look for anything that can assist me in paddling.

"Yes!" I mumble. Long strides lead me in front of a couple strip boards perched against the wall beside the elevator. Dragging one behind me, I head down to the water.

I might not be physically fit, but I'm a survivor. I've proven that every day since I found my mom's corpse at the age of four. Addiction is an ugly thing and I'd love more than anything to erase those memories from my head. After two hours of staring at her in hopes of her waking up, I eventually realized she wouldn't. I kissed her forehead and ran to the neighbor's house. Twenty minutes later, I was put in the back of the car by a social worker and the adventures of foster life began.

I was in and out of so many homes that I lost count. Apparently, it's frowned upon when you're headstrong and speak what's on your mind. Slowly, I learned to keep my mouth shut. That's when I ended up at The Webster House.

The first time I saw Cal, it was like we instantly connected. Kindred spirits, soulmates—call it what you will, but it was special. My heart aches at what he's become. If I'd stayed with him, like I promised, maybe he wouldn't be so angry with the world.

Sucking it up, I swipe away the tears rolling down my cheeks. I drop the piece of lumber in the boat and it lands with a loud thud. The wind becomes turbulent as rain starts to fall. What starts as a light sprinkle quickly escalates into a full-on downpour. A thunderous boom shudders the ground beneath me at the same time a bolt of lightning lights up the sky.

In a matter of seconds, I went from bone dry to soaking wet. More rain comes as the wind picks up, pelting against my bare arms. I look down, trying to stop it from hitting my face.

"Why is this happening?" I cry out as another strike of lightning crackles through the clouds. Twisting and turning my head, I try to look out at the water, but it's a haze of cloudbursts and I can't see more than three feet in front of me.

I give the boat a push and when it doesn't even budge, I throw my full weight into it and push harder. "Come on, you damn thing." I try again, and it slowly begins to slip out of the muck it's lodged in.

Gripping the front of the boat, I crouch down and dig my bare toes into the moss and push with all my might. It slowly begins to slide out into the water, but with each inch that it is engulfed, the crazier this seems. I'm taking a rowboat out on the bay in the eye of a dangerous storm.

It's only a few minutes. I'll be able to dock at the closest island and call for help.

I'm knee-deep in the water beside the boat when I finally jump in. It rocks back and forth as I steady myself on the seat, wasting no time dipping the board in and paddling. I paddle to the left a few times then switch to the right, until I'm moving straight ahead, right into the torrent.

Rain pommels me, coating every inch of my waterlogged skin while the boat begins to fill. I blink away the drops formed on my eyelashes, trying like hell to see clearly, but it's impossible.

I'm not sure that I've ever been so scared in my life, and I've been through some horrific stuff. I just need to go straight out of here and then to the right until I see the island. Hopefully, the rain will let up and I'll be able to see where I'm going.

It's okay. I'll be okay.

Just when I think I'm far enough to begin turning toward the east, I spot dim lights shining through the smog. My heart beats at warp speed when they begin coming closer, and closer. Steadily, I begin rowing backward. Left side, right side, over and over, as if the bright light blinding me is what's pushing me back onto shore. I pinch my eyes shut, but I don't stop rowing.

They're going to hit me. It's not Cal or the storm that will end my life. I'll be pushed into the water by this huge boat.

My life flashes before my eyes. But, it's him I see. The smile he wore the first time I saw him at the age of ten.

At eleven years old, when I saw the first tear that rolled down his cheek when Mrs. Webster told him that his birth parents were dead and never coming for him. He held it together around everyone else in the house, but when we were alone, the tears fell.

That time when he was twelve and got a bloody nose in the middle of the night and I was so worried that he was going to choke on his own blood and die. I didn't sleep at all that night as I held the cloth so his sleepy eyes could rest.

When he was thirteen I caught him staring at me with a new look in his eyes as I played his favorite song on the piano. It gave me butterflies and I never understood why— until now.

At fourteen years old, I never even told him goodbye.

And now, I'll never be able to make him understand. He'll never get a proper apology and I won't know what filled his heart with so much anger.

I can't tell him about my first kiss, or hear about his first dance. I won't know what year he graduated, or from where. All the little things that shaped us into who we are today are left unknown and all we have is the memories of our lives before meeting as kids.

My body goes into shock before reality can touch me.

I'm going to drown.

This is the end.

10

"DOCK US NOW!" I shout over the riotous downpour bombarding us. The boat catches in a gust of wind and sways us too far to the right. "Get it under control or I'll hire someone who knows how to drive a goddamn boat!"

Holding tightly to a limp Bella, I look down at her. She's pallid and unresponsive, but she has a pulse, so I know she's still alive. Her lips are slightly parted and each breath flares her sprinkled nostrils just a tad. She's always hated those freckles, while I'd always told her they were cute as shit. Now, I'm not so sure I like them. I'm not sure I like anything about her. Not her curls that no longer cover her entire head but just the very ends of her hair. Definitely not her pink, plump lips. And most certainly not the way she lies perfectly in my arms like her body was molded to fit with mine. No. I don't like any of it. In fact, I downright hate it.

Months before Bella arrived, I'd remind myself daily that all of this is an act of revenge. I will not fall under her spell. I refuse to be manipulated, just so she can pull the rug out from under me again and send me free-falling into twelve more years of hell. No. Falling for this girl is not an option.

Everything I went through—everything I am—is because of her.

Another gust of wind whirls, sending strands of her hair over her face. I use my forearm to try and sweep them away from her mouth but fail horribly. Hail the size of marbles begins beating down on the boat, so I lean forward, using my body to shield hers.

I'm not sure why I do it, but I don't stop as I tug her closer. Her cheek presses firmly against my chest and I hold her like her life depends on it.

"I never took you to be a complete idiot, Bella," I say, looking down at her. Who the fuck goes out in a rowboat with a board as a paddle in the midst of a tropical storm?

We finally stop at the dock and Leo, the captain, begins tying the boat up. I don't even hesitate to cradle Bella in my arms as I stand. She's ice-cold and if she doesn't get warm immediately, hypothermia could set in.

"Anders," I say to my head security guard who rode along with us. "Page Joel and get him out here." Anders has been with me for a few years, but Joel has only been on my payroll for a short six months, and I should have known better than to trust the reference of a strip club bouncer.

Peter is waiting with an umbrella when my feet hit solid ground. He holds it over my head immediately and I scowl at him as water rolls down my face.

"I'm sorry, sir. We didn't—"

"Don't!" I reply sternly.

Joel comes walking amply down the beaten path, as if we aren't all standing here in the rain waiting on his sorry ass.

Anders joins my side and I abruptly hand Bella to him. He catches her, cradling her in the same manner I was. "Take her to my sitting room and wrap her in a blanket. This won't take long." My eyes are held tightly to Joel's as he comes closer.

Peter hovers over me with an umbrella, and I swat it away. "Cover her. Not me."

I close the space between Joel and me, but before he can even come to a complete stop, I cock my fist back and plant it right between his eyes. He stumbles backward but doesn't fall, so I grab him by the head with both hands and lift my knee straight to his chin. Just as I release him, I look up and see Bella's watchful eyes. Her expression is blank, but she's just bore witness to the monster I've become—the monster *she* made me.

Joel lets out a low grumble but doesn't dare try and defend himself. "Get the fuck off my island." Giving him a push, he finally hits the ground and I walk past him.

Leo will be escorting him off the island. He's lucky he won't be getting dumped in the middle of the bay.

Blood runs down my hand, dripping to the ground as the rain washes it away. My feet move at a leisurely pace as I make no attempt to outrun the storm that's only strengthening with each passing minute. A little rain never hurt anyone. In fact, storms are one of the few things that make me feel alive anymore. There's nothing quite like the cleanse of a downpour while the sky opens up and shouts back at you. I've had my fair share of screaming matches with the atmosphere. It seems to hate me enough to keep me here no matter how many times I've tried to leave.

It was all for this—every beating from the world, every hurdle I've jumped—it all happened to bring me here, with her.

I make it up to my floor and pause in the doorway to the sitting room beside Peter. He's peering into the room with his hands folded behind his back. "As you can see, she's awake. Though, I'm not sure she's totally coherent. She seems to be in somewhat of a disorientated state, likely from being out in the cold rain for so long. I've laid some dry clothes out beside her, but she's made no attempt to change."

We both just survey her as if she's some bizarre lifeform. "Thank you, Peter. Please have the cook make her some soup and hot tea."

Peter acknowledges me with a nod and steps around me.

I press both hands to the doorframe and just watch her. On the floor in front of the blazing fireplace with a white shag rug beneath her. She's curled herself into a ball with a cream-colored throw blanket wrapped securely around her. Her brown hair is now black as water drips, soaking the blanket on her back.

For a moment, I forgot that I'm also drenched. My shoes squeak as I move closer to her, but she doesn't even flinch at the sound of me drawing near.

Vulnerability at its finest. I could choose to beat her down a few more pegs and throw another reminder of the past in her face, or I can savor this serene moment of placidity between us. I've got little fight left in me today and I prefer not to rile her up and risk a slap in the face. No, I'll save that for the morning.

Right now, Bella needs out of these wet clothes. She needs warmth, food, and rest.

Crouching down, I slowly slide the blanket down her back. She offers no recognition of my presence in the room. My head tilts forward and I inhale the scent of her wet hair. She smells of earth and rain.

With a shaky hand, I touch the ends of her hair. Damaged remnants that probably took years to grow to this length. Twelve years, perhaps. Is it possible that these were baby hairs growing all those years ago? The last hair on her head I touched before she left me.

I'll never understand how this beautiful girl was ever a hand-me-down. Passed along from person to person because no one wanted to keep her. She's the epitome of perfection and grace, aside from that dirty mouth of hers.

Bending at the waist, I peer around her shoulder and look at her face. Wide open eyes with dancing flames in them as she stares into the fire. She's completely void of any emotion at this moment. Hands folded neatly in her lap, back straight as a board.

I move to the front of her, kneeling in my waterlogged clothes. Breaking her gaze on the fire, her eyes bore into mine, but she doesn't make a sound.

"I'm going to take these wet clothes off you," I tell her, making her aware of my intentions. I will surely have my way with Bella, but tonight is not the night for that.

In a gentle motion, I grip the bottom of her shirt and lift it up to pull it over her head. She doesn't fight me off as her chest is exposed to me. I drop the heavy shirt on the floor beside the rug and bite hard at my bottom lip as I ward off temptation. Her cleavage peeks out of her black bra and I'm mesmerized by her silky, peach-colored skin. There's an insatiable need to touch her. To taste every inch of her body and remind myself of what I've missed all these years.

It wasn't supposed to be like this. When I found Bella last year, I had a plan. Get her here and make her miserable for leaving me by keeping her forever. She ate right out of my hand when she signed that contract. I wanted to punish her, but not in the same way I punished everyone who hurt us. Her punishment was as simple as giving me the next twelve years of her life to make up for the lost time.

I watched her. I held back as I waited for the right time. Months passed as I witnessed her relationship blossom with that son of a bitch, Trent. I saw family dinners from the yard outside of her house. I stole glances as she slept peacefully in her bed. I fought off the urge to smother her with a pillow one night before the plan of taking my own life, just so we could hold true to the pact—*always stay together, until kingdom come.*

Months of misery that were nothing compared to the years of pure torture.

Now, she's here and the only thing I desire is her.

"I want to go home," Bella finally speaks through a cracked voice.

My fingers slide featherlike up her arm, leaving a foot-path of goosebumps. "You are home," I whisper into the thin space between us. Taking her hand, I lift her up and she follows suit as we get to our feet.

"I'm going to take your pants off now." As I crouch down, I look up at her for approval, determined not to take advantage of her vulnerable state. She peers down at me with sadness in her eyes but doesn't fend me off when I tug at the waistband of her black cotton pants. They slide down with ease, leaving a trail of dampness behind. Her legs part slightly, allowing me to pass her thighs and when they reach the bottom, she lifts her foot and steps out of them. I place a hand on her calf and slide it up, sweeping away the water droplets.

Water continues to drop freely from the ends of her hair, hitting me in the face as she glances down at me. My heart rattles against my rib cage as I slide my hand up farther, stopping at her inner thigh. I squeeze slightly and draw in a deep breath, reminding myself that there will be plenty of time to explore every crack and crevice. And I will. I want to memorize every scar, blemish, and mark on her fragile body.

"Callum, I..." Her words come to a halt when my head snaps back up to look at her.

"You called me Callum. Why?" She never calls me Callum, even when I asked her to.

"I'm cold."

Of course she is. I push myself up and stand, bringing the

blanket up with me. Airing it out with a fluff, I wrap it around her. It hangs freely over her shoulders as she makes no move to hold it.

"Come with me." I place an arm around her neck, holding the blanket in place. We walk side by side out of the sitting room, and my nerves begin to heighten as we approach my bedroom. I stop abruptly a foot away from the door and try to calm my racing heart.

I can't bring her there.

Yes. Yes, I can. This isn't just somebody, this is Bella. My Bella.

Trembling, I reach into my pocket and pull out the master skeleton key that opens every door in this place. I look at Bella before sticking it into the lock. She's still void of expression, but her color is starting to return.

I can't do it.

"This way." I jerk her by the arm and walk steadfast back down the hall to her bedroom.

The blanket falls to the floor and Bella stumbles, almost tripping over it, but I continue to pull her along, picking up my pace. When we reach her door, I open it up, give her a nudge inside, then slam it shut—with me on the other side.

Two hands hit the side of my head as I clench my hair and pull with all my might.

Fuck. That was too close. I was seconds away from allowing her into my sanctuary. The one place that is only mine—a place where I'm untouchable and free to unleash my demons.

I can't let my guard down like that again.

11

IT'S BEEN three days since I miserably failed at trying to escape. I've managed to stumble into this dark cloud that's draining me of purpose. Everything I had hoped for or planned for the future seems so unattainable. All my dreams, as far away as they were, have washed away in a matter of days. What's left of me lies hopeless in this fancy bed, when all I really want is to be home, curled up on my yard sale, full-size mattress.

There's a knock at the door, one of many over the last seventy-two hours. I ignore it, just like all the others. And, just like every other time, the door opens and Peter comes in, against my wishes. I'm not angry with him. He's just doing as he's told by his boss. The person I'm angry at is Callum.

"Ms. Jenkins, Mr. Ellis has requested your presence for lunch in the courtyard."

The courtyard? I roll over to my other side, so I'm able to see Peter. "What courtyard?" As far as I've seen, everything outside of this castle is just unattended landscaping and overgrown weeds.

"I'll show you to it if you'd like."

Rolling back over to face away from him, I tug the blanket up over my shoulders. "Tell Mr. Ellis I kindly said to fuck off."

My stomach growls loud enough for it to ripple through the room, but I ignore the cries of hunger.

The sound of Peter's shoes against the hardwood floor alerts me that he's coming closer. "You should consider eating. You need your strength."

"I'll survive."

When he occupies the space beside my bed, I look over my shoulder. Before I can even speak, he does. "He's very fond of you, Ms. Jenkins. Mr. Ellis is not fond of much."

Curiosity piques my interest as I push myself into a sitting position. "Your boss is an asshole. Not to mention, he basically kidnapped me."

"Legally, yes."

It's obvious whose side he's on.

My legs fold into a crisscross and I use this opportunity to quiz Peter, possibly while earning his trust. It could benefit me in the future. "How well do you know him?"

"Well enough to know that he'll be very upset if he knew we were having a conversation about him. He's a very private man and prefers to keep things that way."

"Okay then, we can keep this our little secret. How long have you worked for him?"

Peter looks at the ceiling, as if he's counting the years, then he looks back at me. "I've been with the Ellis family for seventeen years."

"Oh, wow." That's long before Cal was adopted into the family. I figured Peter came on board after the death of Mr. Ellis Senior. There's a good chance he knows all the secrets to this mysterious man.

"So you knew him when he first came to live with the Ellises?"

"I did. In fact, I'm the one who escorted him from the home he was in to his new home in New York."

"New York, huh? I didn't know that."

"He was such a quiet boy. Had a very hard go at life, but inside of him, there is a heart that beats with good intentions."

"Yeah," I chuckle, "a hollow heart."

Peter glances behind him before leaning forward and whispering, "He can be a bit intense, but it's because he knows no better. He needs you to show him." Peter straightens and takes a step back. "He'll be waiting in the courtyard." He gives a curtsy, nods, and leaves me with my thoughts.

He knows no better. He needs you to show him.

No. Screw that. Cal is twenty-six years old. It's true that he had a hard go at life, but so did I, dammit. I'm not out kidnapping people who pissed me off and belittling them to the point of no return. He knows better and he, or anyone else who says he doesn't, is just making excuses for his behavior. He might be rich and insanely attractive, but he needs to earn back my respect and all the money in the world won't buy it.

Last night, for a brief moment, I looked into Cal's eyes and I saw the boy I once knew. He undressed me with such attentiveness. Never once tried to take advantage of my defenseless state. But it doesn't change anything. Those moments were short-lived before he threw me into my room like I was a naked rag doll and left me in tears.

There's a monster inside of the boy who was once my friend and I'm not sure he'll ever break free from the chains that bind him to his past.

Kicking my feet out in front of me, I get up. My bare feet pad across the floor, then down the hall.

I'm wearing nothing more than a pair of black lounge shorts and a solid gray hoodie, twice my size, but I'm not exactly out to impress. It's apparent with the messy bun topping my head and the lack of makeup on my face.

I stop walking directly in front of Cal's bedroom door, wondering if it could be unlocked. Maybe I could get an inkling into the man he's become if I can find something in his room. Possibly something that shows what he's been doing the last twelve years to become such a deranged man.

Just as I go to reach for the doorknob, my hand jerks back when I see Peter.

"Oh dear," he says in a concerned tone, rushing to my side. He grabs me by the shoulders and walks me toward the elevator. "Never, ever, try to go in that room. Mr. Ellis is a very private man and he'd be very upset."

"Duly noted. It's just a room, though."

"A room that is off-limits. For your own safety, pretend it doesn't exist."

For whatever reason, Peter is very persistent, but it only makes me want to go in that room even more. To be that serious about no one entering, Cal has to be hiding something.

Peter continues to usher me to the elevator. He even presses the down button and makes sure I'm on, before letting the doors close with him on the other side.

Cal has waged a war and I'm prepared for battle—at least, in my head I am. Physically, I've got nothing. He could do whatever he wants with me on this island and I've got no defense.

When the elevator stops at the ground level, I look around, wondering where this meticulous courtyard could be. It has to be out back, possibly beyond the arch I saw when I was out here with Peter a few days ago.

Each step sends my heart deeper into my stomach. Something is different. I'm not outside yet, but I can see that the yard has been manicured. The grass is cut, and...is that the sound of a fountain running?

I pick up my pace and step outside.

My eyes widen in surprise. It's not what I was expecting at all. Everything I envisioned—all the ideas I told Peter I had for this back yard—it's all here. There's a fresh paved patio with a wrought-iron, glass table sitting in front of me with two chairs on either side of it. To the left is a beautiful garden blooming with wildflowers, even peonies, which Cal knows are my favorite. They had to have all been planted because they certainly did not grow.

Walking farther out, the sound of the fountain comes closer. I keep going until I'm on the finished, wood bridge. It no longer looks like it's about to collapse at any moment. It's newly built with a cherry finish with clear water running beneath it. I walk across it and gasp at the sight in front of me.

It's the courtyard. At least, I think it is. This is exactly how I would imagine a courtyard would look. A curtain wall wraps around the circular area. There are bushes with symmetrical tops surrounding the wall. The grass looks like it was laid, not grown. It's far too perfect, not a bare spot in sight. In the center is a large square of mosaic tiles and right in the middle of them is a fountain that takes my breath away. Made of five tiers with water running into sphere-shaped bowls.

"What do you think?"

I jolt at the sound of his voice. Spinning on my heel, I turn to face Cal. "It's beautiful." I continue to walk the grounds, taking it all in. The flowers and live plants offer a sense of calm. Everything here has felt so dead since I've arrived and it's twisted, but it sort of felt like that was my fate. While it's beautiful, it doesn't change that I'm still slowly dying inside.

"The cook has just brought lunch out. Come with me." Cal extends his hand. I look down at it like it's encased with poison.

"No," I say point-blankly, "I'm not going anywhere with you."

I shouldn't have even come down here, but Peter piqued my interest when he mentioned a courtyard. I had to see what he was so buttoned-up about. Well, now I know.

"I'm going back to my room." Crossing my arms over my chest, I hide the fact that I'm not wearing a bra, though it's not noticeable in this large sweatshirt.

"Bella, wait." Cal reaches out from behind me and grabs me by the arm.

"Get off me." I scowl, jerking away from him. "Don't you get it by now? I don't want to be here anymore. As soon as I can get a signal on my phone, I'm taking the first boat out." My words are harsh, but they have to be. Cal has not shown me the slightest bit of decency and I refuse to let him think I will stay here, just so he can make me feel like shit for leaving him twelve years ago.

"You're not going anywhere. Now, quit being a pain in the ass and eat."

"Why do you care so much if I eat?" It's getting really annoying. He treats me like I'm a child who's on the verge of starvation.

"Because you need your energy."

I'm trying really hard to keep my cool here, but I'm two seconds from lashing out at him. After years of therapy, I've learned, quite well, not to wear my emotions, but he's pushing buttons that he has no right to push.

Ignoring what he said, I storm back toward the castle.

"They'll never love you the way you love them," he hollers from behind me, in a last-ditch effort to get a reaction out of me.

Against my better judgment, I give him the reaction he's digging for. "That's where you're wrong. They do love me the way I love them. You're mistaking my family for yours." There's a smirk on my face that I hope he reads loud and clear. He once said he could read my thoughts just by looking in my eyes, so I glower hard at him, hoping he's hearing exactly what I'm thinking. The smile on his face says he's reading me all wrong, so I lay it out for him. "Fuck you."

Long strides bring him in front of me. "Oh, I will, and I'll love every second of it."

"I'd die before I ever had sex with you."

His tongue runs between his lips. "I prefer my women alive while I'm fucking them, but I'm willing to make an exception just for you."

He takes my hand in his, but I pull back, and in a knee-jerk reaction, I slap him across the face.

Unmoved, he warns me with a hard stare and before I can react, he's grabbing me by the waist and walking me backward, as my handprint forms on his cheek.

A low grumble climbs up his throat as he takes both of my wrists and pins them with one hand over my head. "I hate you, Callum."

"Quit calling me that," he bites back.

"Oh, now you want me to call you, Cal? I thought that title was saved for your friends and family." A shiver rides down my body.

"I have neither of those." Hungry eyes dart down to my lips and I lick them instinctively. He wouldn't dare.

I watch his mouth in anticipation and I despise the part of

my brain that wants him to kiss me, just to see how it makes me feel. "Well, you know exactly who to blame for that."

"That I do. You." His face comes closer, and I catch my breath, right before his mouth lands on mine.

I should fight him off, but the pressure he's laying on me is too much. He pries my tight lips apart with his strong tongue. His hard cock grinds into my hip bone while my hands stay anchored over my head, unable to push him away —not that I'm sure I would.

My nipples pebble under my sweatshirt. No one has ever kissed me with such intensity or made my body feel weightless the way it feels now. We could leave the ground and float away and I'd be none the wiser.

Sweet mint seeps into my taste buds as it rolls off his tongue. His free hand slides down, gripping my waist. I'm miniscule and weak beneath him and there's not a damn thing I can do about it.

My pussy pulsates, begging to be touched, while I internally scream that this is not what I want. That deceitful little bitch.

My eyes open and I spot Peter carrying a pitcher of lemonade, but when he turns back around abruptly and walks away, my eyes close again. I try to pull back, so I can stop this, but there's no point. What Cal wants, Cal gets, and right now, he wants me.

So, I fall into the kiss and I give him all I've got. Lifting my knee between his legs, I rub it against his erection. He groans a sound of desperation, then moves his hand up my sweatshirt. I'm braless and he soon realizes that when he pinches the bud of my nipple and rolls it between his thumb and forefinger. My skin tingles and my logic is clouded, once again.

Cal moves his fingers steadfast down my side and immediately sticks his hands in my shorts. "Cal," I whimper into his mouth. He silences me by crushing it harder against mine, deepening our kiss.

I gasp when he unexpectedly shoves two fingers into my sex. A twinge of pain shoots through me, but it subsides quickly. My skin sears as my face reddens from the heat I'm engulfed in, just from his body pressing so closely to mine. Hesitation pokes at me, but I ignore it.

When Cal breaks our kiss, he looks me in the eye momentarily, possibly seeking assurance—something I refuse to give him—then he plants soft kisses all over the crease of my neck.

I'm sure he's confident that I won't try and run at this point, so he lets go of my hands. Unsure what to do with them, I set them on his shoulders.

I push away all hesitation and give in to what my body craves. If he wants to pleasure me, fine. But, I refuse to reciprocate the gesture and do the same for him.

Parting my legs slightly for him, he cups my pussy and continues pumping two fingers inside of me. The swooshing sound of my arousal makes me cringe, but at least it drowns out the thumping of my racing heart.

His venomous breath hits the shell of my ear. "Fuck. You're so wet, Bella."

My cheeks heat up again, but when his thumb begins rubbing my most sensitive spot, all modesty leaves me. I drop my head back and rest it against the stone wall. Cal bends his fingers and hits my G-spot, sending me soaring. My eyes close, my mouth falls open, and I relish in the insane amount of pleasure he's giving me. It's like nothing I've ever felt before. Trent has fingered me before, but it wasn't like this—not even close. At this point, I'm not even sure if I've ever had an orgasm before, that's how novel this feeling is to me.

"Oh God," I cry out when his pace quickens. My spine

grates against the wall, but the pain only arouses me further. "Cal, I'm—"

"That's right. Come for me, Bella." His voice is strained and husky. Holding a lust that sends my body into a frenzy.

Holding my breath, I clench my thighs and feel my insides contract while leaving me powerless. Ripples of electricity course through me and the next thing I know, I'm coming around Cal's fingers.

It takes me a moment to collect my thoughts, but once I do, I'm humiliated. I straighten my back and look to the right of me, avoiding eye contact. "That was a mistake." I pull at his arm, forcing his hand out of my shorts.

Cal puts his hand on my cheek, with the same fingers that were just inside me, and he turns my head to look at him. "It's a good thing you're not a regretful person then." His lips press against mine and nausea pools in my stomach.

"When do I get to go home?"

His eyebrows dip. "I've told you. You are home."

"Cut the bullshit, Cal."

"Oh. I'm Cal again?" He runs his fingers behind my ear and I push him back with two hands.

"You can't keep me here forever."

"Sure I can." His hand grabs mine and he pulls me like a disobedient dog on a leash, dragging me through the courtyard.

I look down and notice a wet spot on my shorts that looks like I've pissed myself. When I look up, I see Cal watching me as we continue to walk.

"Peter," Cal calls out. When he doesn't show his face, he yells louder, "Peter."

At his beck and call, Peter pops out from the archway of the castle. "Yes, sir?"

"Please bring Bella some clean clothes. She's made a mess in her shorts."

I instantly feel my cheeks flush and pinch my eyes closed. When I open them, Peter is gone. I swat hard at Cal's shoulder. "Why would you do that?"

He bites back a smile and my stomach somersaults. *Did Cal almost laugh?* I'd do just about anything to hear that sound again. One of his curled-over belly laughs. It was the best sound in the world.

Cal pulls out a chair and gestures for me to sit. "I'll wait until I change, thanks." My eyes roll as I try hard to maintain this hard-ass facade. I can't let him see how much of an effect he has on me. If he knew that I hated his guts one minute and internally cried to see a humane side of him the next, he'd use it to his advantage. All sociopaths do, and I'm almost certain that's what Cal has become.

It hurts to know that it's partially my fault. If I'd been there...no, I can't go there.

Cal slides a chair out from the table, the metal legs scraping against the cement patio. He takes a seat and sets a napkin on his lap. "I hope you still like spaghetti," he says, pouring himself a glass of lemonade and then another that I presume to be mine.

I press my hands to my hips. "If I eat your damn spaghetti, can I catch the next boat out of here?"

"No." He flips open a Manila folder on the table and takes out some stapled papers. "But you can have your copy of the contract, like I promised."

I snatch it away when he hands it to me. My eyes skim over the first page, then the second, but I'm too riled up to read anything my eyes see right now.

"Thought you might want a copy of this, too."

I look up and see him holding out what looks to be a page from a newspaper. I take it from him. "What's this?"

"Insurance."

The headline on the paper grabs my attention immediately. **Hanafin Incorporated negotiates partnership with Callum Ellis, owner and operator of world-renowned Ellis Empire.**

"Okay," I say with sarcasm. "You want me to congratulate you or something." I hold up the paper. "I've got no idea why you think I'd care about this. You're rich. I get it."

"Keep reading."

I shake my head in annoyance but read the short paragraph.

Hanafin Incorporated, known for their subsidiary company, Office Pro, specializes in custom office furniture.

I don't even continue. Slamming the paper down on the glass table, I rattle the fine china sitting on top. "You son of a bitch."

"I never knew her, but I assume she probably was a bitch. I mean, you'd have to be to leave your newborn child next to a dumpster in an alley."

"Is this some sort of a joke to you?"

Cal re-situates his napkin and casually lays his arms on top of the table on either side of his empty plate. "No joke. Strictly business."

"You bought my parents' fucking company!" I scream, grabbing the glass of the round table and flipping it up.

Cal springs to his feet as the glass crashes against the pavement.

"Why?" I shout, even louder this time. "It's a measly office furniture company. You don't even have offices."

"Sure, I do," he replies, completely calm and collected, and it only pisses me off even more. "But that's not why I bought it. I told you, it's insurance."

Cal begins picking the remnants of my outburst off his shirt. Spaghetti noodles drop off him. Red sauce coats the patio and glass is everywhere.

"Insurance for what? Me? I will never belong to you, Cal."

He stops, noodle in hand, and flings it to the ground as his eyes darken and the rigid cords of his neck bulge. "You already do." His jaw clenches, teeth grinding. "And now it's set in stone. You try to leave and your parents are out of jobs. They'll never find work in that rundown town. They'll lose their house, their cars, everything."

My head shakes in disbelief. "What the hell happened to you?"

I always knew Cal had a side to him that could be dangerous if it wasn't controlled, but I never expected he'd turn out to be this heartless.

"Life happened. When you're forged with no purpose in life, unwanted by the world, and hated by all, this is what becomes of you."

My heart aches. As angry as I am with Cal, I know that gnawing feeling inside that tells you you're incapable of being loved. "You are wanted, Cal. You have a family. A very wealthy family, I might add."

He gives me a side-glance while wiping his sauce-covered phone with a napkin. "I didn't ask for this." Then he goes to leave, hollering over his shoulder, "Peter will bring food to your room."

"No," I holler back, "you can't just leave. I need answers, Cal." He doesn't stop, so I follow after him. "Cal," I try again. He picks up his pace, so I snatch his forearm. "Please." He jerks away and I feel defeated. Tears begin falling down my cheeks and I'm so damn tired of crying. I swipe them away violently. I fall to my knees on the cement foundation in the unfinished area of the castle. "I'll never stop trying to leave. You won't win."

Cal stops in front of the elevator, his icy stare held on me. "Then I'll be forced to destroy everything you love." The doors open and he steps inside, leaving me broken and helpless.

AFTER SPENDING an hour moping around the ground level and seeing if there is anything to help me make my escape, I come up with a plan. It's not foolproof, but it's better than doing nothing. I just have to break Cal down and use my charm to convince him to let me leave. Even if I do get a signal or a phone to use at this point, it's no use. He'll destroy the lives of everyone I care about and I'm not about to let that happen. So, tonight, I'll play the dutiful prisoner.

When I came back to my room, I found a dress lying on my bed with a note on top of it that said, *Meet me in the ballroom at eight o'clock.*

This afternoon I would have crumpled the letter and possibly lit it on fire outside of Cal's bedroom, but now, I'm stepping into a teal gown while Peter waits outside the door to zip me up. Fortunately, I did bring a strapless bra with me, so I don't have to go commando underneath this thing.

"You can come in now," I holler in front of the closed door.

The door opens and Peter steps inside. I glance over my shoulder and notice Peter's rosy cheeks. It makes me wonder how long it's been since this old man touched a woman. He's such a sweet guy and it's a shame his life has been wasted on this unhinged family.

With my hair bunched to the side, Peter zips the dress up, and I turn around to face him. "How does it look?" My fingers run over the satin fabric and I feel like Cinderella. If only I were about to meet my Prince Charming.

"You will most certainly take Mr. Ellis's breath away."

"That's what I'm hoping for." *With any luck, it will be the last breath he takes.* The thought crosses my mind, but I quickly sweep it away. I don't want Cal to die, or even get hurt, for that matter. I just want him to let me leave, so I can go back to my life in Rhode Island and begin searching for a new job. Of course, I'll have Trent telling me how I don't need to work.

Trent. Guilt gnaws at me when I think of what I allowed earlier today. I've always despised cheating and that's exactly what I did. I cheated on Trent. The sad truth is, it's the action that makes me feel guilty, not so much the thought of it breaking us apart or causing me to lose Trent's trust. I'm at the point in our relationship where, I think, 'it is what it is.'

Peter snaps me out of my thoughts. "If you no longer need me, I'll let Mr. Ellis know you'll be down shortly."

"Thank you, Peter. I appreciate your help. It's not like I have a lady-in-waiting here to help me with these things." I chuckle.

"If you'd like one, I'm sure it can be arranged. Magdalene did a lovely job for Mrs. Ellis and she was very fond of the family."

I was only making a joke, but it seems that this family really does hire all kinds of help. Peter is looking at me like he's waiting for me to answer him and I didn't even realize it was a question. "You're serious?" I finally say.

"If it would make you happy, I'm sure Mr. Ellis would be obliged to have her stay."

"No, that's not necessary. I'm fully capable of dressing myself."

"Very well. If you change your mind, please let one of us know. I'll see myself out." Peter goes to leave, but I'm left with a lingering question.

"Peter. What was she like? Mrs. Ellis, I mean." It's only natural that I'd wonder what Cal's adoptive mother was like.

Was she nurturing? Kind? Sweet? Did she tend to him when he was sick?

Peter's face turns ghostly white and it's apparent that I've hit a nerve as he fiddles with his fingers nervously. "Mr. Ellis is waiting. I must go." He turns quickly and leaves the room.

That was strange. It was a simple question, and he couldn't even answer it.

I go into my en suite bathroom, that is actually pretty small for such a large bedroom. It's also old-fashioned with a clawfoot tub in the center and a basin for a sink that's attached to the wall, not the floor.

There's a small square mirror over the sink and I look back at myself while tying my hair into a bun. Remembering that my goal is to entice Cal, I pull it back down and give my head a twirl to fluff my natural curls. I dab on some light makeup and coat my lips in a nude gloss then smack my lips together.

Stepping into a pair of silver strappy heels, I straighten my posture and hope like hell that I don't break a leg in these things. It's been years since I've worn heels and I'm not even sure if I remember how to walk in them. I don't live the lavish lifestyle that Cal does. My life is average, at most. I prefer casual clothes and nights in with movies and popcorn.

Somehow, I manage to make it down the hall to the elevator without even stumbling. My confidence is soaring as I hold my head high and imagine that I'm on my way to some fancy gathering. The elevator beeps and I go to step in but take a step back when I see that it's occupied. "Umm, hi," I say to Byron, Cal's attorney, who's standing in the elevator in a three-piece black suit with a matching tie.

"Wow," his eyes skim over every detail of my body as he presses a hand to the door, keeping it open, "you don't see that on Cori Cove often."

Flattered, I feel myself blush a little. "What are you doing here?" I spit out, likely sounding ruder than I intended to.

"I'm here to escort you to the ball."

This is just far too formal for my liking.

"Back to your original statement. You don't see girls like me here often, or ever?" I step inside and bunch myself into a corner.

"It's probably best if I don't answer that question," he says in a teasing tone, but now he has my wheels turning.

The door slides shut and Byron still has his gaze laser-focused on me. It's not my eyes he's looking at, though, it's my cleavage peeking out of the V-neck of the dress.

"Come on, you can tell me. It's not like Cal and I are dating. Or ever will, for that matter."

Byron stuffs one hand in the front pocket of his black pants and uses the other to run his fingers through his hair. He leans against the back wall and turns his head toward me. "Let's just say Cal isn't as lonely as you might think he is."

I'm not sure why, but my heart drops into my stomach. I guess it's because I never pictured him with a girl. From what I've seen, he's this dark and mysterious loner, who'd easily get annoyed with one. "Wait. Is Cal dating someone?" I suddenly feel foolish for even dressing up to go meet him. I knew I should have burned the invitation. Probably all the dresses, too.

"Cal doesn't date."

The elevator stops, but I wish it hadn't. I hate that all I get are bits and pieces into who Cal is because everyone leaves me hanging.

I swallow my pride and ask the question that's eating me up inside. "So, who are these women that come here?"

Byron extends a bent arm toward me, and I hook my arm in it as we step off the elevator. It's pretty similar to the eighth floor that I'm staying on, but I imagine the rooms here are different. They're few and far between, which leads me to believe they are large rooms. They must be for one to be a ballroom.

"Cal's a single man with enough money to buy an island, obviously." Byron snickers. "You can't expect a bachelor like that to walk the straight and narrow all the time."

I can't imagine Cal walking the straight and narrow, ever. "So, they're hookers?"

Byron shrugs his shoulders with a lopsided grin and I get my answer.

I feel sick.

Of course Cal has sex. Byron's right. He's a single man and he can do whatever he wants, but it still disgusts me. If he'd just be a little less daunting, he could easily get any girl he wants.

"But, you didn't hear that from me," Byron continues. "Callum is a very private person, as you've noticed."

"Yeah. I keep hearing that. What I don't understand is why."

"Between you and me," he whispers, "it's not his fault he is the way he is. He's earned those stripes that allow him to do whatever the fuck he wants."

I blow out an exasperated breath. "So what you're saying is, he's earned the right to coerce people to an island and force them to stay against their will?" Byron goes to speak, but I'm not finished yet, so I hold up a finger. "In layman's terms, he's able to rightfully kidnap people because he's *earned his stripes?*"

"When you put it that way, it sounds pretty awful, but you did sign a contract."

"Ugh," I growl, unhooking my arm from Byron's and stomping, impetuously, away from him.

Everyone is on Cal's side. *Everyone!*

It seems he's forgotten that he's not the only one who's

had a rough go at life. What about all the other kids at The Webster House or in any foster home, for that matter? None of us were wanted, but we don't go around behaving like the world owes us something. I was raised by a single mom who was a drug addict. I loved her fiercely, but my love wasn't enough to keep her sober. I found her dead and can still smell the foam that was coming out of her mouth. For years, I had the picture of her face in my head. Now, I don't even remember what she looks like. Life wasn't easy for me either. But nothing worth fighting for ever is.

"Poor Callum," I mock under my breath, right before my ankle twists and I fall straight to the ground. My legs sweep to the side and I yank off my shoe. "Stupid heels." I chuck it down the hall, then remove the other one. I lift it to aim and throw, but see Byron standing there.

"Whoa," he holds both hands up in surrender, "put down the shoe."

I drop it and go to get up. There's a twinge of pain shooting up my leg, but it's nothing I can't handle. Byron offers a hand, but I push myself up without his help. "I'm fine. But you can throw those shoes in the garbage."

Cal pops out of a room down the hall and it takes me a second to catch my breath. He's probably the most gorgeous man I've ever laid eyes on.

His black hair is messy, as usual, with glossy ends that are flipped carelessly to one side. A few hang in front of his forehead, but he makes no attempt to sweep them away. He's also wearing a black suit, similar to Byron's. A jacket buttoned halfway with a white button-up shirt underneath and a black tie. He stands tall with both hands in his pants pockets. His broad shoulders drawn back and his signature scowl on his face. It does things to me and I fucking hate it.

Regardless of how much I despise him right now, there's

no denying his strikingly good looks or the way his masculine voice makes my pussy throb.

"Bella?" Byron says loudly.

I peel my eyes off Cal and look at him. "Huh?"

"I asked if you were coming. Callum is waiting."

Best not to keep Callum waiting. My eyes roll as I walk down the hall barefoot. It's going to be really hard because I'm stubborn as an ox, but it's time to play nice, if I ever want to leave this godforsaken island.

12

FUCK. She's breathtaking. All I see is her. Around the edges of her sculpted body, everything's a blur. The sounds I hear, all static. Just one look has consumed my entire train of thought. The closer she gets to me, the weaker my knees become.

I knew she was beautiful. Knew this wouldn't be easy, but damn, I never expected it to be this difficult. Every plan I had laid out perfectly. Every angry bone in my body was ready to fuse back together with the undeniable satisfaction of making her live a miserable life on this island with me. Now, it's taking everything in me not to lay her out on the floor of this hall and devour her body with my tongue while shoving my cock so far into her pussy that she walks bowlegged for days.

"Hi," she says with a softness to her tone. Her hands gathered in front of her while her thumbs drum together.

"You look..." my words trail off, unable to fulfill the compliment with the words in my head, "...nice." Giving it will make me appear vulnerable and weak. It's something she can use against me. I can't give her that power—not yet.

"Right this way." I place a hand on the small of her back and my semi-hard cock fully erects instantly, straining against the fabric of my pants.

Bella stops in the doorway and tosses me a glance. "Another piano?"

"We have three. The eighth floor sitting room, here, on the seventh floor, and one in the cellar."

Her eyes shoot wide open. "The cellar?"

"You'll see it someday." I wave a hand into the room. My head designer did a fantastic job throwing this together with only a month's notice. Open, hardwood floors with an eighteen-light, cut-glass chandelier hanging in the center of the room. The grand piano sits to the right overtop an antique Persian rug. The wall is layered with la fleur wallpaper and gold-encrusted vines. It was all part of the plan for the hotel —tailored to Bella's taste—but now, I'm not sure I want to share it with anyone but her.

I look at Bella for a reaction, hoping she loves it, but she gives me nothing. This is what she always wanted. Fancy dresses and formal dances. Is it not enough?

I always knew she was a tough girl, but she's been making this exceptionally difficult. Not just her presence alone—it's her inability to cooperate and let things happen as they are supposed to. She might not believe that this encounter was fate, but it most definitely was. Fate led me to her and I've led her to me.

"Say something," I bark out as an order.

Her fingers trail down the wallpaper and she looks at me. "This wallpaper must have cost a fortune. Is it real gold?"

"Of course it is. Do you like it?"

Her shoulders rise then fall. "It's all right."

"All right?" I snap back. "I did this all for you and all you have to say is that it's *all right*?"

"For me?" She laughs. "Why in the world would you buy expensive wallpaper for me?"

"Isn't that what you always wanted? A life of luxury without worrying about money?" I reach into my pocket and pull out a rectangular box, then walk around her so that her back is facing me.

"What are you doing?" She looks over her shoulder as I take the top off the box and pull out the pearl necklace. Once I've got the clasp unhooked, I string it around her neck and fasten it.

She immediately spins around to face me, fingers rubbing the beads around her neck. There's a sadness in her eyes that takes me by surprise. "Cal, I never wanted any of this. Not the castle, the wallpaper, the fancy dresses, and certainly not the necklace."

"When we were kids, you gawked at the Beckhams' little girl and always said you wanted all the fancy things she had. You'd daydream about dancing in ballrooms to an orchestra. So, tell me, Bella, are you happy now?"

She turns to face me with pinched brows. "What I admired about them wasn't their things, it was their family. A mom, a dad, siblings, love. That's all I ever wanted. Sure, I would have loved to have one decent dress I hadn't outgrown or worn out but that wasn't what I dreamt of. I think you've lost sight of what's important, Cal."

"Me? How so?"

Gripping the sides of her dress so she doesn't trip over it, she walks closer to me. "You hated money, and now you're bathing in it. Ya know, I've always heard that men who flaunt their money have small penises. Is that the case?"

Dropping my head back, I let out a roaring laugh. "Oh, Bella, you're in for quite a surprise."

Her arms cross over her chest and she tilts her head,

regarding me closely. "I've always hated surprises, so I think I'll let you keep that one to yourself."

The lights dim and Beethoven's "Für Elise" begins playing through the surround sound speakers, but it's not the song that was supposed to play. My blood boils at the uncanny ability for that new asshole guard to fuck everything up.

I'm not sure where Byron keeps finding these dumbasses, but if he doesn't get me some help without burnt brain cells, I'll have to do the hiring myself.

Regardless, I offer my hand, placing the other behind my back. "Shall we?"

Bella's cheeks tinge pink and it's a look I haven't seen in a while. She's embarrassed. But, why? "Umm, actually..."

"You can dance, right?" My eyebrows elevate to my forehead. "You've played this song before. Tell me you can at least sway your body to the notes."

She laughs nervously. "My body can do many things, but swaying to notes is not one of them. Hard pass."

"Come here." I point and bend my finger, calling her in front of me. Hesitantly, she takes a couple slow steps. Still too far away, I scoop her by the waist and, in a swift motion, I pull her body to mine. I hold my hand up. "Hand in mine." To my surprise, she doesn't argue. I place my other hand on the small of her back while looking down at her lips as they move.

"I don't know about this. What if I trip myself, or you?"

"It's a quick waltz and it's already half over." I twirl her around to the beat then bring her back to me. "Besides, I've watched you fall at least three times since you've arrived. Once more won't hurt."

Looking down at her, I see that she's smiling. I catch myself doing the same and quickly erase the look from my face by pressing my lips together. Guiding Bella's movements, I do a chair and slip pivot while she follows my lead.

"Curved feather, step," I say under my breath as we glide across the dance floor. "Now chasse." I walk her forward, then to the left, and back around. She misses a step and stumbles, but I grip her tighter, pulling her closer to me.

She looks up, our eyes catching, and it feels as if I'm staring into an open flame. The heat between us is fierce and I'm curious if she feels it too. When her expression becomes thunderstruck, I'm certain she does. Innocent eyes peer up at me, as if they're searching for clarity. Something I'm not able to give because I'm searching for the same in her.

The song stops and so does Bella. Her hands quickly pull back as if she was holding on to hot coal. "All your bones are intact. I'd say you did pretty well."

"Wow. A compliment. From you." Sarcasm drips from her tone. "I don't know what to say."

"It wasn't exactly a compliment but take it as you will."

Bella walks over to the piano and I follow behind her while some Johann Strauss begins to play through the speakers. "Where'd you learn to dance like that?" she asks as she runs her fingers over the piano hood.

"Private lessons for a year."

"Oh," her eyes perk up as she looks over at me, "did your parents make you take them?"

"No. It was my own choice."

Vincent and Delilah only wanted me to do the things that Caden did, and dancing was not one of them. He was into physical sports—football, baseball, basketball. I never took up any them because sports weren't my thing, but if either of them had lived longer than they did, Vincent would probably have forced those hobbies on me.

"I shouldn't be surprised, but I am." She sits down on the piano bench and folds her hands in her lap.

I take a seat next to her, our outer thighs brushing against one another. "Why's that so surprising?"

"Just that you took the initiative to let someone teach you something. You always hated instruction. Always wanted to learn everything yourself."

"Well, there was this girl..."

My words trail off when her eyes shoot to mine. Curiosity piques her interest. "Go on."

I shouldn't have said anything. I want to slap myself for even having this conversation. The last thing I need is Bella prying into my personal life. "Forget it." I go to stand up, but she pulls me back down.

"No. Tell me. Was it a girlfriend? A sister? A cousin? I wanna know about your life, Cal."

"I've never had a girlfriend. Never wanted one. The girl was a dance instructor who I met at a coffee shop a few years ago. We had a conversation about a charity event coming up and I told her I couldn't dance, so she taught me. That's it. That's the end of the story. Would you like to dance again?" I grab her hand and pull her up, feeling flustered.

There is nothing I hate more than talking about myself—past, present, or future.

"Actually, my ankle is starting—"

I cut her off by spinning her around. The tempo picks up and I don't stop forcing her along with me. We move in unison, flying across the floor, not even stopping for a beat.

"Cal, stop," she says, trying to pull away, but I don't allow her to break free.

Why does she ask so many damn questions? Why can't she just mind her own fucking business, live here with me and start a new life without worrying about what I've done in the twelve years we've been apart?

She's a royal pain in the ass and I'm getting tired of her poking and prodding.

"Cal, please. My ankle hurts."

Her dress snares underneath my shoe and she falls backward. I stumble right along with her, but I'm able to catch us before we both fall to the floor. "Dammit, Cal," she yells, jerking away suddenly and freeing herself from my claws. "What the hell is the matter with you?"

I watch her throw her little fit with a vacant expression while I stand there adjusting my tie. It's suffocating me, so I loosen it up a bit.

She's pretty sexy when she's mad. Right now I'd love nothing more than to shut her up with my cock down her throat.

"Say something, dammit!" she snaps. When I don't respond, she comes over to me and pulls my hand away from my tie.

I bite back, "What are you doing?"

"Quit being such a damn robot all the time. You don't have to pretend with me."

"I don't pretend, Bella. What you see is what you get."

She laughs in a mocking tone. "What you see is what you get? I call bullshit."

"You call bullshit? How about if I call bullshit?" I grab her by the waist and kiss her so deeply and so passionately that I can guarantee there's a puddle for me in her panties right now. Her chest heaves against mine as she melts into my arms.

She can pretend she's not affected, but I know the truth. I can see what I do to her. Which means, she can also see what she's doing to me.

It's scary as hell, but when I get into this mindset, where I'm consumed by only her, I don't fucking care. I will let my guard down, just one time, if that's what it takes to have her. And once my cock fills her pussy, there will be no going back —she will be mine.

"I want you to play the piano for me," I mutter into her mouth.

I've waited twelve years for this. Twelve long years wishing I could watch the way her fingers dance across the keys. The way her mouth parts slightly as she concentrates, every now and then her tongue sweeping across her top lip to wet it. The lust behind her eyes as the passion of playing consumes her.

She pulls back, peering up at me. "You want me to play the piano?"

My fingers slide underneath the spaghetti strap of her dress. "Take this off and play me that piece you wrote when we were kids."

Her pupils dilate with her fixed gaze on me. "You want me to take my dress off and play the piano?"

"Not just your dress. I want it all off—now." I pull the strap down, exposing her shoulder to me, then the other, until they're both hanging freely on her arm.

Bella clears her throat and runs her hands down her dress. "You're kidding, right?"

She should know by now that I don't joke, especially not when it comes to matters of her obedience. "No, I am most definitely not *kidding*."

She will do what I say, or the repercussions will be much worse than her ridding herself of her clothes and pouring her heart into a song that I demand to hear.

Her trembling fingers attempt to adjust the strap of her dress, but I grab her hand and shake my head. "Now, Bella," I press.

"Cal," she takes a calming breath, avoiding eye contact as her eyes stay affixed to the door, "I'm not taking my dress off. That's absurd." She takes a step forward as if she's planning to make an escape, but I throw my arm out, grabbing her around the waist.

"Then I'll take it off for you."

Her eyes look into mine, searching for the darkness in

them that tells her I'm, once again, not kidding. I glower, right before running my hand up the back of her dress. I pinch the zipper at the top and inch it down, exposing her bare back.

Shivers cascade down her arms. "Turn around," I tell her, my skin sweltering from the beauty in front of me. She does as she's told and I run my fingers over her shoulder and sweep her hair to one side. My lips press to the skin over her spine as I tug the zipper down all the way. The V of her thong peeks out, showing me a tease of her ass.

"Cal," she whispers, head tilting to her right shoulder.

My fingers skate up both of her arms until they're wrapped around her throat. I bite down hard on my bottom lip, warding off temptation. I could squeeze and force her on her knees right now. Shove my cock in her mouth until she gags on my cum shooting down her throat. Instead, I tug the strand of pearls aggressively, ripping them off her neck.

Her head straightens, body tensing in scrutiny. "Why'd you do that?" she asks with a hint of sadness in her voice.

"I don't give gifts to disobedient houseguests. Now do as you're told, or I'll stay true to my promise. I *will* remove every article of clothing on your body."

She orbits back around to face me, her eyes wide with discontent. "Please, just stop this. You're being so cruel."

"I never claimed to be kind. Now, go."

She takes a step backward, eyes deadlocked on mine. I watch intently as her chest rises and falls with each shallow breath. Tears prick the corners of her eyes, but she finally turns around and walks toward the piano.

She's right. I am cruel. I hate myself for what I've become —the monster the world created.

But she unleashed the monster in me twelve years ago when she broke the first promise ever made to me, and now, she gets to eat from my hand.

13

BILE SWIRLS IN MY STOMACH, threatening to climb up my throat. I'm repulsed. Downright sickened by the way he's treating me.

Get on his good side. It was supposed to be easy. This is anything *but* easy.

Can I really do this? Strip down to nothing in front of this man who is nothing short of a stranger?

I once ate a three-day-old sandwich from the trash. Got slapped by a drunk man my mom brought home when I was three—never even cried. I walked the streets for hours that night and no one even came to try and find me. I also turned my back on my best friend without thinking twice because I wanted a better life.

Hell yes, I can do this.

I take another step, pushing one strap off my shoulder, then another step, pushing the other strap down my arm. The silk fabric of the dress feels nice against my bare skin as it waterfalls off me.

Cal stands behind me, my backside fully exposed to him. I

lift the hood on the piano and position the leg, so it's in place, then rest the hood back down, so it's slightly open.

With my hair bunched to one side, I grip the strands tightly as a tear slides down my cheek. I dart my tongue out, sweeping it off my lip and swallow hard while pushing my pride down.

I grip the sides of my underwear and slide them down, stepping each leg out, then I sit down on the bench.

It's been over two years since my fingers have laid on piano keys. I didn't stop because of a bad experience or anything like that. The passion left me and no matter how hard I tried to force myself to play, the music didn't hit quite like it used to. Not like it did when I'd play next to Cal. I could no longer feel it in my core. The sounds were different, less satisfying.

I look over at him and I'm surprised to see his eyebrows pulled together with an evident crease. He looks as if his mind is tormented, held captive by the past. His Adam's apple bobs as he swallows and I find myself doing the same—swallowing hard, hoping he doesn't notice.

My shaky fingers hover over D and E. I blink away my tears then I press down and begin. It's been twelve years, two months, and thirteen days since I've played this song. Yet, my fingers gyrate across the keys like it was yesterday.

Memories flood me all at once.

"Okay. Are you ready?" I ask Cal as his eyes glide across the notebook. He's gnawing on his pencil and it looks like he's chewed the eraser completely off.

"Mmhmm," he grumbles, not even lifting his eyes from the page.

I don't begin. I just watch him, waiting, because I know he's not paying attention. His lips move as he silently reads the words he just wrote.

"Cal!" I grab his attention.

He drops his pencil into his notebook and closes it. "Sorry. Something just isn't flowing right."

"Don't stress about it. I'll help you. But first, are you ready?"

He nods. "Let's hear it."

I draw in a full breath and begin playing. Everything in the room is silent and still. The only sound is the harmony that surrounds us.

When I glance over at Cal, my heart quivers. He's not just listening; he's staring at me. His lips curl up in a smile and my cheeks flush with heat. I smile back at him then return my eyes to the keys.

I don't have the notes written out. I've been practicing for weeks and I've finally got it down, stored in my memory.

My fingers drum faster as I hit the chorus. My back steels as I pour my heart and soul into the composition.

Cal scooches closer, his leg brushing against mine and butterflies flutter through my stomach. I look over at him, wearing the same smile he is. His eyes light up, and for the first time in a while, I feel seen—heard, rather.

I wrap it up and end the song with a chord progression, then set my hands on my lap.

My nerves are heightened as I anticipate his reaction. "Well?"

"Wow, Bella. That was really good."

I perk up, tucking one leg under the other and turning toward him. "You really think so?"

"Probably the best sound in the entire world."

I open my eyes, not even realizing that they were closed. Cal is now standing to my left, his hand resting on the base of the piano. I stumble over a few keys but get back on track and keep going with it. I can't believe I even remember this song.

Cal takes a step closer and sits on the edge of the bench. I slide over a tad and I'm not sure if it's to get away from him, or to make room for him.

This moment is unlike any other since I've been here. So many emotions invade me and I try like hell to fight against them. My chest feels constricted—my lungs unable to fully inflate.

Another tear falls from the corner of my eye, but it's not because I'm scared. It's because I'm sad. My heart is breaking and it's because of this melody, this moment, and him.

My soul cries happiness for the years together—sadness for the years apart—and fear for the years ahead.

What does this life mean anymore?

I finish the song off and rest my hands on my lap.

Silence engulfs us.

Until Cal breaks it. "Are you going to ask me?"

My arms cross over my chest, hugging myself to hide my breasts as much as possible. "Ask you?"

"What I thought about the song?"

He remembers. I always asked him what he thought every time I played, sometimes, multiple times a day. Once I woke him up just to sneak downstairs and listen, so I could hear his thoughts on a piece.

"Okay. I'll bite. What did you think?"

Cal brushes the stray strands of hair from my shoulder and begins to caress my upper arm. "I think it was the best sound in the entire world."

My heart pangs with agony. I feel dizzy and weak under his thumb.

"Why are you doing this?" I sniffle. "Beyond the anger and possible revenge. Why?"

Cal taps his finger to the C key repeatedly. I tuck my chin to my chest to see his face and there's a glint of a smile. "We were pretty brave back then, weren't we?"

I cover his hand with mine, stopping him from tapping the key. "We were just kids."

His eyes stay affixed to my hand that's touching him. "We were survivors."

There's no fighting the tears that fall from my eyes. *What have I done to him?*

"I'm so sorry, Cal."

Regardless of everything he's done to me the past couple of days—forcing me to strip down and sit here wearing my vulnerability—a mountain of regret has made a home inside of me. Maybe that was the point of all this. Maybe I deserve it. It wasn't until I sat down at this piano that it all hit me, full force, with enough pain to satisfy my worst enemy.

Keeping his hand in place, beneath mine, he tilts his head to look at me. Our eyes catch and a flame ignites inside of me. He has the most gorgeous dark eyes and I'm almost certain they can still read mine. I wish I could read his thoughts. If only I knew what he wanted from me.

My questions are answered when his lips collide with mine. His hands cup my cheeks as he devours my mouth like he's starving for my taste. It's passionate and unruly and I reciprocate by throwing myself into him.

Gripping the side of his head, I tangle my fingers in his mess of hair and give him what he's asking of me.

He tastes sweet, like apple-flavored whiskey. I haven't had anything to drink, but my head is spinning, my body reacting, like I've drank an entire bottle by myself.

Cal slides his hands down to my waist, placing them on either side of me, then lifts me up until I'm on his lap, straddling him.

It doesn't even matter to me right now that I'm completely naked while he's fully dressed. His erection pressing against my pussy alleviates all the humiliation I feel.

Tingles ride through me and I'm at his mercy, internally begging for him to do something—anything. I deepen our kiss, jutting my hips and arching my back.

A low grumble rides up his throat before he dips his hand between my legs and rubs his fingers in circles at my entrance.

God, I want his fingers inside of me so badly, and I hate myself for it.

I need him to touch me. Carry me to that high he took me to the last time his fingers were inside me.

I roll my hips again, forcing friction. He slides two fingers inside of me, giving me what I want, and my body jolts.

"Do you want me to fuck you, Bella?" he asks through a raspy breath.

I pull out of the kiss and look behind him, thinking. I want to tell him to shut up before he ruins this moment, but I don't out of fear of pissing him off.

Although, he's bound to get pissed one way or another. "No," I shake my head, "I don't."

It's the truth. I don't want to have sex with Cal, or any other man, until I'm married. It's a personal decision and one I've never swayed from. I'm all for foreplay and self-care, but when it comes to the unification of sex itself, I choose to wait.

"So, you're just a tease then? Is that what this is?" His fingers reach deeper, almost painfully so.

My heart jumps into my throat and I look at him with narrowed eyes. "A tease?" I breathe out a moan. "You're the one who made me take my clothes off."

He keeps digging, his nails scraping inside of me, but I crave more. "And you willingly did it. You climbed on my lap and spread your legs for me, never once fighting me off or saying you don't want this."

He's taking this conversation too far and I'm no longer in the mood. I go to swing my leg over him to get up, but he slaps his hand on my thigh, hard, leaving behind a stinging sensation.

I try again, to no avail, as he holds me in place. "I'm only human, Cal."

"And I'm not?"

With a crooked grin, I hold his gaze. "I don't know, are you?"

He grabs my hand, laying it on his erect cock. "I have human needs just like you do."

Cal squeezes his hand over mine, forcing me to feel his girth and my God, it is girthy. I can only imagine what that thing would do to my insides. It has the potential to spread me so far open that I would rip.

Cal moves his hand up and down, forcing mine to do the same. I take note of his length. At least eight inches that would fill me up. It sounds satisfying. His big cock sliding in and out of me while his naked, warm body presses to mine. I clench my thighs at the tempting thought.

No. I have morals. Having sex with Cal is the very last thing I need to do. What I need is to find a way to leave.

I jerk my hand away and try one more time to get off his lap, but this time, he grabs me by the throat. "Do my needs not matter? Only yours? You want to come around my fingers, only to have me go jerk off in my room, alone?"

The image of him stroking his cock flashes through my head and I pinch my eyes shut, trying to rid my mind of it.

What the hell is the matter with me?

"No," I choke out, his grip relentless.

"Then get on your knees and prove it."

"I...I can't, Cal. I have a—"

"What, Bella? A boyfriend?"

I nod slightly.

The veins in his neck flex prominently as he clenches his jaw. "Consider your relationship with *Trent* over." He emphasizes his name as if saying it is torturous.

Cal isn't wrong. My relationship is over. It was over long before I left home.

But even if my body is hungry for a man's touch—Cal's touch—as sadistic as it is, I've already been unfaithful once.

Another tear slides down my cheek and I'm so damn tired of crying. "If I do what you want, will you let me leave the island?"

"I can't let you leave, but I can promise I won't hurt you." His voice is tranquil as he observes the tear skating down my cheek. His jaw begins to unclench, the muscles in his forehead relax, and his posture goes slack. His eyes shift to mine and it's almost as if he was under a spell that he snapped out of, because now I'm looking into the eyes of the Cal I used to know. In a matter of seconds, the threat he held has disappeared, taking my fear along with it.

"Forget it. You can go back to your room now," he says, still staring deep into my eyes.

For a moment, I imagine myself leaving his lap and pulling my dress back on and walking out of this room, only to go in mine and spend the evening alone. It's been so lonely, and I think he's lonely, too.

"Maybe I don't want to," I whisper, raising my trembling hand and setting it on his cheek. The touch of his skin feels like fire against my palm.

My eyes close and I lean forward, gently pressing my mouth to his. The feelings that hit me all at once are obscure. So much doubt, but so much desire. Our lips never part as I hold this soft kiss in place. Chills ride up my thighs, never stopping until they spill into our kiss.

A soft, subtle kiss that escalates into two people ripping into each other without giving it a single thought—I refuse to let myself overthink this. Even if I know it's wrong, my body won't allow me to stop.

With both hands pressed to Cal's cheeks, our heads tilt,

our teeth clank, tongues tangling haphazardly in a muddle of passion.

My want for him drips from my pussy onto his black trousers, seeping through them and coating his erect cock.

Cal puts his hands on both of my breasts and squeezes so hard that it hurts, but I want more. More pain, more pleasure, more of him.

He pinches my puckered nipples, tugging at them and stretching them. His teeth graze my bottom lip before he bites down forcibly. I cringe, pulling back to look at him, but he doesn't let my mouth leave his for long. He regains my lip and sucks hard, really hard. I whimper at the rush of pain. "Ouch, Cal."

He doesn't stop, just keeps milking my lip of blood until he licks his lips and I see a streak of red on them. Then, he kisses me, compelling me to taste it. It's metallic, mixed with his sweet, apple tang.

Something about it turns me on even more, causing me to roll my hips against his cock. My breasts perk up when my back arches and his lips work their way down from my neck to my chest before he takes my nipple into his mouth.

My head drapes back, eyes closed. Warm, dampened hands slide under my ass and he squeezes my cheeks while sucking on my nipple. "You should have left when you had the chance." His voice is husky behind an ominous tone.

In a swift motion, he stands, cradling my ass while seducing my mouth once again. My legs wrap around him and he kicks the piano stool backward, causing it to flip over.

Cal takes a few steps, holding tightly to me, our lips never parting. Once we're on the other side of the piano, he uses one hand to knock out the leg holding up the hood, then he sets me down on top of it.

He stands tall in front of me, my knees level with his

abdomen. His hands slide up my legs, separating my thighs. My body infused with desire and lust as I watch him. Biting the corner of his lip, he gapes at my pussy. I should be mortified that he's studying my body like it's a science experiment, but all I want to do is grab his hand and shove his fingers inside of me while feeling his skin meld with mine.

When I go to grab his face to pull his mouth to mine, he retracts, pushing his hand against my chest to move me back. My brows pinch together, wondering why he suddenly won't kiss me. After all this, is he leaving me here unsatisfied?

"Lie down," he demands in an authoritative tone.

I do as I'm told, sliding back onto the piano. I close my legs and bend them at the crease beneath my knees, letting the lower half dangle over the side of the piano. Folding my arms up, I cover my breasts.

Cal slides off his jacket, then unbuttons his shirt, while watching me intently. His chest is exposed to me and I gasp at the sight. Not only at his rigid abs and pectoral muscles, but the mix of tattoos that are covering raised, pink scars. It's like he got them just to try and hide the marks. One side is completely covered in black ink and it looks like the same tree on the stained glass in his office. There's another that rests over his heart of an old pocket watch hanging from a chain that climbs up his shoulder.

Cal grabs both of my ankles and pushes them up until my legs are spread in front of him again. I lift my head to get a look at him, but just as I do, his face disappears between my legs.

His nose brushes my nub and shivers course through me. The stubble on his face tickles in the best way possible.

I lie my head back down on the piano, my chest heaving, legs falling open farther.

Cal runs his fingers up and down my pussy then stops and rubs vicious circles at my clit. He's a master at this technique, possibly even a god. No one has ever made me revel in their touch the way Cal does.

My lower half twitches as my mouth falls open. His stained touch shouldn't feel this good.

His arm reaches under my leg, one hand pressed to my stomach beneath my belly button. My body shivers when he brutally rams his fingers inside of me, He takes no care to be gentle. His force is rough and domineering. As if he's determined to make me come to feed his ego, not to satisfy my desire.

My body fills up with its own greedy needs. I'm forced to grab his hand on my stomach, squeezing tightly as the pressure inside of me builds. Heat pipes through my core, filling my veins, threatening to burst.

I am the greedy one here. Letting Cal get me off, once again, while giving him nothing in return. He asked for this. Dragged me here, forced my clothes off, and laid me on this piano. There isn't an ounce of remorse circling in my head, knowing that I won't fulfil his needs.

The walls of my pussy clench, tightening around his fingers. His tongue continues to flick feverishly at my clit and I wish I could drag out this moment for an eternity.

"Cal," I whimper, eyes closed, mouth wide open. I squeeze his hand harder, holding my breath and trying like hell to make this feeling last as long as I possibly can.

"Don't fight it, Bella. Come for me so I can clean up your mess."

His gravelly voice sends me over the edge. I hold my breath when I reach the height of my climax. A pinched moan climbs up my throat, rippling through the room and bouncing off the walls.

Exhaling my pent-up breath, I lift my head to see Cal's expression. He gasps, his breaths as heady as mine, as he watches his fingers orbit vigorously around my clit. My body twitches, tingles coursing through me as I orgasm again, this time it's like being zapped with a thousand watts of electricity.

My arousal runs down my leg, but Cal swoops down and licks up my inner thigh. I jolt when he begins sucking at my entrance, then my clit, cleaning me up, like he said he would.

I lean back down, my head resting on the piano hood as I catch my breath and steady my heart rate.

Regret begins to trickle through me and I know without a doubt that more is to come. I'll likely lie awake all night beating myself up for allowing this to happen again. The first time, it was due diligence. It had been months since my needs were met, and it was the least Cal could do to begin making up for holding me as a prisoner—not to mention, my hormones took control. This time, though, it was a mistake.

No matter how much I hold on to the moments of seeing the Cal I used to know, he's proven time and time again that he's as ruthless as they come.

I'm lost in my thoughts when suddenly all the air in my lungs comes out in one stuporous breath. I go to close my legs, but I'm too late. Cal grabs me by the waist and jerks me down until my ass is hanging off the piano and the head of his dick is inside me.

Unable to form a coherent sentence, I gasp when he shoves his full length in. It slides in with ease because I'm still drenched from my orgasm, but it doesn't hinder the pain.

"Cal," I finally say, in a raspy croak, "what..." My words trail off when he begins thrusting harder, faster, deeper. I go to lean forward to look at him, but he presses his hand to my chest, bearing weight on me.

No. This wasn't supposed to happen this way. Tears prick the corners of my eyes as I watch him. His mouth agape, his lust-filled eyes staring back at me. His cock strains against my walls and while it hurts, I imagine it would be much more painful had he not just had his fingers delving inside of me.

"Ugh," I cry out at the rush of pain shooting through me. To him, it probably sounds like a plea for more—a pleasurable moan.

I have to stop this. It wasn't supposed to happen. This was meant for my husband, and Cal will never be that man.

"Cal," I cry out again as the tears continue to shed. Just as I'm about to shout for him to stop, our eyes catch and something doesn't allow me to halt his movements.

A breathless groan escapes him as the corded veins in his arms flex. Sweat pools around his hairline, glistening in the dim light. In physical form, this man is an Adonis. He has the ability to make my heart skip a beat by just looking at him. Which is exactly what it's doing right now as we connect on this new level.

This is it. There's no going back.

He will forever be etched in my memory. Not because of our past, but because of this moment right here. Even if it was unknowingly, he stole something from me that I can never get back. But looking at him right now, I'm not sure I'd want it back. Maybe my innocence has always been meant for him.

Now that he has it, I hope he doesn't plan to shred me of my dignity too.

"Fuck, Bella. Your pussy feels so good." He leans forward, hands pressed to either side of me as he hovers.

His words vibrate through me as his face lingers over mine. Having him inside me feels like heaven and hell at the same time. Sin and benevolence. Wrong, yet right.

I'm taken by surprise when he presses his lips softly on mine. It's almost...sweet. Though, his movements never falter. His pelvic bone moves in a rhythmic motion. He thrusts in and out, assaulting my pussy and eventually the pain begins to subside, being replaced with something else. A feeling of contentment. A momentary unification between two people who came from the same broken path. There's a sense of attachment as his waist grinds against mine.

Cal grunts into my mouth, his breaths becoming labored. "God, Bella, I want to make a home between your legs and live inside of you forever."

Forever. Such an indefinite word.

He releases a few more husky moans before his movements slow, until he's motionless inside me.

My heart rate excels again at the realization of what just happened. He just came inside of me.

I push my hands to his shoulders, attempting to move him. His chest rises as he peers down on me with wide eyes. "What's wrong?" he asks, as if he has no idea why I'm suddenly agitated.

I need to get up. It feels like I'm suffocating beneath him. "Move, please."

He does as I ask and climbs down my body until his feet hit the floor. I spring up into a sitting position then hop off the piano and head straight for my dress lying on the floor while cum leaks down my leg.

As he pulls his pants up and buttons them, he walks toward me. "Why are you angry?"

Snarling, I snatch up my dress and wrap it around my naked body like a towel. "You came inside of me, Cal. You should have used a condom. Which I would have told you to do if I'd had a minute to think before you...began."

My heart begins rattling against my rib cage. Byron mentioned frequent female visitors and didn't deny that they were hookers.

I feel sick again.

"Calm down. It was one time." He zips up his pants and grabs his jacket off the floor. "I'm sure you'll be fine."

"You're sure I'll be fine?" I huff, stalking toward him and shoving my hands into his chest.

He takes a few steps back and smirks. "I'll have Peter take care of it. And if you're worried about STDs, don't. I'm clean and get checked regularly."

"Regularly?" I mutter. "How often do you have new partners? Wait," I hold up a hand, "don't answer that."

I really don't want to know because I really don't care.

"We all have needs, don't we?"

"Apparently yours are more important than mine because you didn't even ask before stealing something that was never meant for you."

Cal raises a brow, oblivious to what I'm talking about. "What the hell does that mean?"

Ignoring him, I gather up all my clothes and grumble before storming out of the room.

14

As I wait for the elevator to take me up to the floor I'm staying on, I hold tight to the dress wrapped around me while clutching my bra and panties. There's no need to put anything on since everything would come off as soon as I get to my room. A hot bath sounds perfect right now. A stinging sensation is riding through my insides, and while it's expected after having sex for the first time, I wasn't prepared for that night to be tonight—or that person to be Cal.

My heart feels broken. All these years I have saved myself, just for him to sweep in and shatter every dream and moral I have.

The elevator comes to a stop and the doors slide open, but it's only the sixth floor. I backstep, my shoulders hitting the wall.

"What are you doing?" I ask Cal as he stands with a scorned look on his face. "How'd you even get on this floor?" There must be a staircase that I have yet to see. While the doors are still open, I look into a large library straight ahead. Floor-to-ceiling bookshelves encased in it. Cal always loved reading, so I'm not surprised.

He steps in the elevator and quickly eats up the space between us. His hands hit the wall on either side of me, causing my body to shudder. "Are you starting your period soon?" he asks point-blankly. The doors behind him close and the elevator climbs up again.

My period? "No. Why?"

"What the hell is this?" He holds up a pair of gray boxer briefs and I immediately notice the streak of dried blood on them.

"It's obviously blood, but it didn't come from me. I had my period a week before we got here." I know exactly what it is, but I don't tell him that.

"Then where'd it come from?"

We come to a stop and the doors open. "I don't know." I go to push past him, holding tightly to my bra and panties bunched in my hand.

He sidesteps in front of me, blocking my path.

"The doors are gonna shut. Move." I shove him to the side, but he's quicker than me. They begin to close and I blow out a frustrated breath. "Dammit. What do you want now?"

Cal glares down as he towers over me. "Have you fucked Trent?"

My chin hits my chest as I look down, avoiding eye contact. "That's not your business." I keep my eyes on my toes as I bend and flex them out of nervousness. Although, I shouldn't be nervous. So what if I was a virgin? It's not anything to be ashamed of.

"Have you fucked anybody? Ever?"

"Just get out of my way." I push him again, anger infiltrating my bones. I tap repeatedly at the button to open the doors, until they finally slide open.

I move quickly down the hall, trying to get to my room and away from him.

"Don't walk away from me when I'm talking to you," Cal

calls out. I look over my shoulder and see him hot on my trail.

My pace quickens as I hold tight to the dress wrapped around me. I'm fully aware that my ass is showing, but I don't even care.

Once I reach my door, I glance over my shoulder one more time, and see Cal three feet away. He holds up the boxers and shouts, "Dammit, Bella. Just tell me you weren't a virgin."

I turn the doorknob and tuck myself inside, closing it gently behind me. My back presses to the door and my eyes close.

They shoot back open as my body rattles from Cal pounding on the other side. "Open the damn door or I'll come in without permission."

"Since when do you ask permission to enter? Sure as hell didn't ask permission twenty minutes ago."

"I just need to know because if it's true then I owe you an apology. Hell, I'll owe you a lot more than an apology."

My heart flutters at his words. They're not exactly endearing, but knowing he considered apologizing to me for anything seemed so far-fetched.

"Your first time shouldn't have been like that. On top of a piano, beneath an ice-cold heart. It should have been special. Just tell me I didn't fuck up. Please, Bella."

Why does he do this? This constant push and pull. He says hateful words and glares at me with threatening eyes, and then turns around and shows me the tiniest sliver of decency, forcing me to hold on to that fraction of a moment, where I know his heart isn't completely empty.

Pinching my eyes shut, I say in a placid tone, "You didn't fuck up, Cal."

Silence surrounds me. Not even an audible breath on the other side of the door.

I hear him. Or at least, I think I do. Maybe I just feel him. It's a strong sensation that tells me he's definitely still there.

"Can I come in?" he finally says, startling me. My heart jumps into my throat and I step away from the door.

I'm still wrapped in the dress and my hand is sweating from squeezing it so tightly to hold it in place. Probably shouldn't do what I'm about to do, but I do it anyway. I turn the knob and open the door for him.

I step aside, allowing him in. He glances at me as he walks in, then looks over at the bed and stops in the middle of the room. His hands in his pockets, again. I'm starting to think that's a quirk of his.

He's no longer holding the boxers. God, I hope he didn't give them to Peter to throw away. It's totally something Cal would do.

He turns around to face me and his complexion is pale, as if the very thought of taking my virginity is harrowing to him. "Thanks for letting me in."

"You're welcome. Now get this over with. I'd like to take a bath," I say, while walking to my bathroom. I leave the door open, so I can hear him, but I have to put something on.

"Are you on birth control, Bella?" he asks from outside the bathroom.

"No," I drawl. There's no reason to lie about that. There's also no reason for me to be on birth control right now.

"Why not?"

The dress falls to the floor and I grab a white, silk robe hanging from a hook in the bathroom. I didn't bring the robe here, but I've been wearing it, assuming it was placed in here for me.

I grab a scrunchie out of my makeup bag and wrap it around my wrist. Once the robe tie is fastened around me in a tight knot, I walk back out to the bedroom. "Because I choose not to be."

Cal is now sitting on the edge of my bed, his hands still in his pockets. His shirt is back on, but the top three buttons are undone, exposing a tuft of his black chest hair. "Because you and Trent want a baby?" His voice is strangled as if it was pure torture just saying the words. "Is that why?"

This would be a good opportunity to tell him the truth, that no, I don't want to have a baby with Trent, or marry him, but that really doesn't concern Cal. Maybe once he realizes that my heart isn't on this island and never will be, he'll let me go. "Yes," I lie, pressing my lips into a firm line.

Cal hangs his head and nods, as if he's accepting my lie. The tension in the room is so thick it's suffocating.

"Now, if you don't mind—"

"Actually," Cal stands abruptly, "I do mind." Long strides bring him in front of me. "I do mind because Trent doesn't deserve you. You're too generous and pure to be involved with someone like that. Why the hell are you even with him?"

"I told you—"

"Told me what? That he changed? That he's a good man? He's not, Bella. Trent Beckham was and always will be the enemy."

"I don't want to have his baby," I spit out in a fit of rage. "Dammit, Cal. Quit prying into my life. I'm not on birth control because I don't need to be. Trent and I haven't slept together." The words just spew from my mouth uncontrollably.

His mouth falls open as if my words have surprised him as much as they've surprised me. "Never?" he asks.

"Not yet."

"But you plan to marry him, right?"

I sweep the air with my hand and turn away from him. "I'm not listening to this." I walk over to the vanity set against the wall and open the jewelry box. The ballerina pops out and begins playing a familiar song. Just like the last time I opened it, I slam it shut again. "Why that song?"

"Quit changing the subject."

"No. How about you answer a few of my questions? Starting with that song. I know damn well Peter didn't pick that out and place it in the room I'd be staying in. Are you purposely trying to make me sad?"

He knows that's the tune to a song my mom used to hum to me when I was a kid. Even as she was on the verge of passing out with a band still wrapped around her arm and needles on the table, she'd rub my head and hum that tune.

"I'm trying to remind you who you are and where you came from."

"Why?" I shout, spinning back around. I shove my hands to his chest to push him away because I need some damn space. "Why would I want that reminder?"

I swipe away the tears on my cheeks aggressively, not even realizing that I was crying again.

Cal grabs hold of me and cradles my head while his chin rests against my hair. And I lose it.

I break down, letting it all come out until I'm ugly-crying in his arms.

"How are we supposed to get where we want to be if we don't remember where we came from?" he says, or rather, asks. I'm not really sure. "They took you away and fed you lies. They painted you this picture of a perfect life and stuck you in it then placed it on a shelf so you were out of reach. The world isn't pretty for all of us, Bella. Some of us are forced into ugliness." He brings the back of his hand to my cheek and brushes lightly. "You got Vango, while I got Caravaggio."

Caravaggio was always Cal's favorite artist. His work is Gothic and dramatic, but also full of emotion. Cal would flip through pages of his book and each picture would paint a new expression on his face.

I inhale a deep breath, filling my lungs before I say what needs to be said. "You need to let go of the past. It's the only way you'll ever be happy."

Cal tsks, "Easy for you to say."

"Ya know, it really bothers me that you act like you're the only one to ever have a bad start to life. At least you have a family and a home. Some never got that."

His brows pinch together, back steeled and shoulders drawn. "I didn't want this life."

"Well, too bad. You got it."

"You're right," he takes a step back, "I did.

My voice drops a few octaves as I try to sympathize with him. Something bad had to have happened. "What the hell happened to you, Cal? Please, just tell me."

"I didn't get the parents we always wanted. A year after you left, I was adopted by the Ellis family. A week prior, they lost their son in a car accident. His name was Caden. My adopted mother, Delilah, was a little crazy." His fingers loop around his ear. "Never accepted Caden's death and went into a manic state. So, Vincent took me in and forced me to pretend I was their son, just to appease his wife. Her mind was completely gone and she believed that I was really him. Most days, I pretended. Other days, my hatred for the old man wouldn't allow me to."

"Cal," I say, walking toward him, "I had no idea." I go to place a hand on his shoulder, but he swats it away. "Don't! I don't want your pity."

"I don't pity you. I just want you to know how sorry I am."

"Sorry?" He laughs. "You're sorry? For what?"

"I...I guess I'm sorry that you had to endure that."

"Because you left? Is that what you want to say? You left

me after we made a solid promise to stay together. Do you realize that a week after you left, Nikki and Dante were adopted together? School teachers. If you'd just stuck to the plan, it could have been us. But you didn't because the pact meant nothing to you."

"If I could go back, I'd choose to stay." Am I lying? I'm not so sure. I love my parents and my brother, Mark, but if going back meant taking Cal down a different path, with me, maybe I'd do it.

"It's too late. The damage is already done."

I take a step closer, while he takes a step back. His legs hit the end of the bed and he's unable to go any farther, so I keep walking until we're face to face. "Did they hurt you?"

"Hurt?" He laughs monstrously. "They stripped me of my flesh and exposed my soul and coated it with salt. No, they didn't hurt me. They destroyed me."

My hands grasp my chest, holding tightly as my heart shatters into pieces. This isn't just about me leaving; this is about what happened after I left.

I go to speak, but the words won't come out. Cal glowers as he stalks past me for the door, slamming it shut behind him as he leaves.

"I had no idea," I mutter under my breath, on the verge of tears once again.

15

I SPENT hours crying in bed last night. It finally hit me that my future husband would not be my first. All through high school—many nights of temptation and pressure—I was able to hold on to my innocence and in one split second, it was gone.

Eventually, I sucked it up and convinced myself that it's not that big of a deal. Another part of me, a crazy part, even came to terms with the fact that it was probably always meant for Cal. I'm not angry, at least, not because of that.

I haven't been able to face Cal. Words cannot express how sorry I am for everything he's been through. I don't even know what happened, and I'm not sure I want the sordid details. No matter what Cal does, I will always have love for him. There is still a piece of my heart saved just for him, and maybe there always will be.

I've been sitting at the vanity mirror in my room for almost an hour, brushing my hair and thinking, when someone knocks on the door.

Shaking the thoughts that threaten to keep me under this

dark cloud, I push the stool back and get up. I haven't walked around much today because my body is so sore. It feels like I ran twenty miles and had a jackhammer rammed up my vagina.

"Who is it?" I holler, while making my way to the door.

"It's Peter. I have something for you."

Please let it be food.

I opted out of breakfast this morning. I asked Peter to bring it to my room, but apparently, *Mr. Ellis* said if I didn't eat in the dining room with him then I could go hungry. My stomach has been growling ever since. For someone who worries so much about me eating, he has no problem starving me just to get his way.

I open the door and Peter is standing there with a tray holding a glass of water and a couple packets of pills. "What is this?" I ask, picking one of them up.

"Mr. Ellis asked that I bring you this. He said to take the single pills today and begin the others tomorrow."

I laugh, dropping the packet back down on the tray. "I'm not taking those."

Peter clears his throat. "He said it's a morning-after pill and your birth control."

"Well, you can tell Mr. Ellis that I'm not putting any pill in my mouth that comes from him, and certainly not a morning-after pill."

"If you'll just take the tray, I'll relay the message."

"Or," I emphasize, "you could give me the Wi-Fi password and some service on my phone and I could call and tell him myself."

Peter just stands there, dumbfounded.

"Fine. Gimme the tray." I take it from him, knowing that this isn't his fault. Boss's orders, after all.

Peter leaves and I close the door before setting the tray on my nightstand. I sit down on the bed and look at the little packets. I pick one up, the morning-after pill, and study it while I think.

The chances of me being pregnant are slim to none, but even if they were high, I'm not sure I would take this. I'm also not completely sure that I wouldn't. On one hand, it would be my baby. On the other, it would also be Cal's. We'd be connected for life, even more so than we already are.

Regardless, I drop the packet back down. Just as it hits the tray, the door flies open. "Take the damn pill, Bella."

"No!" I huff, getting to my feet. I'm tempted to pick the tray up and throw it at him, glass of water and all.

He pins me with a stare. "Why not?"

"Because it was your mistake, not mine. I shouldn't have to put something into my body because you couldn't take a minute to pull your dick out of me."

He tsks, "Don't act like you didn't enjoy it."

"Your ego is far too big for your head. You need to get that under control."

"And your mouth opens too much for someone who has nothing to say."

"Oh," I laugh, "I have a lot to say, but unlike you, I'm mature enough to know when to just keep my mouth shut."

"Fine. You want to risk having a baby with me. Don't take the pill."

My fingers tangle in my well-brushed hair. "God, you're so infuriating."

"And you're a royal pain in the ass."

I drop my hands and go to move across the room to get away from him. "Then just let me leave and…" My words trail off when a sharp pain shoots through me. I try to play it off like it's nothing, but Cal takes notice.

"What's wrong? What happened?"

I walk back over to the bed and sit down. "I ran into the bedpost earlier. I'm fine."

Cal comes to my side where I sit and crouches down, looking at my leg. "Where?"

I'm wearing shorts, so I probably should have come up with a better lie.

"There's no bruise. It's nothing." I grab a pillow and hold it in my lap.

"You're lying. You're in pain from last night, aren't you? Did I hurt you?" The realization that he did hits him and I'm shocked at his response. "I did."

"Just drop it."

"Peter," Cal calls out, "Come here, please."

Is this guy just lurking around every corner or what? He seems to always be there.

Peter comes into the room and Cal shifts his attention to him. "Please bring Bella an ice pack. Make it three or four. And some pain reliever and something to help her sleep tonight. Make it quick."

Cal's expression hardens as he kneels on the floor. "Were you a virgin up until last night?"

I take a deep breath and look away from him. It shouldn't matter. And I'm not embarrassed at all, I just don't want Cal to act as if this is some sort of a big deal, even though it is, to me. He didn't take advantage of me and I never tried to stop him, but I also didn't want it. I certainly wasn't prepared for it.

"Yes. Okay. I was planning on waiting until I was married."

Cal runs his fingers through his hair and growls, "Dammit, Bella. Why didn't you stop me?"

My shoulders shrug as I hug the pillow tighter. "Heat of the moment, I guess."

Cal runs his fingers through his hair, deep in thought. Finally, he looks back up at me. "I'm sorry. I had no idea. I'm sorry your first time had to be like that. I'm sorry I hurt you. Fuck!" he shouts. "I'm a monster. I'm a goddamn monster."

"No. You're not a monster, Cal. Not for that."

"I would have never—"

"I know. Or at least, I think I know. Please, don't make this into a big deal." Humiliation begins to take over. I'm no longer angry; I just hope he doesn't drag this out.

Peter returns at the perfect moment with the items Cal requested and I'm instructed to stay in bed for the remainder of the day with both Cal and Peter at my beck and call.

I had breakfast, ice cream for dessert, lunch, pie for dessert, dinner, a brownie for dessert, and even more ice cream before bed.

I really think that telling Cal the truth was the best decision I've made since I've been here.

I'M on my way to the fourth floor to go over some designs with Cal for the guest rooms, and it feels nice to be doing something productive today, although I'm sure the tension between us will be high. Today is all about business and I'm really hoping Cal can behave professionally.

He was so tender and attentive yesterday, so today, I'm holding on to that version of him.

I ended up taking the birth control and pain reliever but stuffed the morning-after pill into the drawer of my nightstand, along with the sleep aid. I suppose it's better to be safe than sorry with the birth control. I'm not sure if I'll ever have sex with Cal again, but if I do, I certainly don't want to have his baby.

The elevator stops on the sixth floor and Cal steps inside, clutching a book under his arm while I grip the notebook hanging from my hand. I take note of his book. "*The Great Gatsby*, again?" I say as the doors shut.

He holds the book out in front of him. It's the same hardcover first edition he had when we were kids. I swear he read it at least a dozen times in those four years.

"*Our past is an anchor and a weight on us, no matter how hard we try to go forward,*" he quotes a line from the book. "Each time reading it is like the first." He tucks it back under his arm when we come to a stop on the fourth floor. "After you." He waves a hand in a gentlemanly manner.

I could debate that line and tell him that we're allowed to let go of the anchor, but I'm picking my battles today and that's not one of them.

When I step out of the elevator, Cal follows, eventually walking in step with me as we make our way down the hall. "Are you feeling any better today?" he asks, looking at my legs to see if I'm walking with a wobble.

"Much better. Thank you."

It's my first time on this floor and it's obvious there's a lot of work to be done. "What made you decide on floors two through five for the rooms?"

"Easy. Eight has the best view. I plan to spend a lot of time on this island and want my own living space. The sixth floor is for staff, as well as the library. The seventh is for entertainment. And you know that the first floor is the kitchen."

"Do you have your own space at all your hotels?"

"No," he shakes his head, "only my favorites."

We stop in front of one of the rooms and Cal opens the door, stepping aside to allow me in first. "All the rooms on this floor will be furnished with a bed, television, and a minibar. All the rooms on the east side have a private balcony. The rooms on the west do not."

They're good-sized and I see so much potential. "Do you

have a theme in mind?" I pull the pen out of the binding of my notebook, ready to take notes.

"I've decided to go with a regal theme. We utilize the same theme at our most popular resort in Eastern Europe. My team thinks that having one in the states would attract American tourists from all over the country."

"Okay," I nod, "and the color scheme?"

"That's up to you. I'm not a fashion guru, or a designer."

"You mean, assuming you'll take my advice?"

Cal gives me a side-eye. "Assuming."

I bite back a smile. "Okay, then. Gold and burgundy it is." I step farther into the room, decorating it in my head. "For the suites, I definitely think there should be working fireplaces. Maybe Tudor windows and clawfoot tubs similar to the one in my bathroom."

"I think we can work with that."

We finish going over some ideas for the guest rooms when my hunger pangs strike. Cal glances at his wristwatch as we're standing quietly in the elevator. He gives me a look. He must've heard my stomach growl. "Damn, it's already four o'clock. We didn't even have lunch. Where the hell did the time go?"

"Guess it's early dinner tonight." I look back down at all the notes I took today. Cal mentioned setting up a conference call with another designer, as well as the contractors who will be doing the renovations. My first week here has been a whirlwind of emotions and it feels good to throw myself into work. I can really use the distraction, and I'm sure Cal can, too.

"To make it up to you, I'd like to take you out for dinner tonight," Cal says as he pulls his phone out of his pocket. He begins tapping on the screen.

"Take me out?" I laugh. "We're on an island away from civilization."

"You let me handle that." He sticks his phone back in his front pocket when the elevator doors open. "Pick out a nice dinner dress and meet me in the sitting room in one hour." He steps out and begins down the hallway.

Stepping out behind him, I hang back, giving us some space.

Out for dinner? Like a date?

I'm not sure what to think. I'm also not sure where he plans to go. He said 'out.' Maybe outdoors in the courtyard. It is one of my favorite places on this property and dinner under the stars sounds perfect; it's the company I'm worried about. Cal and I aren't able to go more than five minutes without butting heads.

Regardless of the plans, I'm excited to do something other than hang out in my room and listen to Mozart while pacing the floors. Last night I asked Peter if there was a television, with possibly Netflix or Hulu; he told me that Cal doesn't watch TV. Who doesn't watch TV? It's insane. I've got no idea what the staff does for fun, or even to simply relax, but it seems they just lie in bed and stare at their ceilings.

I'll never live like that—ever.

The realization that Cal expects me to stay here hits full force. A feeling of dread sweeps through me. Like a dark cloud lingering overhead waiting for a storm to ride in.

No. It's temporary, not a life sentence.

Once Cal is inside his room with the door closed, I continue down the hall to my room. I'm not sure what dress I'll wear tonight, but Cal said dinner, so it definitely won't be one of the ball gowns, even if I am itching to try on the peach-colored one with a sewn-in crinoline.

I get to my room and before I even open the door, I decide on the form-fitting black velvet dress. I've shuffled through all the dresses a few times and they're all so glamorous. Something I certainly am not. Naturally, I dreamt that one day I would be, but all little girls have those dreams. I guess Cal heard about mine, once or too many times, and decided it was his place to try and make them all come true, even if he is going about it the wrong way.

Making a beeline straight for the closet, I head for the black dress. They are organized by color, so it's easy to find since there are only a couple black ones. My fingers run over the velvety fabric and I'm assured that this is 'the one.' I pull it down and drape it over my arm while I search for a pair of shoes.

I pull a couple pairs off the shelf, sticking them all back on when I spot the perfect ones. They're also black with a small heel and straps that ride up the ankle; they'll look amazing with this dress.

This might not be an actual date, and I might possibly despise Cal, but there's no reason I can't have a little fun with it. Lord knows I'm not doing anything else during my stay, especially having fun. Well, aside from the three times Cal fingered me, and the one time he stole my virginity. I wouldn't say that was fun, as much as it was satisfying. The first time, I think he awoke something inside of me. A part of me that was hiding and craving to be unleashed. Not so much a freaky side, but a curious side. When I'm with him, intimately, I feel sexy—powerful and carefree.

Stripping out of my clothes, I drop them in the hamper next to my closet. Every evening when I return from dinner, the hamper is emptied and clean clothes are set neatly on my bed. I assume it's Paulina, although I have yet to meet her.

I step one foot into the dress then the other and slide it up my body. My arms go into the straps and I lift them into place, while admiring myself in the mirror. It fits perfectly, hugging my waist and hips. I'm not wearing a bra, since this one has built-in cups, leaving the perfect amount of cleavage peeking out the top.

My hands slide down my sides and I bite the corner of my lip. Something about this dress makes me feel provocative.

Reaching my hand behind me, I zip the back up as much as I can. I'll have to get some help to get it the rest of the way up.

Fortunately, after soaking in a nice long bath last night and wrapping my head in a towel while I slept, my natural curls are intact, so I opt for leaving it down.

After I dab on some light makeup, I smack my lips together and head out. It's been well over an hour and I'm sure Cal is waiting impatiently for me to meet him in the sitting room.

You'd think I'm on my way to my first date ever with how fast my heart is racing. I'm not sure why I feel so nervous. Maybe it's because I've never had a formal dinner with anyone before. Now that I think about it, Trent has never taken me on an actual date. We've gone to the movies, grabbed dinner, and gone to a few dance clubs, but they weren't dates—at least, it didn't feel that way.

Oh my God, I *am* going on my first date.

16

I GAVE her shelter and she gave me company. I gave her a dance and she opened her legs for me. Now I'm giving her this date, and she will give me a promise—a promise that she'll keep. She can pretend that her relationship with Trent is viable, but it died the minute she stepped foot on my island.

In life, we come across people with needs. We all have them. Bella has big dreams, dreams that I have the ability to make come true, and I can do that, but I never give without getting something in return.

My kindness is not out of weakness, and she will offer up her mind, her body, and her soul for the sake of her future.

We can do this the easy way, or the hard way.

"The boat is waiting," Peter says as he enters the open door of my office.

"Thank you, Peter." I set the contract down in the folder on my desk and close it. "Has she started the pills yet?"

"It doesn't seem so. I will check while you're out."

I give Peter an approving nod and he leaves the room. My hands press to the desk as I look at the door, waiting for

Bella to come in. I can hear the clanking of her heels down the hall, so I know she's close.

I need Bella's cooperation, but more than anything, I need her trust. She needs to realize that I am not out to hurt her. I simply want *her*. Revenge is a broad term and can be carried out in many ways. I can admire her beauty, enjoy her company, and fuck her, all while knowing how much she hates it. I plan to take everything that she holds dear to her heart, everything she acquired over the past twelve years and replace it with me. That's my revenge. Forcing her to live the life I want her to live, instead of the one she wants.

Taking her virginity was not part of the plan. I had no idea she saved herself for me, even if she didn't realize she was. It's obvious, though. It was meant to be. Her pussy was never meant to be tainted by another man. And now, it never will be.

It's a satisfying feeling knowing that I laid claim to her in that way. She truly does belong to me in every sense of the word. My only wish is that I would have done it properly instead of in the heat of the moment.

"Cal," Bella says, knocking her knuckles on the wide-open door.

My back straightens as I take her in. She's as beautiful as the original Mona Lisa. Alluring, tactful, flawless. Primed to perfection in a sleek black dress. An hourglass frame that makes my cock twitch. Rounded ass and plump lips that would fit perfectly around me.

I'm no match for her beauty in a simple black suit with a matching black tie. My hair is in dire need of a cut, but I'm reluctant to bring Sage, my stylist, to the island. We have a history that I worry she will dredge up. It's the last thing I need now that I finally have Bella.

"Cal," she says again, snapping me out of the trance I was in, "are you ready?"

"Yes." I step around the desk and clear my throat. "You look…nice." My arm ushers out, and she hesitantly locks hers around it.

"Nice? Gee, thanks."

We leave the room and I close the door behind me. We get halfway down the hall when my phone buzzes in my pocket. I drop Bella's arm and take the call. "We're headed down," I tell Leo, before he has a chance to speak.

"The chef is getting antsy. Says the food is ready and he worries it will go cold before you get here."

"I said we're on our fucking way," my voice rises, "you tell him to keep it warm or he can get the hell off my boat and go cook for someone else." I end the call and stick my phone back in the front pocket of my pants.

Bella rolls her eyes at me, as if she's disgusted by my cruel nature. "Main floor?" she asks, her hand hovering over the down arrow.

"Yes."

The doors open and we step inside. They begin to close and it hits me that I forgot to lock up my room. "Shit," I holler, tapping the button to open the door, repeatedly. It does no good, we're already moving.

I pull my phone back out of my pocket and give Peter a quick call.

As usual, he picks up on the first ring. "I was in a hurry and left the door to my bedroom unlocked. Please use the master key to lock it up."

"I will do that as soon as I get to the eighth floor. The new guard was giving Paulina a hard time."

"Make it quick." I end the call abruptly.

It's rare that I forget to lock up. Actually, I never have, and the fact that I did goes to show that I'm far too distracted.

"Everything okay?" Bella asks as we exit the elevator.

I place a hand on her lower back and lead her to the main doors. "Everything is fine," I say sternly. "Have you ever been on a yacht, Bella?"

"No," she shakes her head, "I hate boats. In fact, I hate large bodies of water in general."

I look at her, surprised. "Really? Yet, you took a rowboat out in the midst of a storm, in the dark?"

"That was a matter of life and death." She picks up her pace, walking away from my hand that was resting on her.

"You're still here and very much alive. So call it like it is. You were trying to leave me."

She looks over at me with a scowl on her face. "I won't deny it. Of course I wanted to leave."

"Wanted to? Or want to?"

"Both." Her shoulders rise then fall dramatically.

I bite back a smile. "Well, I hope you can hold your stomach because we're going out on the bay."

She stops walking and jerks her attention to me. "We're leaving the island?"

"Leaving, but staying." I gesture to her to continue toward the dock. She presses up on her tiptoes as she walks, trying to get a better view.

The yacht is lit up in a blue ambient glow and I can already smell the Lobster Thermidor.

"So, we're having dinner on a yacht?" Bella walks across the steppingstones and I follow behind her.

"Precisely. How do you feel about that?"

"I feel like there's a good possibility I'll be throwing up on your shoes. But I've never been one to shy away from a challenge."

When we step on the dock, Leo is waiting with his hand held out to Bella. She accepts his offer and steps through the hull doors.

"Good evening, sir," Leo says in his Italian accent, offering me his hand as well, but I snarl at it and step aboard on my own. I'm not a big fan of the guy, but he does what needs to be done, so I keep him on my payroll.

Bella stands in the middle of the deck and looks around. "This is nice."

"Nice?" I laugh.

"Yeah. You know, *nice*? Like the way I look tonight."

Touché. Those were my words. I wanted to tell her that she took my breath away and made my heart race, but I've never been good with words.

I join Bella's side and draw in a deep breath when I see Serena, one of the hired servers, on board. I thought I was strict on my orders with the crew that I did not want any of the ladies working tonight. I requested all men, yet there Serena stands. The last thing I need is for Bella to get a look into my past. I wasn't a womanizer, per se, but I have fucked many of the women who have accompanied me on the island. It was always consensual, and my partners always knew that it was strictly sexual.

"Right this way," Serena says with a glint of a smile. She walks ahead of us, assuming we're following.

I take Bella's hand against her will and lead her at my side. She doesn't fend me off as we head straight for the bar.

"We'll see ourselves to our seats, Serena," I say in a very serious manner. "You may go."

Serena pulls her lips between her teeth and sticks her hands in the pockets of her black waiter apron before spinning on her heels.

I look down at Bella and realize she's watching me back. "What was that all about?"

I shrug my shoulders, brushing her off. "I don't know what you're talking about."

Strips of blue lights run down a large mirror behind the glass bar and I'm able to see Bella's reflection as she stands beside me. Her fingers are still tangled in mine and I'm surprised she hasn't pulled away or pushed me out of her personal space.

Where the hell is the bartender? I lean over the bar and holler, "Can we get some damn service over here?"

"Sorry about that," Arabella says as she walks behind the bar. *Fuck my life.* What the hell is she doing tending the bar tonight? Either Peter or Byron royally fucked up and they're both on my shitlist right now.

"Two dry martinis," I tell Arabella, who is waiting for our order with a smug grin on her face.

"You got it, Boss." Arabella winks, warranting another glare from Bella.

Peering down at Bella while our drinks are being made, I rest one arm on the bar. I opt for a distraction rather than an explanation. "Still just nice?" I ask her.

She smirks then looks over my shoulder. Tipping her head, she asks, "Who was that girl back there?"

I look behind me, fully expecting to see Serena, but she's not there. "Who? Serena? Just help."

"And the bartender? Do you know her, too?"

"Neither of them are of any importance."

"Not of importance?" Bella blows air. "Help is important."

"You know what I mean."

"No. Actually, I don't. And the way you tensed up tells me they're both more than just hired staff."

Arabella sets our drinks on the bar and I release Bella's hand to grab them both. "Let's sit." I nod toward the only table in the open space. On top of the table is a ten-piece setting for a formal dinner. White cloth napkins, stainless-steel silverware, and fine white china.

I set the drinks down on the table, then pull out a chair for Bella. She sits down before I push her in a smidgen. "You're just gonna ignore what I said?" she asks.

Once I take my seat and position all my cutlery the way I like it, I take a sip of my martini.

Bella doesn't seem pleased that I'm brushing her off, and while it's not my intention, I'm hoping she drops this conversation.

"Did you fuck them?"

I cough, almost choking on my drink. "Excuse me?" I lick my lips dry, then set my drink on the table.

Her short, bare nails tap on her glass as she waits for an answer. "Well, did you?"

I believe in transparency, especially if we're going to make this work, so I give her the truth. "Yes. Many times." At this point, I'm mentally plotting the murder of my friend/attorney and butler/friend. Maybe a slow death—or quick and to the point. Either will be satisfying after this fuck-up.

Bella's eyes widen in surprise. "Wow, just a yes would have been fine."

Tilting my head slightly, I observe her with a grin. "Are you jealous, Bella?"

"No!" She says in a huff. "Not even a little bit." She tips her glass and takes a drink, a very long drink. In fact, she's downright slamming it.

"Whoa," I reach across the table and grab her glass, "slow down. Nobody enjoys drunk company."

She mumbles something I can't make out, probably an insult.

Serena joins us, and Bella reaches for her glass again, finishing it off while Serena sets down two bowls of hot soup.

"Could I get a refill, please?" Bella slides the glass toward the end of the table where Serena stands.

"Of course," Serena retorts, her eyes darting over to me. "And you, Callum? Would you like a refill?"

My jaw clenches, pinning her with a glare. "It's Mr. Ellis. And no, my glass is still full, as you can see."

Serena bites her lip and rounds the table. Coming up behind me, she leans down with a hand on my shoulder and whispers in my ear, "You got it, Mr. Ellis." She enunciates my name and my fingers clench around the cloth napkin in my lap.

When she leaves, I notice Bella scowling. I don't say anything because the last thing I want to do is feed into her assumption that there is something going on between me and Serena. It's sex. Plain and simple.

"Help, huh?" She laughs, reaching across the table and grabbing my martini.

"Hey! What the hell are you doing?"

"Excuse me if I need an extra drink. The *help* who has her ass hanging out of her black miniskirt and her tits threatening to break free has given me a complex."

"So this is about confidence and not the fact that I fucked her?"

"Multiple times," she adds. "And no, I couldn't care less that you slept with that hooker look-alike. As long as she didn't give you a disease that you passed on to me, we're good." She lifts her glass, or mine rather, and sucks half the contents down.

"I promise you she is clean and so am I. We have no worries."

Bella laughs and I can tell the alcohol is now coursing through her bloodstream. "Damn straight we don't because it won't be happening again. And how do you know she's clean? Do you have all your 'women,'" she air quotes, "tested?"

"As a matter of fact, I do. You can never be too safe. I also run a background check."

"Wow!" She laughs again. "Nothing like a hard cock

waiting for a fax to come through before you can have a release."

My lips press together to fight back a smile, but it does no good. "You're just full of humor, aren't you?"

She raises her glass. "When life gives you lemons." The rim presses to her lips and I watch intently as she takes a drink then licks them. She notices me watching and darts her tongue out, sliding it around the rim of the glass, sweeping up the grains of salt.

My cock twitches in delight and I'd love nothing more than to have those lips milking me right about now. I could drag her down to the cabins and force her on her knees. The thought crosses my mind and I'm on the verge of getting up when Serena comes back.

Bella would probably put up a fight, but Serena would willingly do whatever the hell I wanted her to. I could sneak off and use the restroom, leaving Bella sitting alone. But that idea doesn't satisfy me. It's Bella I want.

Serena sets Bella's drink down and smiles politely at her. "Anything else, hun?"

"Actually," Bella holds up a finger, "I'd like to hear how you two met. Cal here tells me you're old friends."

My cheeks instantly flush with heat. Damn this girl. I need to get her under control and it needs to happen fast.

"Old friends, huh?" Serena looks at me and winks before returning her attention to Bella. "Yeah, we're old friends."

I actually do have to use the restroom, so I excuse myself while these two have a little heart-to-heart over the monster who's fucked them into oblivion.

As I'm walking away, I glance over my shoulder and see Bella watching me. She seems tense, but she's the one who started that conversation and now she gets to finish it. That'll teach her to keep her damn mouth shut.

Unzipping my pants after making it to the restroom, I

press my hand to the back wall and take a piss in the urinal. My cock is still a fucking semi from watching Bella's mouth fuck that glass, so I point it straight down, taking care not to make a mess. God, she's infuriating and so damn sexy. I knew she was a knockout, but I never expected her to have this effect on me. I had every intention of fucking her when I brought her here, but I assumed it would be basic and partially fulfilling. Instead, I wanna bend her over every piece of furniture in sight. I need to hear her scream my name, so I know that piece of shit, Trent, is out of her head. I will fuck him out of her mind if it's the last thing I do.

I'm walking out the door, tucking my shirt into my pants, when I crash into someone, or they crash into me, rather. A low grumble climbs up my throat and I'm ready to lash out when I realize it's Serena.

"Callum, what a surprise," she says, looking left, then right, before pushing me back into the restroom.

"What the fuck are you doing?" I grumble, shifting away from her.

She grabs me by the collar of my jacket and pulls me close, her tongue skating across her lower lip. "I've missed you, baby."

"You shouldn't be here."

"Oh, come on," she chuckles, "you came in here knowing I'd follow."

"I came in here to piss and now I'm going back to my date."

"Date." She blows air, now gripping both sides of my jacket and pulling me closer. "Since when does Callum Ellis date?"

"Since the last time I fucked you and had nightmares of your saggy pussy. Figured I'd give monogamy a go."

Her hands drop, hanging at her sides. "Fuck you."

"Probably not."

I go to walk around her, but she slams her hand to the door.

"When you break her heart and she leaves, I'll be waiting."

Serena is desperation at its finest. She's a good-looking girl and can suck a mean dick, but it was never about more than a quick fuck for me and a good paycheck for her. She needs the money, but I no longer need the whore.

"Hello," I hear Bella say from outside the door. Serena purses her mouth into a satisfying smirk and moves her hand from the door so I slap mine against it, keeping it shut.

"In the stall. Now!" I mutter through clenched teeth.

Her hands cross over her chest and she just stands there, pleased with herself.

My jaw ticks in fury and I use my free hand to squeeze her upper arm tightly, so tight that the tips of my fingers hide in her skin. "Now! Or I will do very bad things to you."

Serena pushes herself up on her tiptoes and sweeps her tongue across my upper lip. "I like when you do bad things to me. That basic bitch out there, probably not so much. Enjoy your vanilla sex life." She drops down and yanks her arm away, then goes into one of the bathroom stalls, closing the door behind her.

My hands run down my suit, straightening myself out before I move my hand and open the door.

Bella takes a step back when we're face to face. "Everything okay?" I ask her.

"I'm fine. Is everything okay with you?"

The door closes behind me and I place an arm around her and begin to lead her back to the table. She steps away from my touch and stops walking. "I was looking for the restroom and heard commotion. Was our waitress in the bathroom with you?"

I've never had this feeling before—the need to lie to

prevent an argument. I'm always straightforward, no bull-shitting, while taking none in return. Right now, though, I feel ten years old, meeting potential parents for the first time. Only this time, I'm trying not to piss off my future wife.

Since when do I care if I piss her off? I've done it daily, sometimes hourly, since she's arrived.

My fingers run through my hair as I choke on the words that want to come out. "Umm, about that…" Here comes the obvious lie. "She was lost."

Bella's eyebrows hit her forehead, arms crossed over her chest. "Lost?"

"That's right." What the fuck is the matter with me? Why do I feel like I'm on the verge of being scolded?

"Whatever," Bella waves her hands in the air, "let's just eat and get this over with."

Her heels clank against the hardwood floors as she walks back to the table. I watch her round ass rise and fall with each step and I'm suddenly enthralled again.

She's definitely jealous, and I'm highly turned on.

17

WE'RE HALFWAY through dinner and Bella still has a sour attitude. I asked her if she preferred to eat in the dining room in the house, or even in one of the cabins below deck, but she insisted we stay.

"How did you like the lobster?" I ask her as she sets her fork down and puts her hands on her full belly.

She holds up a finger as she finishes chewing then swallows down her bite. "Delicious. A little heavy on the parsley but still good."

I'm surprised she's admitting to liking something that I planned for her, although, it's not a compliment meant for me, it's for the chef.

I pat my mouth with my napkin, then set it on top of the table. "I'll be sure to let the chef know."

Serena comes over and offers to take our plates. I don't acknowledge her, while Bella, on the other hand, glares a warning in her direction. Serena takes notice and lets out a giggle. "Are you two lovebirds having dessert? Possibly something *vanilla*?" She looks at me with a crooked grin.

She wants to stir trouble and I won't allow it. Not with my date.

"We'll be having dessert on the sundeck. Please make sure everything is set and then you may leave for the night."

"But, Mr. Davis said—"

"I don't care what he said. You are finished for the night. See yourself off the boat and Mr. Davis will handle your final paycheck."

"You mean...I'm fired?"

I pick up Bella's plate and place it on top of my dirty one Serena's holding. "Precisely. Goodnight, Serena."

"Because of her?" Serena spits out in a fit of rage.

"This has nothing to do with Bella. This is due to your lack of professionalism on the job, as well as your poor bedroom skills."

Serena's face blares crimson as she stomps her feet like a child. "You know what, Callum, you might be a billionaire with a big dick, but you're the most selfish asshole I know." Her hands cup around her mouth, although she speaks loud and clear. "For the record, you never even got me off. You will pay for this. Mark my words." She storms off in a fury and I shoot Bella a look before she busts out laughing.

"Should have at least made her clean the bathroom first. I imagine she dirtied it while she was *lost*." Bella smirks before finishing off her drink.

She's on her fourth martini of the night and the white of her eyes are now streaked with red.

"Serena," I call out. She turns around to face me with hope in her eyes. "Since you like to wander into restrooms, why don't you clean those before you go?"

Serena snarls in disgust. "You're kidding, right?"

"Do I look like I'm kidding?"

Once she stomps away, probably cursing me internally, I

look at Bella who is laughing hysterically. "Let's have dessert then get you back to your room. You need sleep."

"Sleep?" she laughs, "I'm not even tired, besides, the sun just set ten minutes ago."

I push my chair back and stand, offering her my hand. She looks at it like it's diseased, before breathing out a hefty sigh and accepting it.

We pass by the bar where Arabella wipes down the counter, quietly. I'm sure she just heard the outburst from Serena, and if she wants to keep her job, she'll remain quiet.

"Are you enjoying yourself?" I ask Bella as we walk up the stairs to the sundeck. Granted, the sun has set, but there's an open view of the stars over the bay.

"As much as I can knowing that I'm trapped on an island by a man who hates me and won't let me leave. Oh, and stole my virginity."

"You sure do like to speak your mind."

"I'm not one to hold back, much like you. So, tell me Cal —why are you being so nice to me?"

Once we're at the highest level of the yacht, there's a nip in the air. Bella hugs her chest, shielding herself from the cold. I unbutton my jacket and slide it off, then wrap it around her shoulders. "Just because I'm a forward man doesn't mean I'm not a gentleman. I know what I want and I never stop until I get it."

"And I suppose *I* am what you want?"

Narrowing my eyes at hers, I make myself perfectly clear. "I already have you. What I want is for the people who hurt us to pay for their sins."

Her expression becomes solemn, eyes pinched together, shoulders drooping. "No one hurt us, Cal."

It's best if I just let this go. Bella never needs to know the truth about what happened that day and why I was punished, but that doesn't mean that those who had a part in my demise won't pay. It all begins with her, and here she is.

"Have a seat," I angle my head toward the small round table beside us, "I had the chef prepare something special."

"What?" Bella looks at me sideways as she lifts the lid on the silver platter. Her eyes shoot back to mine. "Blueberry pie?" There's a hint of a smile on her face and hope is not lost for the night.

"It was always your favorite." I grab the pitcher of lemonade—also her favorite—and begin pouring her a glass.

"Our favorite," she deadpans. I give her a look and she repeats herself. "It was our favorite. Don't you remember the day Mrs. Webster baked three blueberry pies for the town's pie cook-off that we weren't allowed to attend? We snuck downstairs in the middle of the night and took a pie to your room and ate it with our fingers."

I sit down at the table and Bella does the same. "And the next morning when we denied it, she noticed your fingers were dyed blue and you took the full blame."

"You had just gotten in trouble for fighting Trent and I knew you were on your last strike."

If only she could have saved me the last time I got in trouble. Did I expect her to? No. But, I never expected her to just leave without even letting me explain what happened. All these years she's been a sister to Mark and a girlfriend to Trent, not even knowing what they did.

"I wrote you letters. A lot of them." Bella scoops a slice of pie onto her plate and I'm surprised when she does the same for me. She digs in while so many unanswered questions swirl in my head.

There's a sting in my chest, but I ignore it, while she keeps talking.

"It took me a couple weeks before I got the courage to do it, but once I did, I just kept writing them, hoping one day I'd find your address and I could mail them. I never did find it. I tried, though."

I had no idea.

This subject needs to change fast because I refuse to overthink this. It doesn't change the fact that she left me. If she did write letters, it was out of pity and that's something I do not fucking want.

"Why did you turn down Juilliard?" I shift to a lighter conversation, at least for me.

Bella grabs the bottle of whipped cream and begins topping her pie. "Why do you always change the subject when the conversation is about you?"

"Because I'd rather talk about you."

"Couldn't afford it. Plain and simple." She takes a bite, her eyes close, and she moans at the deliciousness. "This is really good." She points her fork to the pie.

"You had a full scholarship."

Her eyes widen in surprise. "No, I didn't."

"Bella, you can't lie to me. I did an insane amount of research on you. School records, criminal records, medical records. By the way, I'm happy to see that the scar on your forehead is minimal from that rollerblading accident when you were fifteen."

There's a loud clank when her fork hits the ceramic plate. "Why would you snoop around in my life like that? Those things are private!"

"I wasn't about to let a hard-earned criminal move into my house. Or someone with a nasty venereal disease."

"You're crazy."

"Most of the time, yes. Why'd you turn down the scholarship?"

There's a brief moment of silence between us. Bella picks her fork back up and takes another bite, chewing sluggishly.

"I guess I just wanted to make up for lost time and leaving would only cause me to miss more time."

"Did they ask you to turn it down?"

Another beat of silence.

"No," she spits out. "They'd never ask me to turn it down. We all just thought it would be a good idea if I stayed. Mark was already accepted into law school and preparing to leave, since he was a year ahead of me. I didn't want them to be alone."

"So Mark gets to chase his dreams, but you don't?"

"Music is a hobby, not a career." She jabs the fork into her mouth, ripping off the piece of pie aggressively.

"You've got a career now in interior design, so maybe it's time to enjoy music again."

Bella blows a sarcastic laugh. "I wouldn't call it a career. A degree doesn't give me experience and even you were hesitant on my ideas."

"I think you had great ideas. In fact, when I set up the conference call with Barbara, I mentioned so."

"Can we drop this? None of it matters."

"Sure, it does. What if I told you that I could make your dreams come true?"

Bella slides her plate across the table while licking a smidgen of blueberry from her lips. "I'd say you're out of your mind."

"Maybe I am. But we both know that interior design is not what you're passionate about."

"You don't know anything about me."

"I know enough."

I won't stop tossing the bait. She'll bite when she's ready. If she lets me, I'll give her a good life, as long as she's with me and away from them.

"Are you ready?" I ask, before finishing off my lemonade.

She nods, then pushes her chair back and stands. I do the

same, rounding the table and taking her hand in mine, without her permission. "I hope you enjoyed tonight."

"Aside from the deep conversation about my career choice," her shoulders shrug, "it was all right."

I smile at her snarky response. She's got quite the attitude, and it's due for an adjustment.

We're walking down the dock when my phone rings. I stop, forcing her to do the same by holding tightly to her hand.

Byron's name flashes on the screen. I hold up a finger to Bella, then take the call. "Why are you calling? You know I'm busy."

"Just thought you might want to know that there is a gentleman on the main island waiting to board a boat to Cori Cove."

I look at Bella, brows pinched together, while she stares up at the sky with her head tilted back.

"Who?"

"Trent Beckham. Want me to take care of him?"

"No," I growl. I tuck my phone to my side, covering the speaker, and grab Bella's attention by dropping her hand. "Why don't you go inside and I'll be in shortly."

"Okay," she drawls before turning and walking away.

I wait until she's working her way up the stone path before I put the phone back to my ear.

"Put him up for the night—someplace nice. Have Jeffery escort him before breakfast."

"You're sure?" There's a hesitation in his tone. "Isn't he the boyfriend?"

"Not anymore." I'm about to end the call when I remember that I'm pissed at Byron. "Oh, and I know that the female staff was no accident. I don't know what you're doing, but you know I don't play games."

"Oh, come on." Byron laughs. "One day, Bella might want

to partake in the festivities on the island. I bet she has a freaky side to her. She might enjoy it."

Acid climbs up my throat at the thought. "She will never *partake*. And if you pull a stunt like this again or even have a thought of her in that way, this friendship will be void."

"Whoa. Calm down, Ellis. It was a simple suggestion. Besides, this friendship will never be void, I know too many of your secrets."

Byron ends the call, purposely infuriating me. Gripping my phone tightly in my hand, I growl audibly, feeling the veins in my neck balloon while my pulse throbs in my throat.

Now that Bella is back in my life, she's all that matters. I'd bury my only friend before I let anyone touch a hair on her head.

CAL SEEMED tense when I left him on the dock. Whatever Byron was saying on the other end of the call made his fingers flex around the phone as he clutched it. He can be scary when he's mad, but when it's not directed at me, it's pretty sexy.

As I step off the elevator and make my way down the hall to my room, I unclasp the straps on my shoes and take them off, one at a time. With them dangling in my hand, I pass by Cal's room, but backstep to his door when I remember his call to Peter. Looking behind me and again, in front of me, I give the doorknob a try.

I'm taken aback when it actually turns. My heart begins galloping in my chest and my palm starts sweating against the glass knob. I look around one more time before giving it a gentle push. The door opens, and cautiously, I step inside.

I swear I can feel my pulse around my grip on the knob and I'm fearful to let go. It's pitch-black inside and actually pretty cold for being a closed space. At least, it's colder than the rest of the castle.

Chatter begins carrying from outside the room, so I shut the door quickly, latching it without a sound.

With my back against the door, I draw in a deep breath, quickly exhaling and spinning around in a breathless dismay when I hear a key slide into the lock from outside the door. I back away slowly, thinking someone is going to come in.

This is it. I'm caught.

I stand there frozen, waiting for someone to barge in and drag me back to my room before padlocking it shut so I'm not able to leave.

Seconds pass, until it's been a minute, and no one has opened the door.

Peter must have been locking it.

Taking a few steps back, I catch myself unintentionally holding my breath until my lungs feel like filled balloons. I exhale sharply and continue to step backward. It's completely dark, not even a glimmer of light shining into the room.

I gasp when I bump into the far wall. Reaching behind me, I press my hands to it and realize that it's not a wall. At least, it doesn't feel like it. It's cold—glass, maybe? I turn around, running my hands down it when, at the sound of a threatening hiss, I suddenly jump back.

My heart gallops into my throat as I hurry back toward the door to see if there's a light switch on the wall.

I should try and get out of here. Bang on the door for Peter to let me out before Cal catches me. In my head, I know that. But, something doesn't let me.

I'm running my fingers up and down the wall near the door when I come across a switch.

Please be a light switch and not an alarm of some sort.

It wouldn't surprise me if Cal had this room armed with cameras and sounds.

Holding my breath again, I push up, breathing out a sigh

of relief when the light shines into the room. It's dim and comes from a floodlight in the middle of the ceiling, but at least I'm able to see now.

I turn around, and the next thing I know, I'm screaming at the sight in front of me.

My hand claps over my mouth, shutting myself up. If anyone is on this floor, there is no doubt they heard me. Peter will likely be barging into the room any second.

Moisture coats my hand as I keep it in place, taking small steps toward the wall-sized tank, or cage, or whatever the hell it is. All I know is that staring back at me is the biggest snake I've ever seen in my life. It's all black, thick, and it has to be at least seven feet long.

I walk closer, closing the space between me and the caged reptile. My eyes are locked dead with his, or hers, and I feel like it's warning me off. Practically demanding I leave. But, I don't.

Instead, I go closer. With my hand out, I press it to the glass. The snake stays still, while I do the same.

Once I'm no longer afraid, I look at the other tanks beside it. There are three, horizontally lined up and running from the floor to the ceiling. Each one is at least ten-foot wide. Inside, there are branches, vines, and logs, and it reminds me of a little oasis. There are lights on top, but none of them are turned on, which is odd.

I look closer at the other cages and notice a smaller brown snake. I only see one, but there could be more hiding. In the cage at the end, there's another brown, but smaller one.

As long as they are in there and I'm out here, we're okay. Although, the sight of them does make me feel queasy. I'm not deathly afraid, but I'm certainly no friend to reptiles. If snakes can sense fear, that black monster would probably swallow my entire arm.

I had no idea Cal had a liking for snakes. I suppose there's a lot I don't know about who he is now.

It wasn't until this moment that I even realized that the bedroom walls are as black as coal with a black fleur print. Sconces are placed on all the walls around five feet apart. There's a very dark vibe to the room that slides chills down my spine. A king-size canopy bed sits on top of a black antique-looking rug. It's dressed perfectly in deep red, silk bedding. I walk closer to the bed, my fingers running along the wooden beams holding up the canopy. Engraved snakes slither down the mahogany wood and meet again at the footboard.

Are there no windows in here? I look around, thinking maybe there is one hidden beneath a curtain, but it's confirmed, there are none.

How strange.

Regardless, I still don't see why Cal would be so persistent on keeping people out of his room. Sure, it's Gothic and has me questioning if he's actually a vampire who eats snakes, but really, there's nothing that screams 'secretive' to me. If he were really that adamant about keeping others out, you'd think he'd have a better lock than one made in the early 1900s. Maybe even an alarm system. I suppose he probably doesn't need all that because most people obey his demands and don't sneak into rooms like I do.

There's a couple closed doors that I assume are a bathroom and a closet. Beside them is a floor-to-ceiling bookshelf packed full with classic books. I pick a door and turn the knob. It's the same glass, ancient knob that's on all the doors on this floor. I pull it open and it's a closet. A very large one at that. I step inside and flip on the light switch. There's two tall dressers, and a row of hanging suits, all black. A shoe rack, some shelves with shoe boxes, and...Cal's memory box. It's a weathered, wooden box with a metal clasp that's about the size of a shoe box.

He had that thing when we were at The Webster House. I can't believe he still has it. Pushing myself up on my tiptoes, I try to reach it, but I need something to stand on; it's too high up.

My eyes sweep the closet, looking for something that will raise me a few feet, but all I see that will work is the dresser.

I pull out the bottom drawer to get me a foot higher, then pull myself on top of it. I'm on my knees with my fingers touching the box when I hear something outside of the closet.

Quickly, I jump down and flip the light off in the closet and close the door gently. My heart hammers in my chest as I crouch down in the middle of the hanging suits.

When I hear the door to the room open, I pinch my eyes shut, holding my breath and internally begging for whoever it is to turn and leave, so I can get the hell out of here.

The door closes and I listen to any sound that tells me someone is in the room. My heart begins to steady at the silence, but quickly accelerates when I hear Cal's voice.

"Did you enter my room?"

A beat of silence.

"The light was on so someone was here. Was it Paulina?"

Another beat of silence.

"Yes, she is well aware that it's off-limits but someone was here. I forgot to lock up, but I'm not distracted enough to leave the light on."

I swallow hard, hoping it wasn't audible on the outside.

Cal raises his voice to a near shout. "I don't give a shit. Find out who it was. And check on Bella. She had a little too much to drink."

He obviously doesn't realize I can hold my liquor. Even if

I do feel like I'm about to throw up all over his Brunello suits.

"Who was it? Was it her? Did she wake you up?"

Is he talking to his snakes?

The hairs on my arms shoot up when I see the shadow of his feet outside the closet door. I have no idea what he'll do if he finds me, and I really don't want to find out.

I freeze, unable to breathe, let alone think, when the closet door opens.

I'm still hidden, but if he's looking for me, he will find me.

Cal just stands there, puzzled, as if he's searching for clues as to who was in his room.

A few moments pass before I hear the sound of his belt buckle. My mouth pools with saliva when his pants drop to his ankles, along with his boxer briefs.

Being the curious person that I am, I tilt my head slightly to the right, looking around a hung suit, to steal a peek at his own hung package.

Even soft, he's well-endowed. Thick black hair coats his pubic bone, running down to his smooth cock. Bulging blue veins and a plump silk head. My nipples pucker against my dress at the sight in front of me.

When he unbuttons his shirt at a leisurely pace, I once again find myself holding my breath. I gulp air as he slides off the shirt and is standing before me completely, butt-ass naked.

I don't even care what this man has done to me since I've been here. Part of me wants to dive out of this hiding spot and tackle him to the ground, just so he can shove his fingers inside of me again. I'd probably even let him fuck me—maybe. I'm still a little sore down there, but it's eased up quite a bit.

Cal pulls on a pair of gray sweatpants and I force the

ridiculous thoughts away, even if there's a pool of moisture in my panties.

The light switches off and the door closes. I'm left sitting here, motionless, speechless, and totally fucking stuck.

Cal's phone rings on the other side of the door, startling me. I creep forward a bit to try and listen to the conversation.

"What the hell do you mean she's not in her room?"

Busted.

"Well, find her dammit."

I need to suck it up and walk out there, admit I screwed up and apologize for being nosey.

Just as I'm about to stand up, I stoop back down when Cal lets out a harrowing scream. Everything inside me comes to a halt—the blood in my veins, my heartbeat, the pent-up air in my lungs.

There's a loud bang that has my body shooting back into the corner I was tucked in. I hug my knees to my chest as shivers run through my body.

Cal tears open the closet door. I scooch back against the wall again. All I can see are his bare feet as he jerks open a dresser drawer then slams it shut. He walks back out of the closet, shutting the door behind him.

With my hands pressed to the floor beneath me, I notice my fingers sliding under something—an opening of some sort.

I wait a minute, then two, then three. Then the door outside of the closet slams shut and I'm left in complete silence, once again.

On my hands and knees, I crawl to the door. It's pitch-black and I can't see a thing, so I reach up and grab the handle, inching the door open so I can poke my head out.

He's gone.

I should run for the door, leave unscathed—but I don't,

because I'm an idiot. Instead, I go back into the closet. I have to know what that lip on the floor was.

I flip on the light and push the hanging suits to one side and, clear as day, there it is.

A door.

There's a secret room? Or exit, maybe? I know this castle is old, but I thought those were only in movies.

I don't know what's behind that door, but I plan to find out.

19

"I DON'T CARE if you have to call in the goddamn coast guard, you will find her!"

Fucking imbeciles can't do their damn jobs if their lives depend on it. And they do. If she's not found, I'll bury every staff member on this island.

"I am powerful and I deserve power-filled things," I say under my breath, as I repeat the verse that I learned from my therapist when I was eighteen years old. It's the only useful thing that old wench gave to me. Because, I am powerful, and I do deserve power-filled things.

"I am powerful and I deserve power-filled things."

"Callum, you have to get control of your emotions, or you will do yourself more harm than good," Trudy, my thirty-five-year-old therapist says. Her legs are crossed properly, giving me no view of what's beneath her slate gray skirt.

Coming here was supposed to help me; instead, it's made me realize that I'm beyond help.

"I'm not scared of my emotions. I'm more concerned about the harm they will bring to others, instead of myself. I have this rage inside of me that screams revenge on those who wronged me."

"*Those thoughts are normal. You're not crazy, Callum.*"

"*Wow. Never said I was, but thanks for clearing that up.*"

"*You know what I mean.*" She giggles.

Is she flirting with me? I think she is. "*I don't know what you mean. Care to elaborate?*"

"*Let's just move on. Have you memorized the chant I taught you?*"

"*Mmhmm,*" I grumble, my eyes sliding from her face down to her chest where her nipples pucker against her thin shirt.

"*You are not a victim of your past. You are powerful and you deserve power-filled things.*"

Smirking, I look her in the eye. "*You're right. I am powerful, and I will have power-filled things.*"

I slide my wheeled chair closer to her, my hand sweeps up her leg and separates her thighs. They uncross and both feet plant to the floor beneath her.

"*Callum. This is very unethical. You need to stop this.*" *She pinches her legs together, squeezing my hand between them.*

"*Maybe crazy is the word we should use,*" *I whisper, watching my hand as I pry her legs apart. Her white cotton panties are exposed beneath her skirt and there's a small wet spot on them that has me grinning.* "*Trudy,*" *I tsk,* "*I'm beginning to think that you don't want me to stop.*"

Her chest rises and falls rapidly when I sweep her panties to the side and puncture her pussy. Wetness pools around her entrance and my mouth falls open at the sight in front of me.

"*Do you feel powerless, Trudy?*"

My fingers slide in deeper, working her G-spot. She lets out a breathless moan. "*Yes.*"

"*That's because I have all the power here. Never forget that.*"

In a spurt of anger, I tear open the door to the hall and walk with heavy steps to Bella's room.

"I want them everywhere!" I blow out at Peter, who's working on the installation of the cameras. "Every floor.

Every exit, entrance. I want to see the fucking dock if I need to."

Kicking open Bella's door, that wasn't even latched, I storm into her room. "Bella," I holler, knowing it's pointless.

There's no way she got off this island. She's here, somewhere. Byron is guarding the cellar. At least, he better be, or he's out of here. I told him that this shit stopped when Bella arrived, and it was recently brought to my attention that he's been carrying on as if he's at one of the main resorts.

I tear through the room, pulling blankets back, tipping her dirty hamper to see if she changed out of her dress—which is not inside—scope the balcony and look around the visible grounds from her room.

"Fuck!" I shout, heading back out of her room.

I pull my phone out of my pocket and give my head of security, Anders, a call. "Anything?"

"Nothing, sir. It's like she just…vanished."

"I want security heightened. Get at least three more guys here. With them and the new hire, you dumbasses better make sure this shit doesn't happen again."

I end the call and walk back down the hall to my room with long strides.

My light was on.

It hits me. I never forget to turn off my lights. Peter said he wasn't inside. It had to be her.

"Motherfucker." I stick the key in the lock and turn it so aggressively that it sticks and I'm forced to jerk it out.

I slam the door behind me, rattling the old clock on the wall. I don't even need to flip on the light to see because the closet door is wide open with the light on.

She was definitely here.

20

My entire body trembles as I grip the banister. My sweaty palm slides down it, and even though I know I should turn around, something doesn't let me. There's a reason why Cal is so protective over his room, and maybe this is why. If he's hiding something, this could be my only chance to find out what it is.

Thankfully, there's more sconces on the wall that are lit up, so I'm able to see where I'm going. The lights being on only reaffirms that something is definitely down here.

Fear courses through me when I think about what that something could be. It could be dead bodies—or imprisoned women. Oh my God, what if he plans to take me down here one day and tie me up? Maybe I really don't know Cal at all.

Saliva begins pooling in my mouth with each step down the spiral staircase. There's a familiar scent that only strengthens the farther down I go. It's that lemongrass scent that I smelled my first day here.

When I make the turn down the last few steps, I'm shocked to see that it's just an empty room. The walls are painted all white. The floor is clean cement. There's nothing down here except for a door.

I walk over to it and wrap my fingers around the handle. Drawing in a deep breath, I give it a turn, but it's locked.

Dammit.

As soon as I turn around to go back up the stairs, I'm face to face with a very angry Cal.

"Umm. Hi," I say, stupidly.

Cal makes a growly noise before grabbing me by the waist and flinging me over his shoulder.

"Put me down," I holler, my hands smacking at his back.

I shrill when his palm slaps hard against my ass.

There's a bite to the imprint he left and instead of making me fearful, it pisses me off. "What the hell is the matter with you?"

"Didn't you ever learn that snooping can get you killed?"

I push my hands to his shoulders, lifting myself up as he one-arms me up the stairs. "Oh, are you going to kill me?"

"You'll be lucky if you get off that easily."

Was that a threat? That was definitely a threat.

"Why do you care? There's nothing down there anyways." I chuckle. "Does it make you feel like a villain to have a secret door in your closet?"

"You're about to learn how much of a villain I am. Now shut your damn mouth."

Pushing myself up farther, until I'm stiff in his arm, I block his path with my body. "I'm not scared of you, Cal." I'm not sure that I've ever seen him look this angry. I should be scared, but I don't think he'd hurt me. "Will you just put me down? I can walk."

"You know, Bella. You've proven to be a pain in my ass. Therefore, it's time to reciprocate."

His jaw clenches right before his hand cracks my ass again.

Shrieking, I draw in a ragged breath. We're at the top of the steps; at least, I think we are. I don't even care. I grab Cal by the face and grit through my clenched teeth, "Don't ever fucking do that again."

His nostrils flare, warranting the threat of another blow. His hands wrap completely around my ass, fingers squeezing into the depths of my skin.

"What are you gonna do about it? Fight me?"

Jerking his foot out, he kicks open the door to the closet and carries me in. The suits are all pushed to the side, giving us a clear entry inside.

"I won't stop until I know what's behind those doors. So you might as well just tell me."

"Oh," Cal drawls, "you will stop if you know what's good for you. Would you like a preview of what will happen if you don't?"

Is that a question? Of course I don't.

Cal carries me over to his bed with shaky arms. He seems nervous, which is surprising for a man who exudes so much confidence. I look into his eyes, noticing he hasn't blinked since we stepped foot in his room.

Remembering that Peter said no one is allowed in Cal's room has me wondering if that's the reason for his apprehension.

"Why are you so secretive with your room?"

Cal drops me onto the bed and takes a step back. Standing with an unnatural stillness, he stares straight ahead.

"This is my sanctuary. A place where no one can touch me and I'm in control. Don't we all need our own personal space as such?"

"I...um, I guess." Most people have bedrooms, but we don't treat them as a barrier from the outside world like he does.

Cal drops his gaze on the wall behind me and walks over to the snakes. He takes something attached to the side of the glass cage that looks like a remote. With the press of a button, the aquarium lights up.

It's like he called them to him, because all of the snakes come to the forefront of the glass. My insides shiver. There are so many of the brown ones, but it's that big black one that has my stomach twisting in knots.

Cal pushes another button that slides open the glass on the cage. He looks at me and the darkness in his eyes—the curl of his lip—causes me to scoot back on the bed. Hugging my knees to my chest, my dress drapes over my legs. My heart beats at an unprecedented rate when he reaches his hand into the cage and the sleek, black monster slithers around his arm.

"Cal," I say in warning, "what are you doing?"

He ignores me, walking over to the end of the cage where the other snakes are. He slides the doors open with the press of a button. Instead of letting the snake climb on his arm like he did the black one, he snatches it by the throat and pulls it out.

I gasp at the sight of him squeezing the smaller snake's neck.

The black one continues to slither up his body, its head nuzzling up to Cal's neck while it tangles around his arm.

Cal begins walking toward me. My heart beats faster, ruffling my rib cage. I'm as far back as I can go on the bed, but I continue to squirm, hoping to move further.

"Cal," I say again.

His knees press into the plush mattress as he slowly comes toward me. "You know what I love about snakes?" His brows rise as if he expects me to answer him. When I don't, he continues, "Any other pet would look down, tuck their tail, and run when they've done wrong. Snakes, on the other hand, they'll stand tall and look you right in the eye."

I turn my head, pinching my eyes shut as he kneels directly in front of me. "Please just put them away."

"You've proven my point. You were a bad girl, Bella. You went snooping around where you didn't belong and now we need to make sure that doesn't happen again. Look me in the eye," he says in a demanding tone.

I open my eyes and slowly turn back to face him.

"You're wearing your fear and snakes feed off that."

He comes closer as my breaths become delayed and my head gets dizzy from the lack of oxygen.

The snake stretches his body, stiffening with its head in the air, and Cal brings his hand down to the bed.

"Please don't put it down," I beg him. He doesn't listen as the snake slithers off his hand and onto the silk comforter.

The other one is wrapped around his hand, but that one doesn't worry me as much. It's on the smaller side and looks more like a rat snake.

With the snake in his hand, Cal climbs up the bed to me, getting as close as he can with my knees blocking him.

"What are you doing?"

His hand, while holding the snake, slides up my leg and he pries them apart, but not without a fight on my end. I squeeze them tightly, forcing my knees together.

Cal looks up at me and smirks before allowing the brown snake to slide off his hand and around my calf.

"Cal, please. Get it off me," I cry out, tears rolling down my face.

With my attention on the snake, he's able to push my legs apart, and his body slides between them. "Are you done sticking your nose where it doesn't belong, Bella?"

"Yes. I promise. I'll never come in here again. Just get that damn thing off me."

I look at the other snake that's sliding slowly around on the comforter. It seems docile, but I know they can strike at any moment. I don't know much about snakes, but I do know that.

I'm afraid to move, so I don't fight Cal off as he slides my underwear down, over the snake and off my legs. Long fingers skate up my inner thigh, pushing my knees farther apart. His face nuzzles in, warm breath riding up my legs.

This is really happening. I have a snake latched onto my leg while Cal is preparing to feast on me. I take a deep, ragged breath when his nose brushes my sensitive clit. I close my eyes but open them again quickly when I feel the weight of something on my chest.

"Oh my God. Move it. Please, Cal. Just get it off me." My chin is pressed to my chest as I watch the snake slither over it. Its head level with mine, staring me straight in the eye, as if it's telling me that it is the one with the power.

"Snakes are powerful. And we both know I like power-filled things." His long tongue stretches out, sliding inside me like an unhinged snake, flexing and flicking feverishly while he sucks my clit.

I blow out a breathy moan, hating that I'm instantly turned on by the thrill of this. I don't dare move; I don't dare make a sound, but the way he's licking me up and down like I'm his favorite taste in the world, it's damn near impossible.

Cal pushes my dress up farther until the bottom half is bunched at my stomach. "Get rid of the dress," he barks out the order.

"I can't," my words come out in a quivering whisper, "the snake."

"She'll move. The little guy, on the other hand, he'll latch on for dear life."

My hands shake uncontrollably as I slide my fingers under the straps on either side of my shoulders. I push them down, taking care not to piss off the snake. I'm staring straight into the eyes of danger, gambling with my life. Even if she's not venomous, she could choke me out in two seconds flat.

The straps fall to the side and the snake worms its way up to my bare chest, sliding across my exposed breasts. With a straight back, I push my dress down until Cal removes it.

Two fingers pinch my throbbing clit, causing me to whimper at the mix of pain and pleasure.

The snake writhes against me, resting on my collarbone while Cal works his magic.

All I can focus on is the greedy feeling washing over me. I buck my hips up, needing more than what he's giving me. I feel like a whore at his beck and call. A weak and miserable slut who spreads her legs for the thrill of the ride.

Cal has awoken something inside of me that I didn't know existed—sexual needs, unfulfilled desires. He's a master at his technique and I'm a mere peasant begging for his touch.

When he removes his shirt, I gaze open-mouthed at his shapely chest covered in black ink. A coat of black hair runs down the V of his abdomen and when he takes off his sweatpants, his cock springs free. Hard, with bulging veins and a plump head that I want to wrap my lips around just to see how it feels in my mouth.

Cal leans forward, his hands pressed on either side of me. His mouth falls to my breast and he sucks my nipple in his mouth. He's a man who knows what he wants and I'm so turned on by that fact.

My eyes close as the snake begins slithering again, while the other latches onto my leg like I'm its lifeline.

"Do you like when I suck your nipples, Bella?"

I nod without giving it a thought. I like everything he

does to me. I never know what to expect, but every touch is an electrical current running through me.

He gives my nipple a flick and I shudder while he watches my reaction. Biting his lip, he reaches down and I feel him unravel the snake from my leg. Bringing it up between us, he puts it right in my face, which instantly stirs the black snake. "Kiss it goodbye."

Thank God!

I breathe out a sigh of relief that he's putting them away. But there is no way in hell I'm kissing that thing.

I turn my head in disgust. "Not a chance."

"If you want him to leave then kiss him goodbye."

Chills shimmy down my body. I close my eyes tightly, pucker up, and hope like hell that thing doesn't bite me.

I'm thrown off guard when it's Cal's mouth that meets mine and not the head of the snake. I feel the weight of the snake drop beside me and the one on my chest instantly leaves. Cal cups my face in his hands and kisses me forcefully while I feel the snakes squirm against my side. There's a hissing sound that signals alarms in my head, but Cal doesn't allow me to break free to see what's going on.

Seconds later, he lets me go, and I look to my side but turn away abruptly, burying my face in Cal's neck when I see that the bottom half of the brown snake is hanging from the mouth of the other.

She ate him. She really fucking ate him next to us while we're lying here naked.

"Are you insane?" My words are muffled against Cal's skin.

He doesn't react; instead, he shoves his cock inside of me, causing my lungs to deflate in one breath.

"Do you want this, Bella?"

God, the way he says my name with that gravelly tone makes my pussy twitch.

"Yes. I want this."

He doesn't move. Just holds his cock still inside of me, filling me to the brim while his balls rest against my ass cheeks.

"Say it. Tell me you want me to fuck you."

I don't respond. Not because I'm embarrassed to admit I want him to, but because the words feel degrading, like I'm begging. Maybe that's what he wants.

He pulls back and rams his cock in so hard that my head reverberates off the headboard. "Ugh," I cry out.

"Tell me."

He does it again, kinking my neck in the process.

"I want you to fuck me."

He pushes himself up so that his face is hovering over mine. He's wearing a grin, proof that he got what he wanted.

In one fell swoop, he pulls his cock out. Proof of my want for him drips from its head onto my parted lips.

His body slides down again while the black snake climbs over my rib cage. I can see the bulge in her from swallowing the other snake whole. I hold my breath as she makes herself comfortable in the crease of my neck, like it's a warm bed for her after finishing a meal.

Cal pushes my legs open until they are widespread. He slides one possessive finger inside of me with ease then adds another. Working them just right, I begin to relax and enjoy the feelings coming over me.

Just as I start to get into it, he pulls his fingers out. I brace myself up on my elbows with a raised brow. "What are you doing?"

He pinches my clit again, this time so hard that every cell in my body is alerted. "Do you plan on snooping in my room again?" He doesn't stop as he awaits my answer.

"No. Never again." It's very possible that I lied, but he

doesn't need to know that. He just needs to hear what he wants so he'll give me what I need.

His fingers penetrate me again, long, curled, and deep. His palm cups my crotch as he pumps them inside, hitting my G-spot while his thumb rubs my aching clit.

This time when I relax, he doesn't stop. My hands slide down to my stomach, grazing the soft skin as I lick my lips. Modesty eludes me. Time has stopped, the world has ceased to exist, and it's just this moment of heightened energy. My hips rise, then fall, up and down, while Cal finger-fucks me. The sound of moisture coating his fingers as he fills me to the brim. His palm slapping against my pussy, thumb circling my clit.

"Oh God," I cry out, grabbing his full head of hair and tugging. Everything washes away. I'm filled with a burning agony and a dire need to release. I squeeze my walls around his fingers, arch my back, and... "What the hell? No!"

Why did he stop? My hands begin to shake like an addict in need of a fix.

Cal comes up on his knees, grinning from ear to ear as he grabs the snake.

"You asshole!" I spit out.

"Punishment is a bitch. Now, roll over."

21

I GRAB Bella by the waist and flip her over onto her stomach, then lay Amira on her back. Goosebumps shimmy down Bella's spine as Amira slides across the uneven surface.

My legs straddle hers as I slide my cock up and down the slit of her ass. "Have you learned your lesson yet?" I ask, eyeing her round cheeks that hold a faded imprint of my hand from earlier.

Her toes curl into the bed and she makes her head comfortable on her folded arms. "Yes. Please, just fuck me."

She's lying. Bella has proven that I can't believe anything she says. I tried to give her freedom to roam, but she's proven twice, not once, that she's incapable of being trusted. She tried to escape by boat in the middle of a storm, and now she's snooping around.

I raise my hand and smack it hard against the same cheek of her ass as last time. Her skin welts into the shape of my fingers.

Her head shoots up. "Ouch," she whimpers, but she doesn't move. I'm not sure if it's fear of Amira, or fear of me.

I like to think it's a little of both. The more worry instilled in her, the more manageable she'll be.

"I don't believe you." I part her ass cheeks and slide my cock in between them. "I want you to tell me you're sorry."

She shifts nervously but doesn't try to get up. Bella isn't a virgin anymore, and that I am certain of. I wasn't aware the first time and should have been gentle, but now, I am free to fuck her with everything I've got.

"I'm sorry," she finally chokes out, "I won't come into your room again."

"You're right, you won't. But that's not what I want an apology for." I bite down on my bottom lip, piercing the skin as blood seeps into my mouth. My eyes widen in anticipation as I raise my hand and smack her ass again, only this time, I put all my strength into it.

"Ahhhh," she bellows, shoving her face into the pillow and forcibly gripping the sides of it.

Once the sting subsides, she lifts her head and twists to look at me with tear-stained eyes. "What am I apologizing for?"

"Leaving me."

We can pretend all we want—ignore the elephant in the room every time we're together—but we both felt the pain that day. The only difference is, I still feel it. I tried everything to forget, to diminish the anger and live life to the fullest. I've fucked random women to feel close to someone. I've killed to rid myself of the toxicity. I've cut, I've bled, I've cried. Nothing worked until she came back.

I'll do whatever I have to do to keep her here.

She won't run. She can't hide. She will live this life with me and learn to love the darkest corners of it.

Her fearful expression is replaced with one of empathy. I can see it in her eyes. The sorrow, the regret, the hope that one day I'll forgive her.

Maybe I will.

I grab her by the waist, hoisting her onto her knees, and in one breath, I stick my cock inside her pussy. Her head drops down, back bridged, and ass up. When I begin thrusting, Amira slithers over Bella's side onto the bed.

Pinching her waist, I use it as cushioning to drive myself deeper. "You're so fucking tight. So warm. So wet." She hugs my cock like she never wants to let it go. I push myself up onto my feet, crouched behind her, while crushing her ass with my pelvic bone. My balls swing back and forth, so I grab her hand and pull it between us so that she's cupping them.

She squeezes and releases, repeating the action, and it feels so fucking good. With one hand on her waist, I use the other to grab her hair and tug enough to raise her head. "Does that feel good, baby?"

"Yes."

An electrical charge roots in my cock, releasing and traveling through my entire body. I pull her hair harder, squeeze her waist tighter, and fuck her faster. My cock slides in and out, sloshing in the mess of her arousal. I'm close. So damn close, but I'm not ready.

Stopping my movements, I'm warranted a stink eye from Bella.

I ease my hold on her hair, but still have a good grip as she drops her head down. "I hate you." Her words are muffled by the pillow she's pressed against.

Jerking her head back up, I cover her body with mine. "You wanna come? Get on your knees and say you're sorry around my cock, then maybe I'll let you." I pull her up by my hold on her hair and she gets on her knees. "On the floor." She looks at me, curious to see if I'm serious or not, so I give her a look that says how serious I am. "Now."

She obeys me, and I'm actually surprised.

Kneeled on the floor, she places her hands in her lap. I stand in front of her and grab her by the back of the head, shoving my cock into her open mouth. "Say you're sorry, again."

"I'm sorry," she chokes out around my cock.

"Good girl. Now suck."

My head drops back, hand resting on her head, guiding her motions. There's no way in hell this is her first time sucking dick. Not with the way she's flicking her tongue and using her own saliva to lubricate me as her hand slides up and down with her mouth. The thought of her even looking at another man's dick infuriates me. Never again. She's all mine now.

I grab her and flip her over the end of the bed. She gets on her knees, so her ass is level with my groin, then I feel the heat of her pussy around my swollen cock as I enter her.

My hips move violently as I slide a finger between her ass cheeks and roam around her tight hole.

She whimpers in delight and I'm pretty sure she likes it. "Have you been fucked in the ass before?" I ask her out of sheer curiosity.

She shakes her head no. "Good." Another first saved just for me. But, we'll keep that for next time. I'm too close right now and if I pull out, I'll likely spill all over her when I really want to fill her up with my cum.

I slide my free hand underneath her and begin flicking her clit until it drives her wild. A loud moan rips through her as she comes, sending me over the edge with her cries of pleasure.

"Fuck," I grumble, thrusting deeper and faster. My breaths become heady as she clenches my cock and milks me.

Standing still, I release inside of her.

My hands drop before thrusting a couple more times, then I pull out. Evidence of our orgasms spill onto the bed.

Bella drops down heavily and catches her breath.

I hope she learned her lesson. Then again, part of me hopes she fucks up again just so I can punish her even harder next time.

BELLA IS in my bathroom cleaning up, while I make the bed with a clean blanket. It feels surreal having someone in here. She doesn't know this, but no one has stepped foot in any of my bedrooms since I was eighteen years old. I clean up after myself and set my laundry in the hall for Paulina. Even Peter knows to stay away. She'll also never know that she's the first girl in my bed. I've been with many other girls, but I have different beds for that.

Tonight was a close call. I have every intention of telling Bella about The Grotto and The Dungeon, but it won't be today.

She needs to ease into things here. If I force too much on her too soon, she'll try to escape again and next time, she might not make it out alive.

Bella is a firecracker and I didn't anticipate that. All of my research suggested that she grew up to be a book smart, family-oriented Christian. Her parents are members of the school board, both well-known in their small community. Although they work for pennies and live in a three-bedroom ranch house, they seem pretty normal and happy. Proof that money is not what makes the heart flutter.

I've always hated money. Just because I keep it and use it to my advantage doesn't mean I wouldn't have given it all up for a little normalcy. I didn't want this life. I wanted the life she got—the life Mark got. It was stolen from me, just like my dignity. Now I keep the power because I knew how much

Vincent didn't want me to have it. He wanted to see me fail after Delilah died.

"All done," Bella says, closing the bathroom door behind her. She folds her hands in front of her waist. "Mind if we talk before I go to bed?"

Fuck. She's one of those. A talker, probably a cuddler. What's next—a foot rub?

I blow air out and shrug my shoulders, smoothing my hand over the comforter, black this time.

Bella walks into the middle of the room and stops about five feet away from me. "Are you ever going to tell me where that secret door goes?"

I should have expected this question. "Yes. Eventually you will know everything about the businesses I run."

"Businesses?"

"Did I stutter?" I turn around to look at her, crossing my arms over my bare chest.

I can see her throat bob as she swallows. "You're so rude!" she stammers, eating the space between us.

With her eyes locked on mine, she runs her hands down my arms. I flinch at the foreign sensation. "Let me help you while I'm here. With the businesses, with whatever is eating away at you."

My brows furrow as my gaze drops on her. "What makes you think something is eating away at me?"

"Come on. You're so obvious. You go from hot to cold in the blink of an eye. There's a constant push and pull between us. I don't know if we're friends, enemies, or lovers."

My fingers sweep her ear, tucking her hair behind it. "If I remember right, you have a boyfriend. So, it's certainly not the latter. Friends share secrets and all you tell me are lies. Enemies would be suitable, but the way I make your knees wobble, I doubt that title works on your end."

"I'll tell you a secret, if you tell me one."

Share a secret? I haven't shared a secret with anyone since…her.

"Okay. You go first."

I take a seat on the bed, and she sits down beside me. For a brief moment, it feels like old times, even if we are older. I'm not sure that I've gotten wiser, but I've definitely learned to cover my tracks when I do something stupid.

Her hands fold in her lap, and she looks at me, so I look at her. "I didn't say yes to Trent."

"Wait a minute. You mean you're not engaged?"

She shakes her head. "I care about him a lot, but there has always been something missing between us. A connection, a spark, maybe? If that sort of thing even exists."

"It does," I spit out on impulse.

Surprised, she turns her whole body toward me and pulls her knees to her chest. "You've felt it?"

I feel it now. I don't say it, though. Vulnerability is scary and something I'm not used to.

"No, I haven't."

"Hmm." She bites at her lip. "Well, hopefully someday we both get to."

My heart quivers, another foreign feeling. Our eyes lock and I'm mesmerized by her beauty. Twenty minutes ago I was punishing her and now all I want to do is wrap my arms around her just so she'll do the same. I forgot what it feels like to be held in the arms of another person.

"Your turn," she says, pulling me out of my thoughts.

I wouldn't call it a secret, but since it's heavy on my mind, I give it a go. "You're the last person I hugged." There's a bite in my stomach as the words leave my mouth, and I instantly want to take them back and swallow them.

Her eyes widen. "You haven't been hugged in twelve years?"

I look away, unable to see the pity in her eyes. It will only make me angry. "It's not a big deal. Just drop it."

"Not a big deal—"

"I said drop it," I shout, getting to my feet and crossing the room to Amira. I got her the day of Vincent's funeral. Amira stared me right in the eyes, challenging me. She stood straight up against the glass, exuding power and dominance. I didn't know a thing about king snakes, but I learned quickly that they are one of the few snakes that will eat their own kind, and that appealed to me. Along with her, I purchased a dozen rat snakes to dump into Vincent's final resting place. My hope was that they'd get hungry and feast on his remains.

Everyone had left the burial site and I asked for a moment alone with my father. Well, I paid the undertaker a grand to open the casket and leave me alone with him.

It was just me and the man who took me in and tore me apart.

"You're in good company, you rat bastard, or should I say, you dirty fucking snake. Rest in hell."

Then I dumped the bucket in and told the undertaker to close him up and put him down.

Bella comes up and wraps her arms around me from behind. Her head rests on my back and I freeze. "What are you doing?" I ask in an authoritative tone.

She squeezes tighter, forcing the air out of my lungs. "Please don't shut me out."

"Let go of me."

"No." I can feel her shake her head against my back.

"Dammit, Bella. Let go of me now."

"I'm not letting you go."

"I don't want to hurt you, but I will."

"No, you won't. I told you, I'm not scared of you."

"You're a fool then." I turn around to face her, but she doesn't back up. I walk around her and she grabs me like she's the one with the upper hand. I snarl at her, grasp her bicep and jerk away. "Quit acting like you care."

I don't know what the hell is wrong with me. Actually, yes, I do. I'm fucked up beyond repair and she's the crazy one for thinking she can pry me open and force me to expose my wounds for her.

"I do care. I always have and I always will. Please," she grabs my other arm so that her body is flush with mine, "let me in."

Tears prick the corners of her eyes and I search them, wondering if they're real or if this is all just another act. For all I know, she could be warming up to me so I let her go. Not that I would. But she doesn't know that.

"I let you into my room. I think that's enough for tonight." I walk past her toward the door. "Goodnight, Bella." I pull it open, waiting for her to leave, but she stands there, looking at me like I'm this sad, broken boy in need of twelve years' worth of hugs.

"Go!"

She shakes her head. "No, I'm not leaving you this time." Her feet move, but not toward the door. Instead, she goes over to the bed and flops down like she owns the damn thing.

A low rumble climbs up my throat as I slam the door shut. "Get off my bed."

She was really good at obeying my commands when she wanted to get off—now, not so much.

"You were right," she says, like I'm supposed to know what the hell she's talking about. "I didn't accept the scholarship because they made me feel guilty for leaving. It wasn't their intention, but their words made me feel it anyway."

She's talking about her parents. I do know that.

"I enrolled at a local university. Recognized Trent in a language arts class and I've been under his thumb ever since.

Before I came here, I started to realize my dreams didn't matter to him. He just wanted me by his side while he lived out his own dreams."

Damn her for doing this.

I round the bed and sit down on the edge, my feet still on the ground. "So you turned down Juilliard, stayed with Trent, but still accepted an offer to work on a private island. Why?"

"To finally get away. I was hoping to come here and find myself. I've been searching for the girl with ambition that was heading into foster care—but I still haven't found her."

"I thought you had everything you've ever wanted."

Bella sits up and crosses her legs into a pretzel. "It's not always black and white. I love my family, but I'm more than just a daughter or a sister."

"If you could go back, would you take the scholarship?"

"Without a doubt." She doesn't even think on the question, just spits out the answer like she's known it all along.

There's a beat of silence before I break it. "My adopted mother committed suicide when she realized that I wasn't her son and he was never coming back. I watched her stuff her mouth full of pills and didn't stop her. It was one less person I had to fend off before making my escape."

Her void expression doesn't falter. I see no sign of judgment or hatred in her eyes. "And your dad?"

"I killed him. A little hydrofluoric acid in his evening shot of Scotch and I watched as it ate away at his insides. He screamed in agony as it burned his esophagus, but that was only the beginning."

"Help me," he cries, a harrowing sound that only makes me laugh harder.

"Help you? Why the hell would I do that? I'm enjoying this too much. How's it feel to be burning from the inside out? Not quite as bad as I felt every time you tried to give me a fever because your wife always thought I had one. You're a loyal husband, I'll give you

that. That's why she thought I said those things. Because I was sick! No. The only sick person in this house is you. I almost died three times, but you wouldn't know that."

"He curled over and dropped dead, then I had his own men come and take his body out and make it look like an accident."

This time, I see it. The judgment. The fear. It's written all over her pretty face.

"Go ahead and tell me what a sick bastard I am. Not like I don't already know."

"I...I'm not saying that. It's obvious you went through some things that made you do what you did."

Now she knows the monster I became when she left me. And for that, she can join me in the darkness.

"Get some sleep, Bella. We have a busy day tomorrow." I stand up, thinking she'll jump at the opportunity to run out of here, so she can get as far away from me as possible.

Instead, she slides under the blanket and makes herself comfortable. "Just one night? For old times' sake?"

I've got no fucking idea why she's not hauling ass, and I don't like this unpredictable action, but I also don't make her leave. Instead, I kill the lights, leaving the middle aquarium light on, and go to the other side of the bed.

I don't lie down. I just sit there and watch her until she's fast asleep. Then I watch her some more. Every twitch of her lips and crinkle of her nose. I admire the crease in her forehead when she dreams. I take it all in, wondering how I expect a girl like that to ever love a monster like me.

22

"Good morning." Cal closes the book in his hand and sets it down on the nightstand. He's no longer shirtless and in gray sweats. Instead, he's wearing a white button-up shirt with the sleeves rolled up and a pair of black dress pants with matching socks. The tips of his hair glisten, so I assume he took a shower not too long ago.

I push myself into a sitting position and lick my dry lips. "Did you sleep at all?" I turn my head slightly, trying to avoid him smelling my nasty morning breath.

"Few hours."

The bags under his eyes tell me he's lying. If I had to guess, he stayed up and read all night.

Something feels different this morning. A new excitement inside of me, this feeling of contentment. My heart somersaults when he cracks a smile, and it's a look I'll never get tired of.

Right now, I don't feel like a prisoner kept here against her will. Today, I want to be here. And tomorrow, and possibly the next day. There's something undeniable between Cal and me and I can't wait to explore the possibilities.

Maybe he was right. Maybe fate did bring us back together. It's possible that he was the one meant to fill that emptiness inside of me all along.

Climbing off the bed, I stretch my arms up and yawn while covering my mouth. I would have thought waking up next to Cal would be awkward and uncomfortable, but it's not. Regardless, I feel disgusting and need a shower. "I'm going back to my room to get cleaned up. See you at breakfast?"

"You sure will. In fact, we'll be eating in the courtyard this morning."

"Oh, that will be nice."

There's something about the way he's looking at me. He seems happy, way too happy. He's blazing confidence and I get the feeling he's got something planned for us today. Normally I'd dread it, but now, I'm pretty excited.

I go to leave but stop to give him a double take. Smiling, I finally unlock the door and leave, closing it behind me.

My back presses to the door and I'm lost in thoughts about how much of a breakthrough we had last night. It started off intensely. I thought for sure Cal was going to be furious when he found me in the secret passage. Then came the punishing sex, which I thoroughly enjoyed, aside from the snakes. Cal was dominant, possessive, and so damn sexy. It opened my eyes to a new world of pleasure that I'm anxious to revisit. Not to mention, the passion. God, did I feel it.

That wasn't the best part of the night, though. The best part is when he opened up to me and shared secrets that I don't think he's ever told anyone. It made me feel special and I was able to remember that, deep down, Cal is not a bad person. He never was. He just doesn't know any better. It's no excuse for murder, but I don't know the whole story. I'm not sure anyone does. It's apparent he faced some traumatic events and I'm hopeful that one day he'll tell me all about them. Even if he wanted to, even if I wanted him to, he can't go back and change his past. I just hope that with me by his side, he doesn't have to live there anymore. I want to help him heal—I want us to heal together.

"Good morning, Ms. Jenkins," Peter says, startling me.

I peel myself off the door with a permanent grin plastered on my face. "It is a good morning, Peter."

"I couldn't help but notice your bed was made this morning. And now I see you're leaving Mr. Ellis's room. I assume things are well with you two?"

My lips press together as I try to bite back the smile that won't leave my face. "You assume correctly."

"That's quite a compliment coming from Mr. Ellis. He doesn't allow anyone in his room."

Peter had mentioned that before, but it didn't really register, and now I'm curious what he means by it. "Not even the women he brings home?"

Peter leans forward and whispers, "In all my years with Mr. Ellis, twelve to be exact, he has never had a woman in his room."

My eyes widen in surprise. "Really? That's so strange for a man who entertains women often."

"You didn't hear it from me." He places a hand on my shoulder, steering me away from Cal's door. "The cook has prepared a special breakfast. I'll see you later, Ms. Jenkins."

I thank Peter with a smile and continue down the hall, stopping when I notice the small black camera on the wall outside of my door. I look behind me and see a couple more. They're everywhere.

Just when I think Cal and I are making progress, whatever that means for us, he proves that he's still all about keeping me as his live-in prisoner. I shouldn't be surprised, considering there was a manhunt for me, covering the entire island last night. I'm just hoping that, eventually, I can earn his trust. Now I just have to decide what I'll do when I get it. Now that Cal is back in my life—as much of a roller coaster as it has been—the idea of him not being part of it hurts. Then again, the idea of never leaving the island hurts, too. There has to be a common ground we can reach, assuming Cal is keen on compromise. I'm not holding my breath, but I'm also not giving up hope.

MY HAIR IS STILL wet from the quick shower I took. After I brushed it out, knowing that it would be extra frizzy and curly since I didn't dry it, I put on a pair of yoga lounge pants and my old Hickory Knoll High 'Class of 2016' sweatshirt. I'm hoping Cal doesn't plan to do much work today, because as the morning goes on, the sorer I begin to feel. My first time hurt, but this is a whole new level of pain. Each step has my lower half aching, while a sharp pain shoots from my vagina to my abdomen. Cal gave me quite the beating last night—I'm pretty sure there's even a bruise on my ass from him slapping it three times—but damn if it wasn't worth the pain.

I go over to my nightstand and open the drawer to take my birth control. They're tiny pills, so I'm able to swallow it down without water.

My mind wanders to Trent and how he's going to react when he finds out what I've done. There's no way I can't tell him. It's also going to be my opportunity to end things for good. Being here, away from him, has made me realize that it's time to chase my own dreams while he lives out his. I'll always care about him, but the way my heart is beginning to open up to Cal assures me that I never really loved Trent.

I'm sure by now he and my parents are wondering why I

haven't reached out. I did tell them there was a chance service would be sketchy and not to worry if they didn't hear from me for a while. It's been almost two weeks, though, and by now, I'm sure worry has set in.

Thanksgiving is in two days and I'm not sure what that looks like here, but I know I'll miss the family dinners I have back home. Maybe I can assist the cook and make a good old-fashioned turkey dinner for Cal. I'm not even sure that he's had one since The Webster House. Even though Thanksgiving there wasn't exactly memorable. It consisted of two dozen kids fighting to get the last slice of turkey before we were sent to our rooms, so the adults could settle their stomachs without the commotion of us kids.

Sliding my feet into my house slippers, I leave the room, closing the door behind me. As I'm walking to the elevator and passing Cal's room, I think back to the secret door in the closet. Obviously I know Cal didn't put that door there and, of course, he'd use the extra space that's given through it, but I can't help but wonder what he could be hiding that would require a passcode for entry. Eventually I'll find out, but right now is not that time. Right now, my hunger pangs are reminding me that I need to eat.

The elevator doors open and I expect it to be empty. I'm surprised to see that Peter is onboard. "Oh, Hi, Peter. Going down?"

He's standing next to the panel with his hand hovering over the G, for the ground level. "Yes, ma'am. And you are as well, I assume?"

"Sure am."

He presses the button on the elevator then looks at his phone, there's a static noise and muffled voices coming from it that has me peering over his shoulder.

It's a video of some sort. It looks like camera footage,

which doesn't surprise me since they armed the entire castle last night.

We make it to the fifth floor, then fourth, and that's when I hear Cal's voice on the phone. He sounds angry. Peter immediately goes to silence it, but like a savage child, I snatch his phone from his hand.

"When is this footage from?" I hold up the phone, wondering why the hell Cal is walking out of the mystery door on the main floor with a girl. Wait...not just any girl. That was our waitress—Serena, I think, was her name. She's wearing some sleazy-looking, leather skirt that barely covers her ass and a top that looks more like a bra, with a large black duffel bag hanging over her shoulder. That's not what gets to me, though. It's the way she's rubbing up on him and he's not pushing her away. His head turns slightly as she kisses all over his neck and I can feel the heat rise in my cheeks.

My stomach twists in knots, and for the first time since I've got here, I'm jealous. Really fucking jealous. In fact, I might just go claw the bitch's eyes out once this elevator stops.

"Please give that back to me."

"Is this live?"

"Yes, Ms. Jenkins, and Mr. Ellis would not be happy if he knew you were viewing security footage." He holds his hand out, but I grip his phone like my life depends on it.

I shake my head no. "Not until you tell me where that door goes."

"I can't do that."

The elevator comes to a stop, but I squeeze my body between him and the panel and press the button to hold the doors shut. "Then I can't give you your phone. Where does that door go?" I look back at the screen and both Cal and Serena are gone from the camera's view.

"It's a private room that's off-limits for staff, as well as...you."

"But Serena is a staff member, or at least she was, until Cal fired her." *If he really did fire her.* "Why was she in there if it's off-limits to staff members?"

It seems the cat's got his tongue. I remove my finger from the button and hand him his phone. "Fine. I'll just find out for myself."

The doors open and my heart is pounding. Instead of going to the courtyard, I turn in the opposite direction and walk straight to the door. Knowing that I'll have no luck, I turn the handle anyway.

Locked. Of course.

"Cal," I holler, walking toward the main entrance, curious if that's where he shuffled Serena to in an attempt to hide her. Or maybe he doesn't even want to hide her. Maybe she's here so they can flaunt their past in my face. "Cal," I holler again, once I'm on the front side of the castle.

I can hear Peter talking to someone behind me, likely ratting me out for taking his phone. I spin around and see him talking to Cal as they both move at a steady pace toward me.

"Bella, what's going on?" His eyebrows are dipped into a sharp V. The top three buttons on his shirt are undone and I try to remember if that's the way they were when I left him this morning. Cal stops directly in front of me and places a hand on Peter's shoulder. "I've got things from here. Please tend to our guest."

Rage cripples me. "Your guest? As in, Serena? So you fire her but let her stay as a guest?" Cal lifts his lip in a knowing smirk, only fueling the flames. "Why are you smiling? This isn't funny."

"Didn't you learn your lesson last night? Or do I need to remind you of what happens when you start snooping?"

I give him a shove and he takes a few steps back, but I quickly eat up the gap between us. "Why the hell is that waitress still here and what were you two doing?"

Cal grabs both of my wrists and that cocky grin is still plastered on his face. "Someone's jealous."

"I am not," I huff, "but I would like to know what's behind that door and why you two just came out of it together." I eyeball the door and he looks to our right, acknowledging it.

"More guest quarters." He begins pulling me toward the back exit to the courtyard. "Come on. There is someone here to see you."

"No," I snap, jerking my hand away, "did you have sex with her just now?"

He wears a defensive but also perturbed expression. "What? No!"

"Have you slept with anyone else since I've arrived?"

The door to the mystery room opens and the bartender from last night stands in the doorframe. Her movements freeze as she looks from me to Cal and quickly shuts it. Cal gives her a warning look and clenches his jaw.

"You've got to be fucking kidding me," I grumble. "You really are a manwhore, aren't you? Byron wasn't lying."

Cal instantly becomes agitated. "What the hell does Byron have to do with any of this?"

"He told me you aren't as lonely as I think you are and didn't deny that you sleep with hookers."

Cal laughs. "Hookers? Byron's a damn idiot. I don't have to pay women for their company." His lip curls. "They beg for it."

"Of course they do. Because you're such a catch." I push past him.

"Bella, would you wait a damn minute?"

"No." I look him dead in the eye as I choke back the tears

begging to break free. "This was all a big mistake. We never should have—"

"Nothing is ever a mistake. You coming here was always meant to be. But we all have skeletons in our closet and you can't expect any less from me."

His words hit hard. Like a knife digging into my chest, twisting and turning. I don't know what I expected from him, from us. Certainly not a relationship. That's insane. A happily-ever-after? It's not possible with Cal.

"Now who's this guest you were going on about? A new maid in a skimpy dress with a feather duster?"

He never answered my question when I asked if he's slept with anyone else since I've arrived. He doesn't need to. It's apparent he has had the company of other women, as he'd put it. In my words, he's fucking them.

I'm disgusted as I walk quickly to the courtyard. My hunger has subsided and been replaced with nausea. I was starting to feel settled here. It was beginning to feel like home, even though it's temporary. Part of me was excited that Cal and I were moving in the right direction. The undeniable spark was there and I couldn't wait to see him this morning, ready to spend the day only growing closer. Then I saw the cameras, and after that came the footage.

I'm so lost in my thoughts when I enter the new courtyard that I don't even notice the man seated with his back to me until Peter snaps me out of my trance. "Right this way, Ms. Jenkins."

"Who is that?" I ask, while we make our way to the table.

"Your guest."

My guest? Nervousness sweeps through me. The man sits there quietly in a slate suit, not even turning around when he hears us coming.

Part of me knows before we get there. Call it intuition. I

hoped I was wrong, but my guess is proven to be right when Trent looks up at me from where he's sitting.

"Bella," he stands and wraps his arms around me, "God, I've been so worried."

I'm rendered speechless as I stand there with my hands at my sides. I slowly raise them, embracing the hug while my heart pounds against his chest cavity. "What are you doing here, Trent?"

He pulls back, looks at me, and smiles. "I came to see you. We've all been worried sick that something had happened. I called the ferry company on the main island and they confirmed that you made it here safely, but no one's heard from you."

If he's here, that means Cal allowed it. He let Trent come on his island, even after claiming to hate him. I wish I could have seen the reunion between the two of them. It's possible that they patched up old wounds from the past and are ready to move forward, much like Cal and I were trying to do.

"Let's sit." I gesture to the chairs. "I told you that I wasn't sure I'd have service and not to worry." I force a smile on my face, as hard as it is. It feels like Trent just walked into my new world, but he doesn't fit here.

"I figured you'd be a little happier to see me, considering I took the time off work and came all this way. A thank-you would be appropriate."

"Thank you?" I say it as a question, not a statement.

"You're welcome. Now, let's eat, then you can give me a tour of this place." He glances behind him, looking up at the castle. "It's nothing like I'd expected when you said you'd be designing a hotel."

"It's not what I expected either." The words coming out of my mouth couldn't be truer. I never expected my boss to be the only best friend I'd ever had. I thought I'd come here and put in laborious hours, staying up until the next morning working on designs and having meetings with contractors. I also never expected to fall out of love with Trent and give myself to another man. I came here a virgin, with imponderable dreams. No idea which direction I was headed in. I played the piano again. I looked in the eye of the storm, and I conquered it. My heart began to open and ten minutes ago, I was reminded why I've kept it closed all my life. I was a fool, and I still am.

"I told you it was a pipe dream. Come home with me, Bella. Let's start our life together."

"Trent, can you excuse me for a minute?" I push my chair back, scraping the legs against the cement. I don't even wait for his response as I put a hand over my mouth to stop the sounds of my shattered heart from spilling out.

I'm looking down at my feet when I crash into someone. I peer up, my tear-soaked eyes looking into Cal's.

His hands set on either side of my waist. "What the hell did he do to make you cry?" His gaze shifts behind me, locked on Trent.

"It's not him. It's you." I step around him and walk back into the foyer of the castle. I keep going until I'm at the front doors. With both hands, I swing one open and walk outside. When I think that Cal is going to talk to Trent, he surprises me and follows me instead.

This time, I don't run away. I turn around and shout with a pointed finger, "Why in the world would you bring him here?"

"I didn't bring him. He came on his own free will."

"And you let him? I thought you hated him."

"I do, which is exactly why I allowed it. He needs to know it's over between you two. Now go out there, tell him you're fine, so I can send him on his way."

A dry laugh scales up my throat. "No."

"Excuse me?"

"I'm not telling him that. In fact, I should go out there right now and tell him everything. How you lured me here with the perfect job wrapped in a shiny box with a glittery bow. I can even tell him how you forced me to take my clothes off and stole my virginity from me without my approval."

He gives me a side-eyed glare. "Hey now, you never told me to stop."

"You never asked me if I wanted you to."

"Does a thief ever ask for permission?"

My mouth falls open at his arrogance. "You're such an ass. I can't believe I was actually starting to like you."

"Like me?" He chuckles. "I had you eating out of my hand, Bella." He closes the space between us and presses his body against mine. His groin digs into my hip bone, igniting every cell inside of me with a burning desire.

His way with words is repulsive, but the chemistry that sizzles between us when we touch is undeniable.

"Maybe I should go out there and accept Trent's proposal. Your contract says I have to stay, it doesn't say I can't have company. He can live here with me until my time is up."

Cal grinds against me, his lips ghosting over mine as he cups my cheeks in his hands. "Your time is infinite and if he stays, I'll kill him and make you watch while I do it."

I swallow hard. "You don't have any power over me. I can get out of the contract."

"And allow your parents to lose their jobs. Go for it."

Damn. I forgot about that.

"Now, I want you to walk back out there like a good girl and end things with Trent, so we never have to deal with his uptight ass again. And if you dare tell him anything about our agreement, or anything else that's taken place on this island, your family will suffer." His lips crash into mine in a tantalizing manner. Hard and forceful, as if he's the one I'm kissing goodbye.

He's so bitter, but he tastes so sweet. Like temptation on a platter—a forbidden fruit. But I've bent over backward for him since I arrived. Maybe he needs to bend a little, too. I'll go back out there, and I'll keep my mouth shut because I love my family, but now it's time for Cal to feel the sting of rejection. He's fucking other girls, so why should he care if I have relations with other men? If the other women stay, so can Trent. I might not want him here, but Cal doesn't know that.

I break the suction of our mouths and smile coyly. "Will you be joining us for breakfast?" My fingers sweep across his bottom lip, wiping the excess saliva from our hard-pressed kiss.

"You think I'd leave you alone with that animal? Of course I am."

"Good. Let's get this over with." I walk around him and pull open the door. He presses a hand to it, allowing me to enter first.

"Let's."

23

THAT WAS EASIER than I thought it would be. Bella is becoming more compliant each day, which is a step in the right direction. Last night we had a little mishap when her curiosity got the best of her—and again this morning, when Peter let his guard down—but as long as we're moving forward, we're on track.

It's possible we may be ready sooner than I thought. Regardless of whether or not she has a say in her future, I would like it to be a pleasant one. I've always heard spring weddings are beautiful. It won't be long until she's bound to me forever and the pact is carried out on both our ends—a vow to never part. Until kingdom come.

Before joining them, I make a quick call to Byron. It goes straight to voicemail, which pisses me off more than I already am.

"Get those damn women off this island now or you're done, this friendship is done, and I'll hire a new attorney to change my will. You won't get a fucking dime."

The space downstairs is complete but wasn't supposed to be in use until after the grand opening. Byron, being the nympho that he is, can't seem to keep his dick in his pants long enough to grasp that concept. Serena and Arabella were supposed to be gone after my night with Bella on the yacht. In fact, they were never supposed to be here in the first place, but Byron brought them for his own personal gain. Now I can see that he kept them here and he's been using The Grotto as his own sexual playground.

He was scarce for a while, but now that he's around, it's obvious he's trying to get under Bella's skin. Bringing the girls here, telling her about my previous hookups. He sees her as a threat, so he's making himself one.

I tuck my phone in my pocket and rejoin them in the courtyard.

"Trent," Bella says, grabbing his attention.

He dusts his hands off on his gray slacks and gets up to face where she stands. His mouth is stuffed full of muffin and while I wish he'd choke on it, I prefer he lives to hear what Bella is about to say.

"You remember Cal…Callum, right?"

Looking me in the eye as he chews, his mouth likely becoming drier and drier with each passing second, he seems stunned.

His gaze shifts from me to Bella. "What is he doing here?"

"Cal owns the property. He inherited Ellis Empire when Mr. Ellis Senior passed away. He was adopted by Vincent and Delilah Ellis when he left The Webster House."

Trent looks like he's seen a ghost, and not a friendly one. He reaches his hand out and grabs Bella, pulling her closer to him with his eyes cemented to mine. "You never mentioned that." He still holds my stare, although he's speaking to Bella.

"I had no idea until I arrived."

"Could you give us a minute alone, Callum?" He finally looks at Bella. "My girlfriend and I have a lot to discuss."

"Actually," I reach the table and grab a muffin, peeling

back the paper, "I'm pretty hungry."

"Me, too," Bella chimes in. She takes Trent's hand in hers and I watch intently as she wraps her fingers around his. "Let's eat."

Trent follows her lead and sits back down in his chair. I pull out a seat for Bella and take the one to the left of her. "This is nice. Like a reunion of old friends." I bite into my muffin, challenging Trent with a glare.

"Cut the bullshit, Callum. We were never friends and you know it. Wouldn't surprise me if you purposely hired Bella just to get under my skin."

I hold up a finger, putting him off while I chew the food in my mouth because, unlike him, I have manners.

"Actually, honey," Bella says to Trent, "Cal had no idea."

Honey? Is she buttering him up before leaving him high and dry?

"Here," she hands him a croissant, "try these. They're like no croissant you've ever tasted before. In fact, Cal has the best cook and every meal is divine. Wait until you see what's for dinner."

Dinner? I toss my muffin down on the small round plate. "Bella," I warn, "isn't there something you wanted to tell Trent?"

"Oh yes," she giggles, "how could I forget? Our room has the best view on the island. It's on the top floor. Well," she corrects herself, "there's one floor higher up, which I think is the turret. I've been wanting to go up there, but the elevator stops on the eighth floor and the stairs are closed off. We should—"

"Bella," I snap, "what the hell are you doing?"

"Whoa. Don't talk to her like that." Trent raises his hand, then rests it on Bella's lap like he's trying to comfort her from my outburst.

I clear my throat, steady my pulse, and glower at her. "Do

it."

She sits there poised with a twitch of humor on her lips. "I don't know what you're talking about. I want Trent to feel at home here. After all, he'll be staying. Right, honey?" She looks at him with fluttering eyelashes.

"Well, for a couple nights. I'll have to leave the day after tomorrow. It's Thanksgiving and all. I was hoping to convince you to come home with me."

"Holidays in Hickory Knoll are my favorite." Bella rivets her eyes to me. "There's nothing like being surrounded by people who love you."

I feel like that was a jab. Is she insinuating that no one loves me? That I'm incapable of being loved? If so, she's correct.

I've lost all control of myself when I jump out of my chair and grip her by the arm until she's standing. "We need to talk." I pull her away, although she doesn't put up a fight, and follows my lead.

Trent shifts in his seat and mumbles something that I completely ignore.

"It's okay, Trent. My boss is an asshole and my job is demanding."

"You got that right," I growl in a whisper.

Once we're back inside, I pull Bella into a small alcove. "You've got some fucking nerve."

"So do you. Screwing other girls while you're sleeping with me. Real classy, Cal. And to think, I was starting to feel like I belonged here."

"I'm not fucking anyone else. But if you keep this shit up, I'll lay Serena out on your bed and let her cream on your clean linen."

Bella raises a hand and slaps me across the face. I snarl at the sting, tightening my grip on her. Her shallow breaths hit the nape of my neck when I lean forward and whisper in her ear, "Then I'll put your face in her mess while I fuck you from behind."

"I hate you."

My erection threatens the fabric of my pants and there's no doubt that I could come just by grinding into her while she trembles beneath me. "I don't believe you. I think you hate that you want me."

She doesn't respond, but her labored breathing and the way her heart is vibrating against her sweatshirt is proof enough.

"Get out there and end this now, so I can take you to the turret and fuck you while we watch him leave."

Her head cocks to the side and she thinks hard. A minute later, a smirk grows on her face. "You tell me what's behind that door and the one in your closet, and I won't fuck Trent tonight."

My jaw ticks, knuckles clenched. Just the words—the thought—sends my blood to a boiling point. "You wouldn't dare."

"Try me."

"Don't push me, Bella. I will kill him. I told you what I did to my parents. It's nothing for me to end the life of the guy I hate more than anyone."

"You say you hate him, but I think you're just jealous of him."

I bite down, my teeth grinding so hard that I feel the crunch against my tongue. I always knew I'd tell her, I just didn't want it to be this soon. "It's part of the hotel. A separate area we call The Grotto. All of Ellis Empire resorts have a grotto area. My guests pay a large amount of money for a retreat that offers luxurious accommodations, as well as the opportunity to become a member of a VIP club."

"VIP club? What does that mean?"

"Make him leave and I'll show you. I'll open your eyes to a

world you never knew existed." My eyes wander to her tempting mouth.

"Tell me now or I'll go climb on his lap and ride him right in the courtyard."

I laugh. "Seventy-three hours ago you were a virgin. You're far from having the nerve."

"Watch me," she titters, grinning from ear to ear as she slides out from under me.

"Don't you dare, Bella."

She keeps walking, adding an extra shake to her hips. Trent meets her halfway and his voice raises as he speaks, "Where were you? I looked everywhere. This place is a damn maze."

I adjust my erect cock in my pants and go to where they stand. Just as I'm about to grab their attention, Bella crushes her mouth to Trent's.

Rage consumes me. Every nerve inside me feels obstructed as I join the two of them and rip Trent away from her. "Breakfast is over."

"Get your damn hands off me," Trent barks. "Come on, Bella. Let's go to your room, so we can have some privacy."

I hold up a hand. "Not so fast. Peter will show you to your room." I look at Bella. "We have a scheduled conference call with Barbara in twenty minutes."

Bella cocks a brow. "I didn't know about that."

"You do now." I holler over them, "Peter." A second later, he's there, waiting for my instruction. "Please show Mr. Beckham to his room on the sixth floor. He'll be staying in six-twenty-two."

"Yes, sir." Peter nods.

"We'll see you later, Trent." I enunciate his name, hating the way it sounds. I despise everything about that man, and not because I'm jealous of anything he has. It's because he stole everything *I had*.

24

"THIS IS RIDICULOUS. Trent just got here an hour ago and you expect him to just go off on his own in this huge place?"

"Why do you care? You told me something was missing between you two anyways."

"That has nothing to do with human decency. The guy came all this way because he was worried about me. That means something."

"It means he wants to deflower you then leave you. I know men."

"You know how you are. Not all men are womanizers."

The door to Cal's office closes behind us and I take a seat on the couch against the back wall. I pick up one of the chess pieces, look at it, then set it back down on an empty square.

"Can we just get on with this conference call, so I can at least do some sort of work while I'm here."

He takes slow steps in my direction, each one causing my heart to flutter. "The call isn't until seven o'clock tonight. Barbara is on the West Coast."

"So you lied, even though you claim to be truthful."

"I lied to get you away."

Cal kneels down in front of the round glass table holding the chessboard. Picking up a rook, he moves it up. "He's not staying. You do realize that, don't you?"

I pick up another piece and move it. "You just put him in a room, didn't you?"

Cal moves another rook, likely guarding his queen. "You're making this harder than it needs to be. If you want him to go home and tell your parents about how miserable you seem here, fine. Let them worry. Otherwise, you can send him on his merry way and tell him you'll see him when you get back."

The last thing I want is for my parents to worry or lose their jobs. I truly believe Cal would go to those lengths to keep me here. I still haven't read over the contract because he basically spelled it all out for me. My hands are tied for the next six months.

"He'll be more worried if I make him leave tonight. Give it until morning and I'll break things off."

Cal chastises me when he thinks I screwed up. Now I get one night to punish him, but I can promise it won't be as satisfying as the decree I received.

"Fine. But you stay the hell away from his room. You two will only communicate if I am there."

"Controlling much?"

"Yes. Yes, I am." He sets his pawn down, taking my king. "Check."

I look up at him as he stands, rounding the table with his gaze set on me. My palms dampen as I drop back onto the couch in defeat.

Using his thumb, he tips my chin and hovers his lips over mine. "I didn't like seeing you kiss him."

Tingles ride downward from his touch. "I don't like seeing you leave strange rooms with women."

"So you were jealous?" He smirks against my mouth.

"Were you?"

"More jealous than I've ever been in my entire life. I could have killed him with my bare hands."

Cal drops the weight of his body on me and devours my mouth like he's trying to make me forget my kiss with Trent. Not that it was anything like this. Kissing Cal is like nothing I've ever felt before.

His knee presses between my legs, grating against my crotch. "Let me fuck you so good you never want to look at another man again."

I moan into his mouth when the friction of his knee intensifies. I'm a terrible person for wanting this while Trent is here. Regardless, right now, I want Cal inside of me more than I've ever wanted anything.

I'm anticipating it will be painful. My insides feel bruised and swollen, but I don't stop him as he grabs me by my waist and flips me over onto my knees. My hands grip the back of the couch as he teases the skin of my lower back with the tips of his fingers, leaving goosebumps in his path. My pants come down, along with my underwear, hugging my knees. The sound of his zipper going down has my nipples puckering against my bra.

"Are you still taking the pill?" he asks from behind me.

"Mmhmm."

"Good girl." He groans before curling his fingers inside of me.

My back bends as he pumps them at just the right pace, sending a rush of adrenaline through me. I roll my hips as he swirls his fingers inside, loosening me up for what's coming next.

I reach my hand back in search of his hardness and find it pressed against my ass cheek. My fingers wrap around his girth and I stroke him to the best of my ability in this position. A pleasurable moan rips through me when he uses his thumb to circle my clit.

With the way he's working his fingers, I'll be coming before he even puts his cock inside of me. Cal takes my hand off him but doesn't stop fingering me.

I look over my shoulder to see if something's wrong.

"You keep that up and we'll be finished before we start."

Suddenly, he picks up his pace, bringing out another moan from me, this time louder. No matter how hard I try to quiet myself, even with my face pressed into the couch, it's no use. Everything he does feels so good, and when I think it can't get any better, he flicks his finger just right, sending me over the edge again.

"Scream for me, baby."

He goes knuckle-deep, and I feel my walls close around him. Not holding back, I cry out in euphoria. "Ugh. Oh God, Cal."

"That's right. Say my name." He smacks a hand to my ass and I roll my hips.

Just as I'm about to come, he pulls his fingers out and slides his dick inside of me. "Come around my dick, Bella." His fingers grip my hips, and he power drives himself into me.

He completely fills me up with his dick, and it fits perfectly. It's like I was molded just for him. Arching my back, I lift my head and close my eyes while my nails burrow into the thick leather of the couch.

Something cold on my skin alarms me and I turn my head to see Cal dragging the queen chess piece over my ass cheek. He's wearing a shit-eating grin, and I immediately know he's got something planned.

"Take a deep breath." His voice is raspy and his eyes offer a warning.

I do as I'm told, anxious for him to continue so I can

come, although my hands begin trembling out of worry of what he's about to do.

The tip of the chess piece enters my asshole and my lower half jolts. I tug forward slightly, but he grabs my hips and pulls me back into place and begins fucking me again.

"Cal?" I say in question, "What are you doing?" It's a dumb question. I know exactly what he's doing. I may have been a virgin up until recently, but I do know what an anal plug is, although, I've never had one inside of me and never cared to, but Cal makes me do a lot of things I never thought I'd do.

It's cold and foreign, spreading me apart slightly with a tinge of pain, but nothing unbearable. As he picks up his pace, moving his cock in and out of me, he pushes the chess piece deeper, causing me to shriek. He begins twisting and turning it, but the pain subsides quickly and all I can focus on is his pelvic bone writhing against mine as he fucks my pussy.

My hips roll and I meet him thrust for thrust. He picks up his pace, and I bite down on my lip, trying to control my outburst as I orgasm around his dick.

Cal grunts, his breathing rapid and labored. He digs so deep inside of me that I can feel him in my stomach. Freezing, he fills me up with his cum and stops turning the chess piece.

In a swift motion, he slides his dick out and replaces it with his fingers. I revel beneath him. A new and exciting sensation flows through me and I feel myself gush with liquid into his hand. I'm not sure what happened, but it feels so damn good, and I don't want it to stop.

Sounds I didn't know I could make escape me as I come undone around his fingers.

I feel out of control, like my body is not my own as I'm struck with insatiable heat.

Cal moans in delight and keeps going until I do it again,

RACHEL LEIGH

squirting my juices all over. It hits the couch and my legs and doesn't ease up as he digs his fingers farther inside of me.

"Fuck, Cal. I'm… Oh God," I scream in ecstasy.

He growls like a beast and I finally pull away, stopping him, because I'm not sure my body can take much more. My head is spiraling, my mouth parched.

Once I settle down a bit, I feel embarrassed about the mess around me. I drop my ass and turn around, tucking my knees as I sit on the liquid spill. "I'm sorry."

Cal chortles, which calms my nerves a tad. "What the hell are you sorry about? That was sexy as hell."

"Is that normal?" I feel stupid for even asking, but I didn't know it was possible for a woman to…ejaculate.

"Yeah, it's normal. It means you've got a gift, and I happen to love the fuck out of it. Not all women squirt, but those who do experience the best orgasms."

Squirt? God, just the word itself makes my cheeks blush.

Cal walks into the bathroom and returns with a towel and hands it to me. I fold it in my lap as I tug my soaked pants up and adjust my shirt back in place. I still feel like my head is in a cloud, like I'm stuck in this euphoric state. "I've never felt anything like that."

Leaning forward, he presses his lips to my forehead. "Then I can't wait to make you do it again."

My heart squeezes at the gentleness of his kiss. The softness in his words. It's eye-opening and right now, all I want to do is take a shower then lie in bed and let him hold me until I fall asleep.

One day. Maybe.

"Trent is in his room, so you can go to yours and get changed." He begins tapping on his phone as he talks to me. "Paulina will be doing rounds soon for laundry, so we can get those cleaned for you." He looks up. "I meant what I said, Bella. You are not to be alone with him."

Then he leaves. He just leaves me sitting on his couch in my own fluid.

"Thanks for the multiple orgasms," I mumble as the door latches shut.

25

I'm PACING The Grotto floor, watching my app where I have the live footage pulled up, so I can see Bella's bedroom door. So far, she's obeying me and staying put.

I'm tired as hell. Haven't slept in two days, and it's not looking good for tonight either. Now I've got to watch her ass and his to make sure no funny business is pulled. I want to trust Bella, I really do, but the way I've been duped by her in the past has me wondering if her sincerity lately is a ploy to try and leave. Unfortunately, if she does try that, I'd have to be the bad guy and carry out my threat to destroy her parents' lives.

A call comes through, interrupting the live stream.

Byron. It's about damn time.

"Where the hell are you?" I huff into the speaker of the phone.

"Had to go take care of something. I'll be back later tonight. Where are you?"

My lack of patience gets the best of me. "The same damn place I've been for the last two months. Now get your ass back here. We need to talk."

"I'll be there around ten. Meet me downstairs. And you're right. We do need to talk."

He ends the call. His ass really just hung up on me *again*. I'm getting real tired of this shit he's been pulling lately. I know he's trying to turn Bella against me. He wants her gone, and he's making it known.

I get to the dining room, just as the cook is setting the table for dinner. Nothing like a nice dinner with my future wife and her boyfriend to end this day on a good note.

"Good evening, Mr. Ellis," Peter says as he enters the room with his hands behind his back. "Ms. Jenkins has informed me that Mr. Beckham refuses to join you for dinner tonight."

My fists ball at my sides as I try to remain calm. There is no one I hate more than Trent Beckham, and nothing I hate more than an ungrateful guest. "Then you can relay to *Mr. Beckham*," I growl his name, "that he can go hungry tonight."

Peter tips his head. "Very well."

I walk so fast out of the dining hall that my body can barely keep up with my feet. Bypassing Peter, I head straight for the elevator and jump on, not even holding the door for him. He's much more agile than most men his age, but he still moves slowly and right now, I'm in a hurry.

Instead of stopping at the sixth floor to confront Trent, I go to Bella.

My knuckles pound against her door repeatedly, until she finally pulls it open. Brushing past her, I enter her room. "It seems your…" I stop, completely caught off guard when I see Trent sitting on her bed. "When did he get here?"

I watched the cameras and didn't see him come up. *Dammit!* It must have been when I was on the phone with Byron. Two whole goddamn minutes and he found a way to weasel his way into her room.

Trent stands up, his shoulders drawn back like he's challenging me. "Is there a problem, Callum? I am Bella's soon-to-be fiancé, and guest, and to be honest, I'm not too happy with the way you've been talking to her. Seems a little unprofessional, if you ask me."

"I didn't ask you, but thanks for your input, *Trent*." His name alone makes me want to break things.

It's ironic that the boy I've hated since I was eleven is now standing in my kingdom, telling me I'm unprofessional.

Trent takes a step forward and places an arm around Bella's waist. "I think you need to leave this room. It's Bella's private space and you shouldn't be in here."

Gnashing my teeth, my gaze skates from his hold on her to his eyes. "Actually, I think you need to leave. Your trip has come to an end. Bella, please see him out."

"What? No!" she stammers, stepping away from him and into my space. "Please, Cal," she whispers, "let me handle this."

I stare into the eyes of my enemy before looking down at her. "You're not handling it very well. End this," I mumble.

Her doe eyes peer up at me and it's hard not to fall under their spell. "I will. I just need some time."

"Fine. I'll see you both at dinner. The cook will be off duty in an hour and if you'd like to eat, now is your chance. Otherwise, you can both starve, for all I care."

Bella glances over her shoulder. "Is that okay?" she asks Trent.

Why the hell is she asking his permission to eat?

"No," Trent retorts with a glowering look. He takes another step forward and pulls Bella back by her hips. Her back hits his chest while his hands stay locked on her waist, his eyes on me. "Bella and I will be eating in here tonight."

Don't kill him.

Not yet.

Look at Bella.

She can calm you down.

She can end the deranged thoughts swirling in your head.

I look at her and see those sad, begging eyes. There's a tremble to her bottom lip that tells me she's scared. She should be. She knows what I'm capable of and I won't hesitate to show them both.

Collecting my composure, I stand tall. "You eat downstairs or you don't eat at all. You sleep in your own room or you get the hell off my island. Got it?" I'm talking to him, not her, but there's a good chance he thinks I'm speaking to both of them.

"Who the hell do you think you are?" Trent grumbles. "You get a few bucks in your bank account and, suddenly, the orphan has all the power?" Bella turns around and begins whispering something, but Trent snaps at her, "Don't interrupt me when I'm talking."

Unable to refrain any longer, I step up to him. Moving Bella out of the way, I get in his face. "Do you have a death wish, Beckham?"

I reach out and grab Bella by the hand, trying to get her away from this lunatic. "Come on, we're going to eat."

Her eyes beg for mercy as she tries to free her hand to no avail. "Just give me a minute. He needs to eat, too. Please."

"You've got two minutes." I drop her hand, throw Trent a warning glare, and head out the door, leaving it ajar.

My back presses to the wall beside the open door and I kick my foot up behind me. One night. One more night and she will never see him again.

"We're leaving this place right now or I'm going back and telling your parents you're working for a psychopath."

I reach into my pocket and pull out a tube of toothpicks, then pop one in my mouth with a smirk on my face.

Oh, if you only knew, Trent. Bella isn't going anywhere with you.

"Trent, please just stop this. This job is important to me."

"You don't need this job, or any job, for that matter. In fact, once we're married, I'd like to start our family right away. You can stay home with them and I'll work."

"Don't I have a say in what I want? Maybe I don't want kids yet. Maybe I *want* to work."

"My future wife will not work some ridiculous nine-to-five job for little pay while someone else raises our kids."

There's a beat of silence that has me leaning closer to the door.

"Trent, this just isn't working anymore. I think you should go."

Trent laughs menacingly. "You're kidding, right? I take time off work to come here and you think you're going to break up with me. For what? This lousy job? For him? He might have money and connections. But I do, too. If you're scared of him, we can take him down. I know a guy—"

"Why are you talking like this? Are you seriously talking about having Cal killed? Have you lost your damn mind?"

Instead of an answer, all I hear is the shuffling of feet. "Let's go. We're leaving this damn place."

She stops in her tracks, not allowing him to usher her any farther. "I'm not leaving with you."

The scuffing sounds against the floor has me pulling the door open the rest of the way. Just as I do, I watch as Trent raises his hand and flattens it across Bella's cheek. The National Guard couldn't even stop me as I make a beeline right for Trent. I grab Bella, who's cupping her tear-soaked cheek, and give her a push to the side. My fist cocks back and I lay it straight on his nose.

"You're a dead man," I scream, as I continue to hammer his face with my fist, rotating from left to right as he falls to the ground. My legs wrap around him. His arms cross in front of his face as he tries to stop me, but I'm unstoppable. Blood splatters around the room. Bella cries out, begging me to stop, and Trent moans beneath me, but I don't stop. I keep going. Punch after punch. Blow after blow. Hearing bone meet bone as my knuckles grind into his flesh. Feeling the slippery mess of his blood—tasting it, smelling it. I'm a man hell-bent on retribution, especially from the asshole who took everything from me.

"Help. Someone help." I hear Bella holler from outside the room.

Trent reaches up, trying to grab my throat, but it's useless. He's too weak. The strength and the power are all mine. His demise will be my dawn. My fresh start. A new beginning. A life with the woman he claims to love.

I've waited years for this. Years of knowing he was living his best life. He had it all. The perfect family, unconditional love, inherited wealth. Then I found out he got her. He got the girl that was meant to be mine. He stole her from me in a dirty power play.

Now, I'm taking it all back. The sweet taste of revenge sits heavy on my tongue as I watch him crumble beneath me.

"I lost everything because of you," I scream so loud my words echo off the walls. "For twelve years, you and that asshole lived a life that should have been mine. Everything we wanted, everything we dreamt, you stole. Now you get to pay. Bella is mine and there isn't a damn thing you can do about it."

I hear her.

"Please stop, Cal. I'm begging you."

The voice of an angel.

"Please," she cries out.

My blows become sluggish. The pain in my hands begins to creep in.

"Please," she says one more time, her hand resting on my shoulder.

I look behind me and see her standing there, tears streaming down her face.

"Please don't kill him."

My chin hits my chest and I sit there, on an unconscious Trent, for what feels like minutes.

"Would you like me to take care of him, sir?" Anders asks from behind me.

"Take care of him?" Bella howls. "I know what that means. No, you will not *take care of him*."

I push myself up, feeling lightheaded from the sudden adrenaline shift. Looking at Anders, I nod. "Take him to the cellar. I'll be there in five."

"No!" Bella screams. Her fists hit me over and over as she cries before falling into my arms. "I won't let you kill him. He's a person, Cal. He might be cruel, but he doesn't deserve to die."

"Now," I say to Anders, before scooping Bella up and tossing her over my shoulder.

She fights me the entire walk down the hall. Her fists whale on my back. Legs kicking, mouth running.

We stop at my room and I squeeze her body tighter, so she's unable to get away. Reaching in my pocket, I pull out my key, unlock the door, then open it. Once we're inside, I go straight to my closet and pull open a drawer.

Bella stops moving, watching as I pull out a thick bundle of rope. "What are you doing?"

"It's for your own good. With him gone, we can finally live."

"No!" She begins kicking and punching again while she screams at the top of her lungs.

"It has to be this way."

I set her down on the bed and bind her wrists together.

She doesn't make it easy as she jerks and squirms to try and free herself. Once the rope is tight enough that she can't get free, I tie the loose end to the pole on the footboard of the bed.

"Why are you tying me up?" She sniffles. "I already know you're planning to kill him. Why are you doing this?"

"Because I don't want you to stop me. He hurt us. Everything that happened is because of him." I give the rope a pull to make sure it's secure. Once I'm sure it is, I kneel in front of Bella. "Everything will be okay. I promise."

Her lips curl in a snarl. "If you kill him, I'll never forgive you."

"With time, you will." I stand up and head for the door. "Scream all you want. This room is soundproof, so no one will hear you."

I walk out and lock the door behind me. Vengeance awaits.

26

"Nooooo!" I repeat, over and over, until my cries feel helpless. I'm sure he didn't mean to slap me, and it's not like he ever has before. It couldn't have been easy for him to step into this environment. Me, his girlfriend, along with his former enemy, who is suddenly so jealous he can't even blink out of fear someone will touch me. I should have just told Cal no, that we weren't eating in the dining room. I was scared, though. He's hanging my parents' careers over my head—he holds my future, and theirs, in his hands.

Sometimes I see the person he used to be. It's a miniscule amount, but he's in there. I was ready to end things with Trent and make myself live in this world Cal created for me. After six months, maybe I could fall in love with him. I might not want to leave once he sets me free, and even if I did, I'd know I at least tried everything I could to repair what was broken between us.

My body is depleted of strength as I twist and turn, trying to break free from this rope that binds me. I look over when I see that black snake looking at me. I hold her stare, challenging her to look away first.

A minute passes, then another, but she wins.

I'm weak.

All my life I've done what everyone else wanted. The one time I made a choice for myself by taking this job, it was the wrong one.

I try again. Tugging and twisting the rope, hoping it will snap and I'll be free. It digs into the skin of my arms with each pull, but I don't stop. Not even when it burns. Even when I begin to bleed, I keep going.

"Ahhhh," I scream, yanking harder and faster, cutting myself while trying to free myself.

I look back at the snake who's still fixated on me. It's like she's laughing. Mocking me and telling me I can't do it.

I will get out of here. I might not be able to save Trent, but I swear if Cal kills him, I'll leave. He can make good on his threats against me. I'll buy my way out of the contract and my parents can get new jobs. I will not live with a man who kills someone just because they upset them. Yes, he killed Vincent, but the man tortured him and left him no choice. If anything, Cal was brave in that moment. Right now, though, he's being a coward.

With my eyes deadlocked on the snake, I pull again. My body crashes to the ground, and I realize I did it. *I'm free.*

In that instant, the snake looks away and slithers down a branch. I'm not sure why, but I smile.

I won.

Without wasting another minute, I go straight to the closet where the secret door is. Pushing the suits to the side, I turn the handle and open the door. My feet get away from me as I hurry down the winding staircase.

For whatever reason, Cal told his guard to bring Trent down here. He mentioned a club of some sort. *Oh my gosh!* My stomach clenches. What if Cal is involved in some shady organized crime that involves killing people, or even torturing them?

I'm fearful of what I could potentially walk in on. But when I turn the handle on the door to the room at the end of the staircase, I'm reminded that I won't be walking in on anything. This door is locked with a passcode.

"Dammit!" My hands fall from the door in defeat. Just because I never want to see Trent again doesn't mean I want him to die. If I don't get in there soon, that is a very real possibility.

I hurry back up the stairs, feeling like time is running out. If there are plans for a club down there, then there has to be another entrance. Surely guests won't be going through the secret door in Cal's bedroom closet. This isn't *The Lion, the Witch and the Wardrobe*.

Wait a minute. The door on the ground floor by the main entrance had the same keypad. Serena and the bartender both came out of that door. It has to go somewhere important. That must be it. It has to be. I can't imagine the password is the same because there is no way Cal would let anyone have immediate access to his room. There is no lock on the closet door, so it leads me to believe Cal is the only one who uses it. He may be the only one who knows about it.

Tearing through the closet, into Cal's room and out the door to the hallway, I don't stop moving. I go straight to the elevator and hit the down arrow, over and over, until the doors slide open. I'm in full-blown panic mode and don't even notice it's occupied when I step in. Taking a step back, I stumble over the edge of the door.

"Cal. I...umm—"

"I can see I didn't put enough faith in you. You're free."

I look down at the elevator floor and notice the blood

dripping from his hands. It's been almost an hour since Cal attacked Trent. The blood from their fight should be dried.

Cal scratches his neck, leaving a trail of the fresh blood on his skin. His white shirt is covered, all the way down to his shoes.

"Well, are you getting on or are you just going to stand there and stare at me?"

Swallowing hard, I step in with apprehension.

"Where are you going, Bella?" His expression is desensitized, hands in his pockets.

I hit the G for the ground floor and press my back to the wall. My arms cross over my chest as my eyes scan his body. He's acting very strange, but that would be expected after murdering someone.

"I just need some fresh air." My fingers graze over the rope burns and deep gashes on my wrists.

Cal takes notice and grabs my arm. "Why the hell did you do this?" He looks at the marks, then to me. "Don't you know stubbornness can get you hurt?"

"Did you kill him?" I spit out, my arm still in his hand.

He just stares at my wrists for a second, deep in thought. Finally, he snaps out of it. "Trent won't be bothering us again."

"Us?" I laugh tensely. "As if there is an us. I told you if you killed him, I'd never forgive you and I meant it."

Snapping my arm away when the doors open, I step off the elevator. Cal follows behind me at an amble pace. I know he's waiting to see what I'm doing, so it looks like, right now, I'm just going for fresh air.

I head straight for the exit, glancing at the keypad on the mystery door as I pass by it.

"You can go clean up. I don't need a babysitter."

Cal joins my side, walking in step with me as the fresh, cold air hits my face. I take a deep breath and keep walking.

"You've proven that you do. First the snooping and now the disobedience. I told you to stay put, yet here you are."

When the sound of a boat engine roars to life, I pick up my pace. Walking steadfast down the steppingstones. "That's a boat. Where is it going?"

"Somewhere you're not." Cal grabs me by the arm. "You can't escape me, Bella. We were so close to where we're supposed to be until Trent showed up. We will get there again, and you will forgive me. He's gone and now you can move on...with me."

I stop moving when Cal holds me in place. A ripple in the clouds tells me another storm is coming. Dread washes over me. I'm so confused and so lost; I have no idea what to do.

"Please just tell me he's okay."

"He hit you, Bella. He talked to you like you were a dog and he struck your face. He wants to control you."

"And you don't?" I shout. "Isn't that what this is?" I jerk my arm away and look at his blood-soaked skin. "Look at you, Cal. You're obsessed with this idea of us living here and falling in love. So much so that you're willing to kill anyone who gets in your way. If anyone is controlling, it's you."

His shoulder shrugs while he stands there, still lacking any emotion that says he's remorseful for his actions. "You're right. I am. It's because I know what I want and what I want is you. I will bleed for you, Bella. I will kill for you. I would walk to the darkest depths of the world to carry you to safety. They don't deserve you."

"And you think you're protecting me by keeping me away from *them*? Or is this just your way of punishing everyone who wronged us?"

"Both," he simply says. He takes a step forward, his chest flush with mine, and he looks down at me with his hands at his sides. "Together forever, until kingdom come."

"Let the past go, Cal. We don't live there anymore."

Cal chuckles obnoxiously. It's his way or the wrong way. "I can only overcome the past by facing it head-on. Only then will I be able to focus on the future. We're getting closer. Now," he says, turning me around toward the castle, "I need to take a shower and get some sleep. It's been a long day. Peter will bring dinner to your room, you have a call scheduled with Barbara in an hour, and I'd appreciate it if you stay there for the remainder of the night."

"But it's only six o'clock. I don't want to sit in my room alone."

"Fine. I'll allow you to go to one of the floors to play the piano. Or, you're welcome to visit the turret."

My eyes light up. "I am? But the elevator doesn't go that high. How do I get up there?"

"Peter can take you."

I'm furious right now, but I've wanted to visit the turret since the day I arrived and saw it sitting so high in the clouds.

"This isn't over. I will get answers, if it's the last thing I do."

Cal smirks. "I don't doubt you'll try."

27

DINNER WAS…MEH. Cold and not exactly what I'd call a meal. Once I lifted the lid on the platter, I knew Cal had it made special for our guest, Trent. Clam chowder, which Trent hates, salad covered in onions—he also hates onions—and dry rolls.

I'm not even sure how he knew the foods Trent despised. Then again, Cal seems to know everything about everyone, so I shouldn't be surprised.

My call with Barbara went great and I'm really excited to get the contractors here after the holidays, so we can begin the renovations on the guest floors. We even went over some plans for the ground level that include an indoor swimming pool and a cozy entrance with an ornamented welcome center.

Hearing a knock has me dropping the book I've been reading—*Wuthering Heights*—and fleeing for the door. Peter is taking me to the turret and I'm grateful I let my phone charge, so I can take pictures. Not only that, but it's also an opportunity to try and get a cell signal. I just need to call

Mark and have him try and reach Trent. I imagine if Trent is alive, he's in a hospital being treated for broken bones in his face, possibly even some ribs, but eventually, I'm hopeful Mark can reach him.

Mark and Trent have been friends since I left The Webster House, although it wasn't until college that Trent and I got together. It was exciting at first. I saw him in a new light. He was sweet and attentive. When the honeymoon stage ended and things got difficult, my family pushed me to try and patch things up. They didn't know how controlling Trent was and only saw what they wanted to see—a good man who could take care of me.

Unfortunately, that doesn't result in love, and I now know Trent is not the man I want to spend my life with.

"Are you ready, Ms. Jenkins?" Peter asks when we come face to face in the doorway.

"Yes, I am. I can't wait to see the view from up top. So, how do we get there?"

"Follow me and I will show you."

A few minutes later, we're standing in front of the mystery door downstairs. My palms are sweating as I push myself up on my tiptoes, peering over Peter's shoulder. He punches in the code without a care in the world, but his fingers move so fast that all I caught was the first number —six.

The door buzzes, then opens. We're standing in, yet another, empty room. Although, this one has an elevator. The door is exactly the same as the one I've been using every day since I arrived. It's eerie to think that after weeks here, there is still so much of the castle I have not seen. There could be just about anything behind these walls. Bodies, killers, ghosts.

Peter calls down the elevator with the push of a button.

We step inside and I notice all the floors are on the panel. There must be access to each floor from this elevator.

"So this can take us to any floor?" I decide to ask, rather than wracking my brain trying to figure things out.

"Yes, and no. It's only accessible to people with the passcode, which is very few. This elevator stops behind the door at the end of each hall where the staircase is and the only way through the door is with a passcode."

So this entire time people could have been coming and going into the cellar and I wouldn't have even noticed. It really has me wondering how many different women have been down there.

"It has to be hard to remember all these codes."

"This is the only one here at Cori Cove, but there are others at the various hotels. After you punch them so many times, though, they stick. I'll probably have them all in my memory until the day I die."

"Aren't you worried you'll forget? I mean, you have to keep a record of them somewhere."

"Mr. Ellis doesn't believe in a physical trail. But, between us, I keep them in a notepad."

I smile inwardly. *That's exactly what I wanted to hear.*

It's a short ride up to the turret level, and even though the main reason I want to be up here is to check the signal on my phone, I am excited about the view. I haven't traveled much, well, at all, really. In fact, I've only visited two states and never left the country. There is so much I've missed out on and as I step out of the elevator and immediately look at the view, I'm reminded of the beauty in this world that I have yet to see.

At this moment, everything slips away from me. My feet take me to the covered balcony and it's like I'm staring into the sky. There is so much out there that I want to explore. Our world has so much appeal and I feel like a caged animal, getting her first nip of the fresh air. As much as I love the life I live, I want more. More of this. More of everything. I want to travel and find beauty in the little things. Seashells and rare flowers. Untouched land and geodes.

All along I thought I was selfish for wanting to leave my parents and Trent, to follow my dreams, but now I realize that I wasn't selfish. I have to live my life for me, not them.

I hold my phone up to look for a signal, but as I should have guessed, nothing.

"What do you think?" Peter asks, standing next to me. I didn't even realize he was there while I was lost staring into the abyss.

"I'm speechless. It's...amazing."

"Sometimes I come here alone when the nights get lonely. My late wife and I loved to travel and of all the bell towers I've been in, this one reminds me of her the most."

Peter has never mentioned his wife and now that he has, I want to know more about her. About him. About them.

I take a step back and look at Peter. "Why this one?"

"Because it's where we fell in love."

My heart squeezes and chills slide down my back. "You mean, you were here before Callum bought the place? I thought you'd been with his family for years?"

I know that sometimes a groundskeeper will stay at a location, even after the property sells, but Peter has been with the Ellises since before Cal was adopted, so how was he here all those years ago?

"When I shared the story about how Carolina and I met, Callum, err, Mr. Ellis," he corrects himself, "was intrigued. He was only fourteen, maybe fifteen years old, and I think it gave him hope that true love really does conquer all. He's not as hard on the inside as he is on the outside. The boy has a heart. In fact, sometimes I think it's too big for that small head of his." Peter chuckles.

"Tell me. Please tell me the story of you and your wife."

Peter gestures toward a concrete bench beneath the giant bell that hangs overhead. "These old legs can't handle my weight as long as they used to. Mind if I sit?"

"No. Go right ahead."

Peter takes a seat and I join him on the bench. "She was the most beautiful woman I'd ever laid eyes on. I was thirteen years old when my family came to work for the Bromley family. My mother was a maid and my father tended to the landscaping. My brothers and I were always causing mischief and I'm pretty sure we almost cost my parents their jobs a time or two."

Peter smiles at the memories and my heart floods with happiness for him. "Carolina was an only child and her father was adamant that she was not allowed to fraternize with 'the help.' So we steered clear. One day, my father became ill and missed his chores for the day, so I wanted to help him. I snuck out in the night and tended to the garden, collecting all the vegetables for the next day's dinner. That's when I heard her. My name whispered in the wind and it was like an angel singing. I looked up and saw Carolina on that very balcony. She was a mere shadow in the night, but I knew it was her. She called me up and I flew up those stairs so fast that I'm pretty sure I tripped at least a dozen times. But it was worth it. We stayed up talking all night. Then each night after, we met up here, until so much time had passed that it felt like our conversation had just started.

His hands slap to his legs and I assume he's finished with the conversation. I need more, though. "And then what happened?"

"When Carolina was sixteen years old, me being eighteen, we were caught. Her father forbade us to see one another, so we planned to run away together. She was the love of my life and the thought of never seeing her again was too painful to bear. We never got away."

The sadness in his eyes sends a tear sliding down my cheek. I quickly wipe it away so he doesn't see how emotional his love story is making me.

"Her family moved and took her away before we could make our own escape. Before they did, though, we made a promise that we would meet back here exactly two years later when she was eighteen. It was still owned by the Bromley family, but there were no plans to occupy the space."

"You did, right? You came back?"

"I came back," he smiles, "and so did she. She escaped the clutches of her father and we married two weeks later and moved to Boston where we lived until she passed away seventeen years ago, and I've missed her every day since."

"So that's where Cal lived? Boston?"

All this time he was so close. I swear there were times where I could feel him near and I just knew he wasn't on the other side of the country, or the world.

"Carolina and I were fascinated with castles and historical landmarks. We traveled the world together. When I heard that the Ellis family was looking for a footman, I contacted him immediately."

"And then Cal's father bought Cori Cove?"

"No. It wasn't until Mr. Ellis Senior passed away that he purchased the island. And here we are."

"And you're okay with him turning it into a tourist hot spot?"

"I'm just happy to be here. It doesn't matter what I see on the outside, it's the feeling this place brings me on the inside."

"It is a beautiful place. It's just a shame that you have to share it."

"If I had to share it with anyone, it would be Mr. Ellis. He, too, deserves to find his one true love."

"That may be true, but, Peter, I don't think that person is me."

"Oh?"

"I'm not emotionally equipped to handle his mood swings or his possessive nature."

"You slept in his room, did you not?"

"Well, yeah—"

"You've gone against every rule he's set in place and you're still here. Something tells me, you're stronger than you think. The heart wants what the heart wants, Ms. Jenkins. Don't fight it."

The heart wants what the heart wants.

Butterflies swarm in my stomach when I think of Cal and his unruly ways. He can be irrational and monstrous, but I suppose he's always been that way. He was always gentle with me when we were kids. Always wanted to protect me and save me from hurt feelings. Time changes people, but people are part of that change. My Cal is in there somewhere and I'm not going to stop until I bring him back.

I don't even think as my arms fly around Peter and I pull him in for a hug. He reciprocates with a gentle pat to my back.

"Thank you, Peter."

Peter has been such a blessing in this scary place. He's a reminder that I'm not alone, even when I feel like I am. He might work for Cal, but I'm starting to think I have a friend in him. It's unfortunate that tonight, I have to do what's necessary to steal from him.

"It's getting late and I'm pretty tired. Would you like to have a bedtime cup of tea with me?"

"I'm not sure Mr. Ellis—"

"Oh, come on," I chuckle, "it's just tea. He won't mind, and if he does, I'll take full blame."

Peter thinks for a moment but finally says, "Okay. That would be lovely. I'll prepare some now and meet you in the sitting room."

I smile at his response while my heart is crying at the fact that I have to swindle this sweet, old man.

28

AFTER A QUICK STOP at my room, I'm headed down the hall to meet Peter for tea. I don't even drink tea, but I've seen him drink it a couple times, so I knew it was a good call.

I stick my hands in the front pockets of my sweatpants and roll the sleeping pill between my fingers. It's been in my drawer since Peter brought it to me the day after Cal and I first had sex. It was a rare time that Cal was catering to my every need, and it was actually pretty sweet.

No matter how much my heart tells me that Cal is not this monstrous guy he wants the world to see him as, it still doesn't change the fact that he's keeping secrets. He should know by now that I don't roll over when I suspect something is going on. I dragged him on so many wild goose chases when we were kids that there's no way he's forgotten. I once suspected the mailman was having an affair with Trent's mom and made him go with me to peek in the window. It turns out it was her brother. I laugh at myself for being such a nosey little shit every time I see Trent's Uncle Bob at his family gatherings.

Peter is sitting on a chair in front of the fireplace. Startled at the sound of my footsteps, he turns his head quickly. "Goodness, dear, I didn't hear you come in." He's clutching a cup in his hand and brings it to his mouth.

"Sorry about that." I reach down and grab my tea then take a seat in a chair on the other side of the fireplace. I stretch my hand out in front of me, feeling the heat of the flames from the blazing fire. "Feels nice."

Peter nods. "It does."

I take a couple sips as we sit there in silence, my anxiety getting the best of me. Maybe this is a bad idea. Knocking the poor guy out, disarming the cameras on this floor, and stealing his key just so I can go search his room for a notebook of passcodes. Maybe I am in too far over my head.

No, I have to do this. If I ever want to find it in my heart to move forward with Cal, I need to know the secrets he's hiding.

"Peter, would you mind fetching me a blanket? Even with the fire, it's still so chilly."

My eyes follow Peter's teacup to the small round table. "Of course."

He stands up slowly and walks behind me. I peer over my shoulder, and once he's out of the room, I get up quickly and walk over to drop the pill in his tea. It sinks to the bottom and I begin to panic when I can see it through the light caramel-colored liquid.

"Dissolve, dammit." I look at the door and back at the tea. It's still there.

Peter comes back in with a white blanket in his hand and I jump back into my chair. There's no way he missed my speedy movements, but he doesn't even bat an eye.

"Here you go." He hands me the blanket and takes his seat again. He picks up the tea and to my surprise, he takes a sip without noticing.

I watch intently as the minutes go by and he drinks at the speed of a newborn baby, never once noticing the pill.

A few more minutes pass and Peter lets out a big yawn.

This could take a very long time, but I have to wait it out.

Watching Peter continuously yawn while he stares into the fire like he's under a spell from the glowing embers, I yawn myself.

I'm about to just give up and go to bed because it's apparent this guy is *not* falling asleep.

I look back at him again and notice his eyes fluttering.

It's working.

The next thing I know, they're closed and he still has his cup in his hand. I give it a few minutes, letting him fall into a deep sleep, then I stand up quietly and tiptoe over to him. I take the cup and notice there are just a few more sips left of tea so he must have drunk the pill. I set down the cup and take a deep breath before patting his pants pocket. I can feel the bulge from his phone, so I slide my hand and grab it, being very cautious not to stir him.

I breathe a sigh of relief when I see that his phone doesn't have a passcode. It seems to be the only thing in this place that's not protected.

After swiping through his apps, I finally find the one used to view live streams and saved footage. There are twelve different cameras, all numbered by floor. Once I've disarmed all three of the cameras on the eighth floor and the one on the sixth floor, I reach in his pocket and pull out the key. If I remember correctly, this is a master key. Right now, though, I only need it to get into his bedroom. I tuck his phone back in his pocket and haul ass out of the room.

Ignoring my rapid pulse and the sweat collecting on my forehead, I go straight to the elevator. I don't even blink as I pass by Cal's room. Hopefully he's asleep. He looked exhausted, so I'm sure he is.

I make it to Peter's room on the sixth floor and slide the key in, internally cheering when it unlocks. As soon as I'm inside, I close the door behind me, flip on the light, and begin my search. It's actually pretty empty, aside from a twin-size bed, a dresser, and a nightstand. There's a somber feeling to his room. Poor Peter is so lonely.

I'm a terrible person for doing this. But, I do it anyway. It doesn't take long before I find a notebook, well, it looks more like a journal, in his nightstand drawer. I begin flipping through the pages when I realize that this isn't just any old notebook, it's a journal. My eyes skim down one of the pages, reading the passage quickly to myself.

Dear Diary,

I saw him again today. My heart fluttered in my chest and the feeling of a thousand butterflies danced through my stomach. We sat at the tower and counted the stars while holding hands and sipping on a bottle of Father's bourbon. Just as a star shot across the sky, he leaned over and kissed me. It was at that moment that I knew nothing would keep us apart. We were meant to live this life together, or we would die trying. Never in a million years would I imagine going against Father's wishes. That's what love does to you. It makes you crazy. You do things you never thought you were capable of. All I know is, I am crazy in love. Tomorrow we're carving our names into the tree at the backside of the island. Maybe one day, it will show proof that love existed here, and true love conquers all.

I clutch the diary to my chest and hug it tightly. Someday I hope to find a love like Peter and Carolina had.

I continue to flip until I'm at the very end and that's when I see them. An entire page of passcodes with various hotel and island names. I search for Cori Cove and there it is. One passcode for one door. That's all I need.

I memorize the numbers in my head, repeating them over

and over again, as I put the diary back and close the drawer. *Six-three-two-eight-eight.*

With hurry behind my steps, I leave Peter's room and go straight to the end of the hall where the door to the private elevator is located. I punch the code in, and the door buzzes. I shriek, looking behind to make sure none of the other staff heard it. The coast is clear, so I go inside.

The elevator doors open for me, and I press the C, which I assume means cellar. I feel like such a rebel, knowing that if Cal catches me, I'll be punished again. After I'm done with my search, maybe I'll get caught on purpose—assuming Cal isn't some crazed killer or rapist. No, Cal is many things, but he's definitely not a rapist.

When the doors slide open, I feel like my heart is about to jump out of my chest. My entire body is shaking and I'm suddenly afraid of what I might find. What if Trent is dead down here? What if there are others?

Cautiously, I step out. That's when I realize I'm in another empty room. *How many empty rooms does this castle have?*

There's a door straight in front of me. I creep over to it and I'm happy to see that there is not a passcode for this door; it's also more modern than any of the others here. It's all white with a silver knob. I give it a turn and slowly pull it open.

I never would have guessed that what I'm looking at right now has been down here this entire time. It's so fancy and well-lit. Everything is blood red and crow black. Red lights are strung around the room. A large bed that looks like a triple-king-size is pressed against one wall. There are curtains separating one section to the next.

Keeping on my way, I take it all in. There's a large swing hanging from the ceiling. "Oh my gosh," I mumble, running my fingers down a floor-to-ceiling pole. There are three of them. Dancing poles. Velvet sofas are positioned around the room. A bar with a lit-up sign that says *The Grotto*. There's even a dance floor. This looks like some sort of club, but not just any club. If I had to guess, it's some sort of sex club or swingers' area.

A VIP club.

I keep walking deeper into the room. There are a few more private sections with small beds. All the bedding is either black or red. My fingers graze over the back of a chair and the touch of the velvety fabric gives me this sexy feeling inside.

I immediately stop walking when I hear voices. Someone is down here. It's coming from behind a curtain at the end of the wall. I slowly walk a little farther but stop when I hear the conversation.

There's two men, at least.

One is definitely Cal.

The other sounds like Byron.

The smell of cigar smoke invades my senses and I almost gag but stop myself. My biological mom's boyfriend always smoked cigars and the smell alone makes me nauseous.

"I know what you're doing. You know what you're doing, and it ends now," I hear Cal say in an aggressive tone.

"It's all for fun," Byron laughs, "besides, I think she'd be a good fit next to this ass here."

There's a quick sound of skin slapping skin, then a girl howls. "Damn, baby. Do that again."

My heart jumps in my throat. *There's a girl with them.*

"You just do what you're told and keep sucking her clit, then maybe I'll give you a little attention."

A moan ripples from behind the curtain and I have the nagging desire to look and see if Cal is with another girl.

"Mmm. That feels so good." It's a different girl and it sounds like Serena.

That bitch is still here.

I creep closer until I'm only inches away from the thick curtain. It's the only thing separating me from them. The only thing hiding me. If I'm caught, I could be forced into the receiving end of Byron and Cal's little sexcapade. I grip the key in my hand so tightly, the sharp edges dig into my skin.

This could be Cal's entire reasoning for me being here. He wants to train me to be one of their little toys like these girls are. With a club like this, there has to be more of them. Hell, it wouldn't surprise me if this is going on beneath every one of the Ellis Hotels.

"One more stunt and you're gone. This is the last time I'm telling you," Cal finally speaks up. "She's off-limits and will never be part of the club.

"Never know, she might love it. These two sure do."

There's a small opening and I lean over to try and get a better look, and that's when I'm able to see Byron and the two girls. He's fucking one from behind, moving at a slow pace while sucking on a cigar, while another girl is spread out on the bed with her legs bent at the knees. The girl he's fucking is feasting on the other girl's pussy.

"She's not ready. And when she is, she will only be with me. You touch her, you're a dead man."

Something doesn't let me stop watching. It's not that I'm into that sort of thing; in fact, a small-town girl like me has never even seen it. But, my body reacts in a way I can't even explain to myself. I can feel my panties dampen as the girl begins swirling her tongue at Serena's entrance while Serena squeezes her own breasts.

"You can throw out all the threats you want, Callum. We both know I'm your only friend and you need me."

"Need you?" Cal laughs. "I don't even like you. You're not a friend to me. Not anymore."

I try to get a better look to see where Cal is and I'm terrified that I'll find him in a similar position as Byron, so much so that a lump lodges in my throat.

Leaning over a tad more, I see him.

He's there. Sitting all by himself in a chair, watching Byron and the girls with a cigar of his own.

"Like me. Hate me. Doesn't matter to me. Doesn't change the fact that I'm one-half of the beneficiary of your entire estate and there isn't a damn thing you can do about it. I helped you, remember?"

"Oh, but there is. Once Bella is my wife, you lose that title."

My hand claps over my mouth, muffling the sound of my gasp. *His wife?*

"Yeah. Good luck getting Mary Magdalene to marry you. Even with the contract, you'd have to drug her to say, 'I do.'"

"If needed, that can be arranged. She will marry me and then she will give me a child."

Ignoring all the moans and groans, I think about what I just heard.

I back away from the curtain slowly. *Marry him and give him a child?* Am I some sort of business transaction? Is this all about his revenge against the people who he claims hurt us? Whatever it is, it's not love.

It's never been about love.

I'm on the verge of breaking down when I hear a phone ring.

"Yeah," Cal says. "What? Well, you better fucking find out why."

"What'd she do this time?" Byron asks.

"Cameras are out on the sixth and eighth floor. Peter is passed out in the sitting room."

"That bitch is trouble and you're a fucking idiot for even thinking about marrying her."

"Shut your damn mouth," Cal shouts. "I'm warning you.

Now get your dick out of her ass and do something productive or get the hell off my property."

I tuck myself into the corner, between a couch and the curtain, and hide when Cal storms past me.

"Don't worry, ladies. We'll all get a little piece of what that bastard owes us." Byron lets out a deep grumble and I can hear the sound of him smacking the girl's ass again. She moans loudly and I find myself looking again. He's moving at lightning speed, ramming her from behind. Her mouth drops open as her tongue slides up and down Serena's pussy. Her fingers spread her lips farther apart, in the shape of a V, and she uses her other hand to shove three fingers inside of her.

They all three expel cries of pleasure as their orgasms tear through them. The sudden urge to touch myself has me looking away. No. I can't.

If I watch any longer, I just might cream my panties and come right along with them.

Just as I go to get up, I hear Byron. "Get your asses cleaned up and go out the back door. Callum will have a fit if his girl sees you around again."

His girl? Or his forced, future wife?

Bile climbs up my throat.

I sit there waiting impatiently while they all get dressed. I can't risk leaving this spot until they're all gone.

Once the girls are gone, Byron walks past me, leaving out the door I came in. I stand up, stretching my body that's tense from being curled into a ball in the corner. I play it safe and give Byron a minute to get farther ahead of me before I leave.

Using this time, I look around the place. It's most definitely some sort of sex club. If what I just watched wasn't proof enough, then the wall-sized shelves of lube sure are.

I'm not bothered by this. If anything, I find myself curious. What bothers me is all the secrecy and lies. I've dealt with enough shady people in my lifetime. I refuse to let one of them into my heart. Cal plans on us getting married, but at this point, that's impossible.

I turn around to leave when the door behind me flies open. I gasp when I'm face to face with a very large, very angry-looking man.

"Don't be scared, little girl, I don't bite...hard." A devilish smirk spreads across his face and alarms sound in my ears.

He's at least six-foot-five with a full beard, yellow teeth, and a mullet cut. His arms are three times the size of my thighs and if it comes down to having to fight this man off, I will lose.

"I was just—"

"Just what? Coming down for a little fun?" He grabs his dick and shakes it. "I've got some fun for ya right here."

"Get away from me," I say, taking a few steps backward. My legs hit the end of a bed, and I fall onto it.

I've seen this guy around. He's the new guard Cal hired. He keeps coming closer, and fear sweeps over me.

"Mr. Ellis is going to come down here. He's going to find me."

The guy laughs. "Mr. Ellis is searching outside. No one's coming down here, baby. They're all looking for his little runaway."

His knees hit the bed and I scooch backward until I can't go any farther. He crawls to me with a scary smile on his face.

"I'll scream."

"I like when they scream. Make it loud for me, okay?"

The sound of his zipper dropping has me holding my breath. The next thing I know, his hard but small dick peeks out.

"Stop." I hold up my hand, not letting him near me. I'll die before I let this man touch me.

With a hoarse breath, he grabs me by the waist and fights to pull my pants and underwear down. "Stop," I scream, tears rolling down my cheeks. The scent of stale beer and cigarettes rolls off him and repulses me even more.

My legs kick and my hands flail around, but he's relentless. They make it all the way to my ankles and, at this point, it's no use. The full weight of his body crushes me. His gross dick, ready to go in. I pinch my eyes shut and internally cry tears of hate for the world. Hate for him. Hate for mankind.

"Get off me," I scream again. Using the key in my hand, I bring it to his face and scream as I slide it down, digging as deep as I can while leaving a trail of blood.

Suddenly, a loud *pop-pop* rings through my ears, and he drops down on top of me. It's not until I open my eyes that I see Cal standing there with a gun at his side.

He jumps onto the bed. "Jesus, Bella. Are you okay?" He rolls the guy onto the floor, but I'm frozen in place.

I go to speak but nothing comes out as I look down at my sweatshirt and see the round blotch of blood. My stomach sucks in, trying to stop the liquid from seeping into my skin. My hand clutches the key in my hand as if my life depends on it.

"Did he..." Cal turns his head and bites his bottom lip, "did he touch you?"

"He...he touched me, but he didn't...you came just in time."

Cal scoops me into his arms and lifts me off the bed. "Dammit, Bella. What were you thinking coming down here?"

Suddenly, coherency returns. "Are you saying this is my fault?" My words come out in a hushed choke.

"No. God, no. This isn't your fault. If anything, it's my fault."

"I...I'm sorry, I—"

"Don't you dare apologize. I'm taking you upstairs and drawing you a bath. I'll have Peter... Never mind, Peter is passed out. But you probably know that, don't you?"

I don't respond. My words keep getting away from me and I'm not sure I could explain anything right now.

"You can sleep in something of mine tonight."

Cal carries me up the winding staircase to his room and I stuff Peter's key into the front pocket of my hoodie. My head rests gently against his chest, and as angry as I am with him, I feel safe. He killed a man to protect me. Aside from the whole arranged marriage talk, I think he really does want to keep me safe. Or at least, away from all other men.

THE IMAGE of that man's face keeps popping into my head as I soak in the bathtub—Cal's bathtub. In his room. Every minute or two, he pops his head in the door and checks on me, but my response is always the same. "I'm fine," I tell him when he does it again.

Am I, though? Will I ever be *fine?*

Cal plans on us getting married, which means one of two things: he always planned on keeping me forever. Or, he just needs the title for his self-image, and/or final will. If that's the case, it's possible he planned to let me go as long as I maintained the title of his wife.

"Cal," I holler, calling him back in here. I'm soaking under white suds with only my head above the water. It's the perfect temperature and seems to be helping me calm down. I've never seen a dead body before and I'm not sure I'll soon forget what happened. I was centimeters away from being raped and the thought alone makes me never want to leave Cal's side again.

"I'm here. What's wrong?" His eyes are alert, and I can tell he's ready to take action at whatever I need.

"Tell me about the contract."

He steps through the opening of the door and into the bathroom. "You got a copy. You're free to read it." Pressing his palms to the sink vanity behind him, he watches my hands as I scoop bubbles and drop them down, repeating the process.

"It's over a hundred pages. You know damn well I didn't read that thing. Honestly, I thought I knew the terms after it was made clear I wasn't here for just a job. Lay out the main points. Why am I here and for how long?"

Cal grazes his chin with his thumb and thinks before he finally speaks. "You're here as long as I decide for us to stay."

"Ugh," I growl, "you're so frustrating. Just tell me the damn truth. Do I have to marry you?"

He looks stunned. Completely caught off guard. "Why do you ask that?"

"I was down there while you were talking to Byron. Also saw him fucking your old flames. Now tell me the truth."

"Yes," he says point-blankly. "You will be my wife."

"And if I don't marry you?"

"Then you breach the contract and pay me a lump sum of two million dollars, plus punitive damages."

"You know, I could fight that. I was coerced into signing the contract."

"You could," he shrugs, "but good luck finding a lawyer that will top mine or a judge that's not on my payroll."

Fuck. He's probably put so much thought and planning into this that I really will have to marry him.

Cal pushes himself off the vanity and takes slow strides toward me. His sweatpants hug his hips so perfectly and the eye-level bulge in his pants has my nipples puckering beneath the suds.

"Is the thought of being married to me really that bad?"

I laugh in a sarcastic pitch. "You just shot one of your men, who was trying to rape me. I just found a secret swingers' club in your basement and you have a secret staircase that takes you to it. For all I know, you're sneaking down there and screwing girls every night. I don't trust you anymore and I can't marry someone I don't trust. And let's not get started on love."

Kneeling, he puts his hands on the ledge of the clawfoot tub. "You don't love me?" The way he asks the question—the look in his eyes—it's like he thought I loved him all along.

Maybe I did.

Maybe I do.

"I've always loved you. I'm not sure I ever stopped. What we had as kids wasn't your normal elementary/middle school friendship. We were closer than that. We were closer than siblings. It's like you were my—"

"Soulmate?"

I nod. "Yeah. Exactly."

"That's because I am and you are mine. I told you, Bella, fate brought you back to me. I'm righting my wrongs while you're doing the same. Words can never explain the pain I felt the day you left me. I wasn't sure I'd ever get past it. Even once you arrived, I still felt the sting of that day. But I found a way to move on and it's in my own selfish way, but it's the *only* way. Marry me, Bella."

"But why? What does marriage solve?"

"Because I have to get married and you're the only person in the entire world I'd even consider taking as my wife. And because it will allow me to finally forgive you while also getting my revenge on the people who hurt us."

Each day I get more and more confused. The more I learn, the more confusing things become. If I'd just stay in my room and ignore all the cracks and crevices in this damn place, my mind wouldn't be going a million miles a minute, trying to decode what this man is saying.

My head rests back and it hits me that Cal just proposed to me and I totally blew him off. I'm not even sorry because it was the worst proposal in the history of proposals. "Please stop beating around the bush. Just say the damn words."

"If you were downstairs when Byron and I were talking, then you heard about my will and how he's one-half of my beneficiary. Vincent never intended to leave me a penny. Everything was left to some woman he knocked up years ago and his bastard son that Delilah never knew about. Byron wasn't only Vincent's attorney. He was also his business partner."

"Business partner? Byron's only like five years older than you."

"Nine. He sees a damn good esthetician and has the best plastic surgeon in the country. Anyways, eight years ago, I went to Byron's office and I struck a deal with him. Change Vincent's will and leave me everything, continue the 20/80 partnership, and pay him a lump sum of three million dollars. It wasn't enough for him, though. He called me reckless and savage and was sure I'd get myself locked up or killed before I turned twenty-one and the business would suffer. He countered and requested he be the sole beneficiary on my will. I agreed to his demand with a clause that rescinded the deal if I were to marry."

"You're saying when you die, Byron gets everything?"

"Half of everything. Peter is a joint beneficiary. Everything will be split between the two of them."

"And you hate him that much to go to all this trouble just to get him out?"

Cal leans forward and the expression on his face sends chills down my spine, even in the one-hundred-degree bath water. "Byron's playing dirty, Bella. I caught wind of some shit he's involved in and if he's not out soon, I risk losing everything. I didn't take this empire from Vincent. I earned it, and I'll be damned if some washed-up attorney, who fell into luck, is going to take it from me."

"You're scaring me, Cal."

"I'd die before I let him or anyone else hurt you. I promise you that."

The look in his eyes, the expression on his face, I believe him.

There is still so much I don't know or believe, though. His answer to this question could make us or break us. "Did you kill Trent?"

There's a long beat of silence as Cal stares at the floor. He knows the answer, so his hesitation has me wondering if I should even believe what he says.

"No. I didn't kill Trent."

I'm not Trent's biggest fan but a rush of relief washes through me. "And the club downstairs?"

"They've been part of Ellis Empire long before I came along. We're known for our top-notch resorts as well as the unique experience we offer. Sex is a natural and beautiful thing, Bella. It's nothing to be ashamed of."

"But with complete strangers?" It just seems odd to me. Granted, I'm a small-town girl who's been blind to this lifestyle. It just seems degrading. Then again, I did see Byron with those girls and there's a part of me that was slightly turned on.

"Some guests just like to watch, some prefer to engage, and others prefer not to take part in the club aspect at all."

"I know for a fact I'll be avoiding that part of the hotel once it opens." At least as a participant. I'm not completely opposed to watching—maybe learning.

"It's not for everyone and I actually prefer you stay away from there. We do extensive background checks on members, but it doesn't mean I trust them." Cal rests a hand on my thigh and looks at me with a quizzical expression. "Unless, of course, it's you and me."

My interest is piqued. "While others watch?"

"Or while we watch them."

My heart jumps into a frenzy at just the thought. The thing is, I'm not sure if it's because I'm surprised he'd suggest such a thing or intrigued because I'm interested.

29

BELLA ASKED if she could sleep in my room tonight. Before the complete sentence left her mouth, I was immediately hit with a rush of panic. She slept in here before, but I stayed awake the entire time. A handful of caffeine pills and a book and I stayed awake with no problem. Although, I did pay for it the next day.

Tonight, I have to sleep. If I'm not at my best tomorrow, things could go very bad. I need to be alert and focused and make sure my plans are made clear at my meeting.

Bella comes out wearing nothing but the white tee shirt I gave her. If I thought she was beautiful before, then there is no word for the way she looks right now. She's a mixture of terms rolled into one perfect body. Stunning, alluring, bewitching, and beddable. The way her wet hair hangs down, dampening the shirt until it's see-through. Her perky tits look at me like a delectable dinner waiting to be devoured. And don't get me started on those long legs. They're squeez-able, bitable, and fuck if I'm not rock-hard.

She walks toward the bed and I straighten my back

against the headboard. My book slowly closes and drops to my side. I clear my throat. "Feeling better?"

She shrugs a shoulder and sits down in the same spot she claimed last time she slept in my bed. "Little bit. I think my nerves are just shot for the night. Hopefully sleep will help."

I wanna grab her and claim her. Pull her on my lap and let her ride my cock. But, it's not the right time. She's depleted and she's right, she needs sleep, as do I.

Her head rests against the pillow and her eyes close. Sitting there beside her, I watch her, wondering what thoughts are circulating through her mind right now. Is she remembering the attack of that sadistic man? His body falling lifelessly on hers? Is she thinking about marrying me? Or running away somewhere I'll never find her?

That last thought is like a knife to the chest and I think I'd take the knife over the possibility of never seeing her again. I know things can get dangerous here, but I'm fixing it. I'll make it safe. I'll protect her at all costs.

Minutes later, she's fast asleep. I slide down on my side and lie there, watching her. Until I can no longer keep my eyes open, and she drifts into my dream.

"No!" I scream at the top of my lungs. "Put it down. That's mine!"

Vincent holds up the picture and shreds it, piece by piece by piece. I watch as fragments of my picture fall slowly to the ground.

"You're delusional if you think any girl will ever love you. You're unlovable. But mostly, you're nothing but a fuck-up. You can't even follow one goddamn rule, Caden!"

"My name isn't Caden. I'm Callum."

"You're Caden Ellis," he shouts so loudly his voice echoes through my head, leaving me with a splitting headache.

My head wobbles as I try to brace it on my neck and I realize the pain isn't from his screams, it's from the punches he's laying on my skull.

"You're worthless. Scum. A piece of rotten shit. Now pull yourself together and get your ass downstairs. Your mom wants to have dinner with you."

"Cal," I hear Bella say, "Cal, please. Stop."

I blink a few times, adjusting my eyes to the light she must have turned on. "I'm awake," I spit out. "It's okay. I'm awake."

"What just happened?"

I can see her chest heaving and it tells me all I need to know. She just witnessed me at my worst.

"It was just a bad dream." I take her hand and lead her back to the bed.

Instead of lying down, she sits, so I do the same. "Dreams happen when you're sleeping. You were not sleeping. You were scrambling through the room like you were trying to get away from someone. You were crying, Cal." I notice a tear slide down her cheek and I sweep it away with my thumb.

Cupping her face, I look into her eyes. "I was sleeping."

She shakes her head, not buying it. I was sleeping, though.

"I have night terrors," I tell her. "It's happened every night since I killed Vincent. Nothing I do makes them stop." Bella throws herself into my arms and begins sobbing. "Hey, it's okay."

"No," her head rests on my chest, "it's not okay. It's all my fault. If I'd never left, you wouldn't have endured all this pain. He destroyed you."

I tip her chin up until she's looking at me. "He broke me, but I'm putting myself back together now that I have you."

Bella presses her lips to mine. The taste of her salty tears seeps into my mouth and I welcome them because they're hers. I welcome all of her as her hand slides down my pants, grabbing hold of my cock.

Then I remember what she went through tonight, what she just witnessed. "Are you sure?"

"More sure than I've ever been about anything." She presses her lips to mine again, chastising my mouth like it's not meant to speak. As if it's only meant for her to kiss.

Slowly, I lie her back, blanketing her body with mine. Her hips buck upward, seeking friction from me as I rest between her legs.

"Yes," she says. I pull back and look at her with questioning eyes. "I'll marry you, Cal."

Every thought escapes me as I fall into her.

I'm not even sure when I got rid of our clothes. Lying there on top of her, naked and hungry, I need to give her something she should have gotten the first time. As rough as I'd like this to be, as much as I want to sink my claws into her flawless skin, she deserves to have what she should have gotten her first time.

Her legs are bent at her knees around me, arms draped at her sides. I pick one up and press my lips to her wrist while watching her. Curious eyes stare back at me as I softly kiss my way up her arm.

Bella sucks in her bottom lip. "What are you doing?"

"Shh," I say, pressing a gentle finger to her lips.

I'm not sure if I know how to be tender, but since I am the only man Bella will ever be with and she didn't get sweet her first time, I'm going to try like hell for her.

My mouth glides to the shell of her ear. I set her arm back down then move to the next one. Sliding up and down, my cock rubs against her. My attention is all on her—on us.

I don't want her to be miserable. I need her to take me out of my own misery. I set her other arm down and draw in a deep breath, filling my lungs with her scent, then I exhale into her mouth. She reciprocates the kiss, sliding her tongue in and tangling it in a web of desire with mine.

Sliding down her body, I kiss every inch in a trail until I get to the parted lips of her pussy. Sucking hard on her clit, I don't stop as she cries out in moans of pleasure. Her fingers tangle in my hair, tugging and pulling as I push two fingers inside of her.

She's so wet for me. Just for me. Only ever for me. Mine.

My tongue sweeps up and down, my taste buds smoothing against the sensitive skin.

Her back lifts off the bed and she pushes my face further into her. My fingers move faster, pumping in and out, and I let out a low growl when I feel her clench around them. I catch myself grinding my dick against the mattress, but it's not enough. I need to be inside of her.

"Come for me, baby."

And she does, proof of her orgasm spilling out of her. I keep my fingers moving and she keeps riding my face as I lick up her sweet juices.

Once I pull them out, I slide up her moistened body and give her a taste of herself. She takes what's given to her and pulls my head closer, tangling her tongue with mine.

My hand moves up her side sluggishly, her skin shivering beneath my touch. "Fuck me, Cal." Her words whisper against my lips.

My hand keeps moving until I'm cradling her head in my palm. With my other hand pressed to the mattress, I line my cock with her entrance and slide in.

I move in slowly and subtly. Taking in every second of the warmth surrounding me. Moving in and out, up and down, circling my hips and letting her pussy engulf me.

"Fuck, Bella."

My senses become keen. Every touch is like fireworks igniting inside of me. Every taste is like a gourmet meal after starving for weeks. She's inevitably the most perfect, most beautiful thing I've ever seen in my entire life.

Our sweaty bodies meld together as we move from the bed to the floor until she's pressed against the wall and I'm behind her naked body. My hands lay over hers on the wall as I slide out, slow and steady, then fill her back up. Her head drops back onto my shoulder and I suck at the thin skin of her neck.

"Cal," she groans when I fist her hair and pick up my pace.

My entire body fills up, ready to combust, and we release together.

Slowing my movements, until we're both standing still with me inside of her, it hits me that she said yes. It might not be for love, yet. But one day, Bella will love me the way a woman loves her husband. She will give me kids and I'll give her an heir to a billion-dollar fortune. They will never want for anything.

"So, we're getting married?" I smile through a kiss on her shoulder.

I pull out and Bella turns around to face me while my hands rest on her hips. "It seems I don't have much choice. I'll help you free yourself from Byron's chains, under one condition. You have to tell me everything. About your family, about my family, about Mrs. Webster. I need to know where Trent is. I don't like him, but I want to know he's not dead. I need you to tell me what you meant when you said Mark and Trent were the reason we weren't together."

I kiss her again and again, speaking against her mouth. "I'll tell you everything you need to know tomorrow. I have to take a short trip to the main island in the morning, and when I return, we will talk. Right now, you need sleep."

She nods in agreement.

I will tell her everything. *Tomorrow.*

That night, I fell asleep and slept through the night for the first time in eight years.

30

I ROLL over to my side and feel the crumple of paper under my cheek. My eyes blink open, and I realize I'm alone. Pulling the paper out from under me, I read it.

Last night was amazing and I look forward to many more nights with you. Breakfast is waiting in your room. When I return, we will talk, as promised. It's time to live! -Cal

A smile grows on my face as I clutch the paper to my chest. Last night was amazing. It felt like the first day of the rest of my life. I have no idea what's in store for me, but that's the beauty of it. I've always planned everything out perfectly and end up disappointed when things don't go my way. When Cal and I talk, he needs to know my family will still be a big part of my life. This marriage of convenience needs to benefit us both. Is that what it is? A convenience? I said yes to Cal because I want to help him. In some ways, I think I owe it to him. But I also said yes because I cannot imagine my life without him. I love Cal. I really do. This thing we have going on is unconventional at best, but it works for us and that's all that matters.

After lying in Cal's bed, thinking about the future for a

good twenty minutes, I have no regrets as I get up and leave to go shower and have breakfast in my room.

Sometime today, I plan on apologizing to Peter for last night. I feel so bad for manipulating such a sweet person. He seems like the forgiving kind, so hopefully it won't change things between us. Peter has been good to me while I've been here, and I don't want that to change now.

As soon as I open the door to my room, I'm grinning from ear to ear. I walk to my bed where a tray is placed on top and run my finger over the stem of a single peony in a crystal vase.

I planned to take a shower first, but the rumble in my stomach has me lifting the lid of the platter and diving into a stack of pancakes, bacon, and fresh fruit.

All I need is some Netflix and this would be heaven. I make a mental note to tell Cal today that I want a television and the Wi-Fi password. If I'm going to be his wife, I'm not going to be treated like a prisoner.

One more bite and I move the tray to the side and get up to take a shower. A knock at the door has me turning around. I pull the door open and Peter is standing there.

The disturbed look on his face tells me he's upset about last night. I never put his key back and he has to know I stole it.

"Hi, Peter."

"Ms. Jenkins," he acknowledges me with a nod. "Mr. Ellis has given me strict instructions to escort you off the island immediately. You'll need to pack your things and meet me at the dock in ten minutes."

"Wha...what? Cal didn't say that." I'm so confused that I'm not even able to form a coherent sentence.

"Something has come up and I'll explain on the way. Please, hurry, Ms. Jenkins."

"Peter, if this is about last night, I'm sorry."

"Last night?"

"Tea in the sitting room? Your—"

"If anyone should apologize, it's me. I was more tired than I thought and it was rude of me to fall asleep in your company."

Huh? He doesn't know about the key or any of the events of last night? Peter thinks he fell asleep because he was tired.

Now I feel even more guilty, but if this isn't about last night, then why am I being forced off the island?

"No time to waste. I'll see you at the dock in ten minutes." He turns and heads down the hall.

I step out the door and holler behind him, "But, Peter. I don't want to leave."

He doesn't respond, just continues walking at a steady pace until he reaches the elevator.

"What the hell?" I grumble under my breath. Is Cal really letting me leave? Not just letting me, but making me?

I begged for this for weeks, but now that it's happening, I don't want to go. I want to stay and be with him. Something isn't right. There has to be an explanation.

Peter disappears into the elevator, so I go back to my room, wondering if I should do as I'm told and pack up my things or if I should just stay here and wait for Cal to return. Unless…unless Peter is taking me to meet Cal somewhere. That has to be it. He wants us both to leave the island.

After carefully deciding to pack my bag and follow instructions, I'm standing in the doorway of my room, staring into it. I hope we get to come back someday. This place has begun to feel like a home away from home. The thought of leaving and not returning has me fighting back tears.

One last look, and I'm closing the door behind me, dragging my suitcase down the hall to the elevator.

I make it to the ground level and see Peter waiting for me.

"Peter, please tell me what's going on," I say as I hurriedly drag my suitcase to where he stands.

He takes my suitcase and drags it behind him but doesn't say a word as I follow. There's a small boat waiting for us and I see it's Jeffrey, the same guy who brought me here.

"Take care, Ms. Jenkins. I hope to see you again soon, for Mr. Ellis's sake. He needs someone like you in his life." He presses a chaste kiss to my cheek and walks past me.

"You're not leaving with me? But where am I going? What happens next?" I chase after him, refusing to leave without knowing why I have to.

Peter stops, turns slowly, and places two hands on my shoulders. "You're in danger, Bella. Don't ask questions. Just go."

My eyes widen, chills cascading down my body. "Danger?"

He nods. "Mr. Ellis will keep you safe if you let him. So, please, go."

Peter disappears and I'm left as confused as ever while Jeffery lifts my suitcase on the boat. "Do you know what's going on?" I ask him.

He shakes his head. "I just do drop-offs and pickups, dear."

I feel like I just got here and now I'm leaving. I want to stay. I want to stay here with Cal. There's a pinch at my heart, a nagging and painful pinch that stays with me the entire ride to the main island. My fear of water doesn't even touch what I'm feeling inside. I'd swim back if I knew he'd be there waiting for me.

If I'm in danger, that must mean someone wants to hurt me. Or, what if someone wants to hurt Cal? Oh my God! And

I just left without doing anything to help him. I have no way to contact him. No way to find him. All I have is his name, an island, and the number to the assistant who set me up with the job. That's all I know about the man I've falling in love with.

AFTER JEFFERY DOCKED and I was handed a ticket for the ferry, I ended up back where it all began. The parking lot of Falcon Ferry. I didn't go home to Hickory Knoll. There was nothing I could do from there. Instead, I took the first flight to New York and I'm walking up to Mark's apartment door, ready to find at least one of the answers I need.

With no call letting him know I was on my way, I came completely unannounced. I knock a few times before the door flies open.

"Bella? What's wrong?" he asks, likely noticing my red, puffy eyes from hours of crying.

"Can I come in?"

He steps to the side. "Of course."

Sheer exhaustion has me wanting to plop down on that white leather couch in the middle of the living room, but Mark and I aren't close. We don't invade each other's space. There's never been a solid friendship, hangouts with friends, or even small talk. Everything we did together was as a family and we sort of just existed together. He's not cruel, by any means. In fact, he's always been kind to me. Don't get me wrong, I love my brother, but he's always been a very stand-offish person. I suppose we all deal with our past lives in our own ways.

"How's law school going?" I ask as I look around the small apartment.

Mark closes the door and enters the room, standing next

to me. "Look, if you're here because you heard, let me start off by saying I planned to tell them."

I've got no idea what he's talking about and I'm sure the expression on my face says so.

"It's only been three months and I was just giving it some time until I got my fitness club up and running. Things are going slow—"

"Did you quit law school, Mark?"

"Yeah. Isn't that why... Why are you here, Bella?"

My hand falls from the handle of my suitcase and I'm unable to hold it together anymore. Tears start falling and I sniffle. "I found Callum."

His eyes perk up. "Callum, Callum?"

I nod. Saving time, I get straight to the point. "We reconnected and things have been...well, weird, but that's beside the point. I need you to tell me what happened before we left between you, him, and Trent."

"Wait a minute. Does Trent know about this?"

I nod again. "He came to see me. I'm sure you'll hear all about it." And of course, he'll go and tell our parents and they'll sit me down for a talk about self-respect and making good choices. "Did you know Cal got in trouble that day?"

Mark runs his fingers through his hair and blows out air. "Damn, Bella. This all happened ages ago. I don't even remember." He walks over to a coffee pot on the counter and fills a mug in front of it. "Want some?"

"Yes, please." I'm not a big coffee drinker, but I could use some caffeine right about now.

Mark gets me a cup and we sit down at a small, round table. "So where'd you find him?"

"Ever heard of Ellis Empire?"

He shakes his no, and I'm not surprised.

"He owns a ritzy hotel chain. Inherited the company and billions from his late father."

"Damn, he made out well." Mark looks around his tiny living space. "If only we could all have that luck."

I don't tell him what Cal had to go through to get where he's at in life, but I don't need to. None of it matters. "I accepted a job and he ended up being my boss. Talk about a surprise."

"No kidding. That couldn't have been a coincidence."

"It wasn't." I take a sip of my coffee, burning the tip of my tongue. "While I was with him, he mentioned a couple different times how you and Trent were the reason for some things that happened. Obviously, you left Mrs. Webster's when I did, so I know it wasn't after the fact."

Mark is silent for a minute. He takes a few drinks of his coffee, taps his fingers to the mug, then finally says, "Trent would be pissed if he knew we were talking about this."

"Fuck Trent."

It seems I've caught him by surprise. "Aren't you two getting engaged?"

"No. I never told him yes and I was never going to. Trent and I are done."

"Wow," he nods, trying to read my expression, "so are you and Callum like a thing now?"

Ignoring his question, I get to the point. "Tell me what happened before we were adopted, Mark."

"Come on, Bella. You're putting me in a really shitty spot."

I don't want to play hardball, but I will. Pulling my phone out of the pocket of my hoodie, I hold it up. "Tell me now or I'll call Mom and Dad and tell them you quit law school."

Mark pushes his chair back and gets up, pacing the small space of the kitchen. He fidgets with his fingers, then stops at the chair he was in and rests his arms on the back of it. "It was all Trent's idea. We were out back following deer tracks late at night and saw Callum sneaking through the living room window into Trent's house. I made some snide remark about how I wouldn't have to deal with the asshole much longer because you and him would probably get picked and go off to live your best lives while I was stuck for another four years."

When he stops talking and begins fidgeting with his hands, I push for more. "Okay. What happened next?"

He looks up and continues, "We confronted him and he told us some bizarre story about how he was doing it for you. Trent knew Callum was always getting into trouble, so he had the grand idea to tell Mrs. Webster he broke into his house and stole a wad of cash from Mr. Beckham's safe. It was supposed to be a joke, but we also thought maybe it'd help my chance. Which it did."

My jaw drops. "So you lied?" I should have known someone stirred the pot and intentionally ratted him out.

"Yeah. Sort of. I mean, he did break in, but he didn't really take money. Trent went to his parents with the money *he* actually took and convinced them to go to Mrs. Webster. Sure enough, she punished him to his room for three days, making him miss out on the meeting."

I take a deep breath, trying to process all this. My heart hurts so bad for Cal. He didn't do anything wrong.

"Wait. What was the bizarre story? How was he doing it for me?"

His shoulders rise and he throws his hands out. "No idea. He said he needed to get something for you to impress 'your new parents.'" Mark laughs. "Even though they were never his parents and never will be. We didn't see anything in his hands, so he must've been hiding it."

"He never told me about that."

"Probably never got the chance. Two hours later, we were on our way to new and better things. Come on, Bella," his voice rises a few octaves, "don't sweat it. We have a good life —good parents. Leave the past where it belongs. Leave that loser where he belongs. Trent is your future. Go make things right with him."

I shake my head, getting angrier and angrier with each passing second. "First of all, I never want to see Trent again, let alone make things right with him. Second, Cal is the furthest thing from a loser. He is a man who is honest and loyal. Unlike you and Trent," I snarl, curling my lip before grabbing my bag and storming out.

I END up in a hotel about a block from Mark's apartment in the Upper East Side of NYC. I'm physically and emotionally drained and right now, I'm not sure I even have the strength to take a shower. I've cried, I've screamed, and I've dropped to my knees and begged for a sign of what I should do next.

Everyone in my life has been lying to me. Mark, Trent, Cal. The three men I thought I could trust. I have no close girlfriends, I have no cousins I grew up with, or grandparents I talk to. I have my mom and dad and those three guys, and that's it. But now, all I have is my parents.

Somehow, I manage to stay on my feet as I wash this horrendous day off me. I've been on a boat, a plane, and walked down the streets of the city, carrying my damn suitcase. I haven't eaten, I haven't slept, and I'm on the verge of throwing up from coughing through the tears so much.

My mind has gone over so many scenarios of what I should do and it's come down to the final two: go home or go back.

I finish cleaning up and crawl into bed, lying there for hours with my eyes wide open.

The next thing I know, I wake up and the sun is peeking through the blinds. My body jolts up when something outside the window catches my eye.

"No way," I mutter. My feet hit the floor and I walk over to the window. Pressing my hands to the ledge, I look at the sign directly in front of me. *Snake Pit Lounge and Bar.* It's not the name or the sign, it's the snake head looking back at me. With emerald green eyes and a challenging stare. Its tongue is out in a hiss and I realize, this is my sign.

I'm not giving up.

31

"THANK YOU, Jeffery. I promise, this stays between us."

"I trust you, dear. But, please be safe."

I give Jeffery a smile before getting off the boat and practically running up the path to the castle. It feels good to be back, and I'm anxious to see if Cal is here. I'm just as nervous as I was the first time I arrived on this island, but this time, my nerves are for good reason. I'm ready to tell him I love him. That, really, I never stopped. Our futures have been carved in stone since before we even met and this is the way it's meant to be. It was always him. It was always us.

Pulling open the door, I step inside the main entrance. "Cal," I call out. My feet don't stop moving as I go to the elevator. "Cal," I try one more time, just in case he's out back somewhere.

The elevator doors slide open and I step inside. It feels strange, but it also feels right.

With no hesitation, I go straight to Cal's room with the key I stole from Peter. The door unlocks and I shove the door open. "Cal, are you here?" I scope out the entire room, the bathroom, even the closet. But it's useless. He's not here.

Just as I'm about to leave and go search the rest of the place, I turn back around and go to the closet.

I pull out the bottom drawer of the dresser and stand on it, pushing myself up until I'm kneeling on the top. Stretching as far as I can, I grab Cal's memory box and jump down.

Carrying it over to his bed, I take the top off and sit down. That's when I see it. My heart squeezes as I begin to sob.

It's been here all along. If I'd only just looked.

I pull out the pink dress and it's exactly as I remember it. Baby pink with ruffles on the seam. Lace embroidery that hangs around the collar.

Cal broke into the Beckhams' house that night to steal this dress for me. He knew how much I loved it and he wanted me to have it for the meeting.

"Come on, Cal. You can't tell me you don't think she's beautiful."

He looks over at Lucy, who's jumping rope in her driveway while we sit on the porch sucking on homemade Kool-Aid popsicles. "She's not ugly but I wouldn't say she's beautiful."

"I want a dress like that. Maybe then I'll look pretty, too." I look at Cal's purple popsicle and my, almost gone, red one. "Trade?"

We switch popsicles, but I don't stop looking at Lucy.

"Bella, she might not be ugly, but she'll never be as pretty as you."

I look over and smile at Cal. "You're just being nice because you want your popsicle back."

"If I wanted it back, I'd take it. I happen to like red better, anyways."

Lucy stumbles a bit but gets back on track with her jumping. "Do you think they won't choose me because I don't have nice clothes like her?"

"No," he laughs, "people don't choose family because of their clothes. But, if it makes you feel better, I'll ask Lucy if you can borrow a dress."

"No!" I spit out, "that's so embarrassing. She'll know I'm poor."

"Bella." Cal levels with me. "We're orphans who live in a group home. She knows we're all poor."

"Please don't ask her. I'll just wear the dress I always wear. Maybe I can sew the hole in the armpit."

"I like that old dress better anyways. It's unique."

"Unique," I chuckle, "more like an antique."

Cal snatches back his popsicle and takes the last bite. "You know, maybe purple is better."

Hugging the dress tightly to my chest, all my emotions spill onto it. My eyes swell from crying so hard, and my throat aches. I have to find him. I have to tell him thank you. He lost out on the life he wanted because he was trying to make me happy. Trent and Mark set him up and he took the fall. Then I left and he was sentenced to misery.

With the dress in hand, I leave the box and the room, searching high and low, but Cal's nowhere to be found.

I go to the sixth floor to Peter's room, and when he doesn't answer, I use the key to go inside.

It's at this moment the world stands still. My heart stops beating, the tears stop falling, and I hold my breath before screaming at the top of my lungs, "Nooooo!"

Still clutching the dress, I snap out of the state of shock I'm in and hurry over to Peter's lifeless body, lying in a puddle of blood on the floor.

Maybe it's not too late. Maybe I can save him.

"Oh, Peter," I choke out as I reach down and place my fingers on his cold wrist. It's no use. He has no pulse.

Peter is dead.

I sit there next to him, crying for minutes before I finally get up to try and call for help, then it hits me. Someone did this. Peter didn't die of natural causes. The puddle of blood is enough proof that he was murdered. Whoever did it could still be here.

He was such a good man with such a big heart. Who would do this to him?

Pulling open the drawer to his nightstand, I get out the diary and go to his page of passcodes, hoping like hell the password for the Wi-Fi is there. I'm pretty sure I'm the only one left here and making a call to the water transport company is the only way I'm getting off this island.

"Dammit!" I slam the diary shut and go to put it back but stop. Instead, I lay it on top of Peter. "You're dancing with your Carolina now." I smile through the tears, then hurry out of the room to try and find someone to help me.

An hour later, I've searched every part of the castle and no one is here. I'm completely alone.

Somehow I have to get off this island.

If anything happened to Cal…no, I can't think like that. He's somewhere safe. He has to be.

My only option is to walk the property and try to somehow find cell phone service. It's a hopeless option because I tried for weeks to get service to no avail.

I go out back to the courtyard and hope washes over me when I hear someone talking. "Hello," I call out, "Cal, is that you?" Keeping on the path I'm on, I follow the sound of the voice I heard.

"Byron?" I say his name in question. "Why are you still here?"

He ends a call on his phone and sticks it into his pocket. "Hi, Bella. I wasn't expecting to see you." He seems calm, which leads me to believe he has no idea that Peter is dead in his room. "What's wrong? Why are you crying?"

"I need to use your phone. Peter...Peter is in his room. He's dead."

Byron's jaw drops. "What?"

"I said Peter is dead. Someone murdered him."

Byron retrieves his phone from his pocket and begins tapping into it. "That's ridiculous. I'm the only one here."

He's right. I've searched everywhere. Byron is the only person I've found. Paulina is gone. The guards are gone. Cal is gone.

But if he's here and Peter is dead...

I backstep a few times until I bump into the glass table on the patio. It tips over and the sound of the metal hitting the cement startles me. I don't take my eyes off Byron.

"Bella," he says, closing the space between us, "I didn't... you don't think it was me?"

I steady myself and take a step back for every step he comes forward. "How long have you been here? Where's Cal?"

His eyes widen and he suddenly wears a look of displeasure. "I just got here. I've been searching everywhere for Callum. He's missing, Bella."

My heart drops into my stomach. *No. He can't be.* "What do you mean he's missing?"

"No one has been able to reach him since yesterday morning when he left the island for a meeting. Peter got a call to send you away, so you were safe, but we've got no idea what's going on."

"Have you talked to the people he had a meeting with? Maybe he's still there?"

Byron shakes his head no. "That's the thing. We don't know who he met up with. I came in on my private boat to see if maybe he came back. Bella, if someone killed Peter, that means we need to leave, like right now." Byron wraps an arm around my shoulder and leads my hesitant body toward the entrance of the castle.

I shake uncontrollably as we walk to the front doors. "We have to find him, Byron. What if—"

Byron's phone buzzes in his pocket and he holds up a finger to me then pulls it out. I stop, listening intently as he takes the call.

"What? When? Where?" Byron looks at me as he speaks into the phone. "Shit." He rubs his hand over his forehead. "All right, keep me updated."

"We've gotta go." He steers me quickly down the path to the dock.

"Who was that? What happened?"

Byron swallows hard and there's a look of fear in his eyes. "They found a body. Apparently, it washed up at a public beach on Bradburn Isle."

"No!" I gasp, slapping a hand to my chest, "please tell me it wasn't him. Dammit, Byron. Tell me." I choke out the words that are barely audible.

"They haven't identified the body yet, which means you need to go home to your family where it's safe, and I'll call you if I hear anything."

I HAVEN'T STOPPED CRYING. Can't catch my breath. I can't even think as I ride in the back seat of my parents' car. They picked me up at the ferry docks after Byron had his captain give me a ride. We exchanged numbers and he promised he'd keep me updated if he hears anything.

So far, I haven't heard anything, but I haven't stopped staring at my phone, waiting for it to ring. I've even searched the news for reports on the body found, but so far, it's all hush-hush.

I refuse to believe it was Cal. He's out there somewhere, and I will find him. I'll do whatever it takes because, as Peter once said, the heart wants what the heart wants. And my heart wants him.

Together.

Forever.

Until kingdom come.

EPILOGUE

ONE MONTH LATER

"Darling," Mom says, peeking her head in my bedroom. "We're heading to Luciano's for pizza, would you like to join us?"

I close the book I was reading and set it down beside me. "No, thanks. You all enjoy."

Mom steps into the room, drawing closer to the bed. Each step has me wishing she'd turn around and walk out. I know she's worried about me, but nothing has changed. I'm still here, and he's still missing.

"Mark is only home for the holidays for a few more days. You already missed Christmas dinner. It would really be nice for us to all have dinner together before he goes back to New York." She sits on the edge of the bed and begins tracing her fingers over the cover of my book.

"I'm really not up for it. I'll try to see him before he leaves." It's a lie. The truth is, I'm still angry with Mark.

"Have you heard from Trent at all?"

I shake my head no. "Nope. And I hope I never do again."

"Mark said he's living in New York now, apparently your

friend threatened his career if he ever came back to this state again."

"Good. And if I know that friend of mine, he'll hold true to his threat."

"Bella, honey," Mom says in an attempt to swaddle me like a baby. "It's time to let go. If he was out there somewhere and wanted to be with you, he would find a way."

Pinching my eyebrows together in frustration, I speak loud and clear, "He is out there, Mom! And we will find a way to be together."

I didn't tell my parents everything, but Trent told Mark about his visit to Cori Cove and everything that happened, then of course, Mark told our parents. I told them about Cal and our past and how we reconnected before he went missing.

They were anything but receptive after hearing what Cal did to Trent. In fact, they insisted I fix things with Trent. I know they just want to try and help and I love them for that, but sometimes, I wish they'd let me make my own choices.

She places a calming hand on my arm, but it does anything but soothe me. "Did you make it to therapy this morning?"

I shake my head and press my chin to my chest, fighting back the tears. "It doesn't help, so I'm not going anymore."

"I wish you'd give it more time. I think it could help."

Mark comes into the room, interrupting us and, for once, I'm happy to see him just so this conversation with my mom can end.

"Hey, Ma. Do you mind if I talk to Bella for a minute?"

She nods, then presses a kiss to my forehead. "I love you, honey, and I'm always here for you." With that, she leaves Mark and me alone.

Mark presses his lips together and rubs his fists as he

walks over, avoiding eye contact. "Look. I know you're pissed about the whole Callum thing from twelve years ago, but we were kids and made a stupid mistake."

"If that's your apology, then you can shove it up your ass and leave my room."

His eyebrows hit his forehead, probably surprised that I grew a bit of a backbone while I've been gone.

"He didn't suffer. He's a billionaire who has everything anyone could possibly want."

"Everything except for a family," I snarl at him in disgust. He doesn't know Cal. No one does. "Cal was severely abused, Mark. His mind was tortured and he's been through things he can never come back from. If you and Trent would have just left everything alone…"

"Then he'd be here and I'd be the one missing."

I never thought of it that way. If Cal would have gotten adopted with me, then Mark would have likely ended up with the Ellis family.

"That's not what I meant."

"We can't change the past. All we can do is try to make better choices in the future. I'm sorry I fucked things up for you two. But I'm not sorry I got you as a sister."

He's got a point. We can't change the past. Not mine, not his, not Cal's. All we can do is move forward.

"Tell Mom I'll meet you guys at Luciano's for dinner."

Mark smiles and I do the same.

I smile while I internally cry. My heart screams for Cal. No matter how much time passes, I will never get over him. Even if he's never found, I will die loving him.

I reach under my bed and pull out the box of letters I wrote him during all the years we were apart. Inside is the dress he stole for me. On top is the master key to the castle.

Byron never called me to give me an update on the body, and when I went to call him, the line was disconnected.

There was never a news report done about the body being found, but I tried like hell to get answers. In fact, I lost sleep and ten pounds because I tried so hard. I called the number to his assistant who set me up with the job and left dozens of messages with no return call. I went to the police on the main island, the mortician, watched the obituaries, and did countless searches. In the end, I never got answers, but I still don't believe it was Cal. I can feel him. He's out there, and he's alive. My heart would know if he was gone.

I look down at the priceless items and draw in a deep breath. "I'll find you. One day, I will find you."

Pulling myself together, I throw on a pair of jeans and a tee shirt and head downstairs. Everyone has left, so I take my time getting out the door.

When I go into the kitchen, I notice a stack of my mail sitting on the counter.

The first couple aren't of any importance. One from a local college, the other an unpaid credit card bill. It's the third one that catches my eye. It's from Carnegie Hall. The odd thing is, it's not addressed to Isabella Jenkins; it's addressed to Bella Jenkins.

Wasting no time, I tear the top of the envelope off and pull out the letter.

Dear Bella Jenkins,

Thank you for your interest in performing at Carnegie Hall. We've received a sample of the song you sent in two weeks ago and we'd love to invite you to perform on Saturday, January 1st, 2022, in a solo symphony, performing *Our Song.*

I don't even continue reading at this point.

I never sent them a sample. I've never even recorded "Our Song." In fact, I've never even told anyone about it. Cal is the only one who knows the title.

The letter says they received the sample two weeks ago.

Cal did this.

This means…Cal is alive.

Read book two, Her Broken Pieces!

ALSO BY RACHEL LEIGH

Bastards of Boulder Cove

Book One: Savage Games

Book Two: Vicious Lies

Book Three: Twisted Secrets

Wicked Boys of BCU (Coming March 2023)

Book One: We Will Reign

Book Two: You Will Bow

Book Three: They Will Fall

Redwood Rebels Series

Book One: Striker

Book Two: Heathen

Book Three: Vandal

Book Four: Reaper

Redwood High Series

Book One: Like Gravity

Book Two: Like You

Book Three: Like Hate

Fallen Kingdom Duet

His Hollow Heart & Her Broken Pieces

Black Heart Duet

Four & Five

Standalones

Guarded

Ruthless Rookie

Devil Heir

All The Little Things

Claim your FREE copy of Her Undoing!

ABOUT THE AUTHOR

Rachel Leigh is a USA Today bestselling author of new adult and contemporary romance with a twist. You can expect bad boys, strong heroines, and an HEA.

Rachel lives in leggings, overuses emojis, and survives on books and coffee. Writing is her passion. Her goal is to take readers on an adventure with her words, while showing them that even on the darkest days, love conquers all.

www.rachelleighauthor.com
Rachel's Ramblers Readers Group

facebook.com/rachelleighauthor
instagram.com/rachelleighauthor
goodreads.com/rachelleigh
amazon.com/author/rachelleighauthor

Made in United States
North Haven, CT
01 October 2023

42190326R00174